MOVING ON

Sometimes love is not <u>enough</u>

DOROTHY AL KHAFAJI

PROLOGUE

It's funny how I can't remember what I did yesterday, she muses, yet events long past and forgotten are as vivid and real to me as if I am watching an old movie. She settles more comfortably in bed, switches off the bedside lamp and sinks back into sleep.

For Linda
Best wishes
Dorothy Chapman

CHAPTER 1

The hot weather is set to continue so Maggie and Linda are going to cycle down to the beach on Saturday morning. Maggie is looking forward to being outside after a week cooped up in the office. It will be such a relief not to have to parry the advances of that pervert from accounts. He always seems to be hanging round the photocopier.

The two friends set off early on Saturday morning, wearing shorts and sleeveless blouses over their swimwear. Linda's is one of the daring new bikinis which have become all the rage. Maggie would love to have one, but her mum says that, with her curvy figure, she will feel more comfortable in a one-piece.

'You don't want to be showing off a builder's bum every time you bend over, do you love?' Mum had said in the swimwear department of Marks and Spencers. Maggie knows that her mum is probably right, but it does nothing for her self-esteem. She envies Linda her lean, straight up-and-down body. She could easily be mistaken for a boy from behind and she doesn't have much to put into the top half of her bikini at the front either.

Linda is faster on a bike than Maggie so she reaches the sea front first. 'Pier end or sand dunes?' she calls out as Maggie comes round the corner, red-faced and out of breath. The dunes are a long way from the pier end with its fairground and fish and chip van but only a short walk from the ferry landing. This makes the ferry end a popular spot for teenagers coming over from Portsmouth. The dunes also provide cover for anyone who wants to sneak away for a snog, sometimes more than a snog if the rumors about Sophie Tattler and Geraldine Morris are true. Maggie would have preferred the pier end, which is more popular with families, but she knows

Linda would rather go to the dunes in case her boyfriend, Tom, turns up after he finishes work. She hesitates,

'You choose, I'm easy.'

'Yea, so I've heard. Sand dunes it is then' Linda grins as she pushes off with one foot and leads the way down the road and onto the sandy track that leads to the ferry port.

When they reach the dunes, the beach is practically deserted so they have first choice of all the best spots. Half-way between the grassy dunes and the water's edge are best for sunbathing because you don't have to keep moving when the tide comes in. Being mid-way also gives you a good view of the football or beach ball games which will inevitably start up later. Most boys usually start off by sunning themselves but soon become bored with lying still and doing nothing. Once a game gets underway, groups of girls will casually prop themselves up on one elbow and pretend to chat while scanning the players from behind their dark glasses. Some of the boys are already known to them, either from school, work or nights out at the Savoy, although they don't know all of them personally. It's those mysterious half-strangers that they'll be looking out for: who knows, one of them might just possibly turn out to be "the one".

The girls spread out their towels and strip off, carefully folding their clothes and storing them in their large canvas shoppers. Linda's has a large CND logo on it while Maggie's announces 'Peace and Rock' in capitals but neither girl has the remotest interest in politics or world affairs. The bags are simply in fashion. Maggie sits down and ties on her silky white headscarf peasant style, a la Audrey Hepburn in "Roman Holiday". She hopes it will help prevent her thick dark hair from frizzing in the sea air.

Linda doesn't need to worry about her hair, it's straight as a die and looks even better when it's windswept than when it's tidy. Once they're settled, both girls begin smearing a mixture of olive oil and vinegar over their bare skin. It's supposed to speed up tanning and probably will for Linda, but Maggie always goes home from the beach with bright red skin which keeps her awake at night and involves her mum in applying lashes of calamine lotion to her shoulders and back. Despite this, Maggie has never given up hope of achieving the beautiful golden tan which seems to come naturally to most of her friends.

A steady influx of young people begins walking onto the sand, clearly just off the ferry. The beach is getting quite crowded now so when Sophie Tatler and Geraldine Morris appear, Maggie turns her back and pretends to be looking for something in her bag. 'Oh no, I hope they don't come and sit near us, pretend you haven't seen them Linda'. Unfortunately, they've been spotted and they're in a prime position, so the newcomers come over and throw their bags down on the sand next to them.

'Hi girls, this is lucky. We can all sit together, can't we?' Sophie and Geraldine were at high school with them so neither Maggie nor Linda feel able to refuse. Actually, Maggie rather likes Sophie. They were in the same sets at school and Maggie never knew her to be nasty or take part in the bitchiness which seems to increase as girls get older. The teachers liked her too, she was hard-working, helpful and always cheerful, something which must have been a refreshing change for teachers who spend most of their time with grumpy teenagers. Sophie and Geraldine are both going off to university soon; Maggie wishes she could go too, but university is not an option her parents would ever have considered. Once she turned sixteen, she was expected to get a job and contribute to the family income.

In fact, it was her father who helped her get her present job at a large medical supply company. He works there as warehouse manager, and he put in a word for her even before he asked whether she was interested in applying for a job at his firm. Maggie knew there would be an atmosphere at home if she said no, and anyway she didn't want to appear ungrateful, so she reluctantly filled in the application form Dad brought home for her. It was sod's law that she was offered the position of a filing clerk immediately after her interview, but Dad was delighted so she felt obliged to accept it. She's been working there for two years now and spends her days on an excruciatingly boring treadmill of copying and filing documents which seldom see the light of day. While she's occupied in these mind-numbing tasks, she dreams of changing her job to something more interesting and productive, but she has no idea what she would like to do instead. Now she feels a twinge of envy as she listens to Sophie and Geraldine chatting about book lists, accommodation in halls and what they're going to do on fresher's week. Maggie has no idea what they're talking about.

Turning away, she notices that a group of boys have separated into teams and are now playing a noisy game of volleyball. Whenever the ball lands near a coterie of girls, one or other of the boys throws himself to the ground in in front of them in a dramatic attempt to catch it. How they can still run around in the scorching heat is beyond Maggie, she's already succumbing to drowsiness and only half listening to the desultory conversation of the other girls. Just as she's drifting off, she's hit by a spray of sand thrown up by the ball, which bounces over her and nearly hits Linda on the head. 'Hey, watch it' she yells at the Cliff Richard lookalike who Is chasing it, 'You nearly landed on top of her'.

'Oh, don't be mean Maggie, he's cute' simpers Linda, but Sophie embarrasses them both by yelling 'Oi, you can land on top of me any time'.

The boy gives her a thumbs-up, grinning, then turns a jubilant cartwheel on the way back to his mates. It's just the kind of high jinks Maggie's mum disapproves of. She definitely would not like her hanging round with Sophie and Geraldine, she's always reminding her of the dangers of mixing with the wrong crowd and getting a "reputation." Geraldine obviously finds the boy's response hilarious:

'You do know who that is, don't you Sophie? It's Lennie Gray from school, he was always in the lowest set for everything? I used to help people in set five with their reading in the lunch hour and he was the worst, he could hardly read anything. He's a postman now, though God knows how he manages to get the letters to the right address.'

Maggie stands up and shakes the sand from her sensible swim- suit, pulling the fabric away from her body and letting it twang back into place.

'Oh well, might as well have a swim now I'm up. You coming, Linda?'

Several of the boys abandoned their game and sprinted down to the water. That's the cue for other girls to stand up, adjust their bikinis and follow them to the water's edge. They soon move out to deeper water, making way for the toddlers playing in the waves. They don't go deep enough to get their hair wet, just enough to cool off. There are several boys a little further out, ducking each other then swimming away in a vigorous crawl. A couple of girls indulge in a little gentle splashing until a boy gets involved as he makes his way out of the water. The ritual has reached the point where anyone can join in and a splashing match develops, accompanied by a lot of screaming as girls are soaked and pushed under. By the time they return to the sand the little groups of sunbathers have re-formed as boys settle down to the serious business of chatting up the girls.

Linda's boyfriend, Tom, arrives and throws his towel down before stretching out beside her on his side. He places his hand on her bare midriff and moves closer, nestling his face into her shoulder, but she pushes him away.

'Get off me Tom, I want to get a tan, not white fingerprints all over me.' He moves away and sits up, checking on his mates' progress. A dark-haired, very handsome boy comes over and sits down next to Sophie.

'Hi Soph, I didn't expect to see you here. Sophie turns on her side and the boy starts running his hand up and down her thigh. She turns on her back and he begins stroking her stomach, but she grins

'You're out of luck, Mick, it's 'time of the month'. After a while Sophie sits up and begins rubbing cream on her shoulders and arms, then she stands, picks up her towel and makes her way into the sand dunes. The boy saunters after her: When he re-emerges from the high grass of the dunes, he doesn't join them but heads straight down to the sea. A few minutes later Sophie returns, shakes out her towel and sits down cross-legged. She exchanges a knowing smile with Geraldine as she pulls out a hair- brush and begins brushing sand from her hair.

Maggie follows the boy with her eyes until he's waist deep in the sea. He stands motionless for a moment then he begins scooping up handfuls of the water and pours it over his back and chest. She has no idea that she's looking at her future husband, Michael Johnson.

Over the next couple of years Maggie has several boyfriends but none of them last very long. The contraceptive pill isn't widely available yet, so the fear of an unwanted pregnancy still hovers over every relationship. Consequently, most young men are preoccupied with sex. At the end of a date a girl knows that the goodnight kiss will end up with her being backed into a corner, or against a wall, while her date pleads, 'Come on, please, I can't stop now' or similar cajoling. Sometimes, if she really likes the boy, Maggie is tempted, but there's no way she's going to have her first time up against a wall. Because she always says 'no' her relationships never last long enough for a boy to take her home to meet his family, usually the only place where young couples manage to find a little privacy.

Linda surrendered her virginity to Tom on his mum's sofa over a year ago while his parents were out at the pub. She gave Maggie all the details the next morning when they met at the bus stop. 'Come over here, Mags, I've got something to tell you. You won't believe what happened last night'.

'Hurry up then, my bus will be here in a minute.' Linda has a habit of making a mountain out of a mole hole, so Maggie doesn't expect what comes next.

'Well, me and Tom were having a snog, but I let him go too far. He was so worked up that I couldn't stop him, so we went all the way. It hurt like hell, but he was so sweet afterwards that I didn't mind'. Linda has always said that she would wait until they were engaged, but it doesn't sound as though she'd had much choice in the end. Maggie thinks that the incident sounds like the least romantic thing she has ever heard, but she doesn't want to upset her friend, so she keeps quiet.

After that, sex becomes a regular event for Linda and Tom, who snatch a few minutes for a quicky whenever the opportunity presents itself. The girls have a good laugh one night when Linda describes the scene a few days earlier at Tom's house:

'It was a lovely evening, and his mum and dad were working in the garden. Tom told them we were going for a walk and his dad said they would probably go to the pub for a drink later. He invited us to join them when we got back. Anyway, we ended up going to the park for a cuddle on the grass but there were too many people about because of the fine weather'.

'Don't you two ever think about anything else?'

'Just listen, Maggie, you haven't heard the best part yet'.

'So we went back to the house, expecting it to be empty, but his mum and dad were still working in the garden. They said they didn't want to waste such a beautiful evening. Tom didn't want to waste it either, so he bolted the kitchen door, plonked me down on a stool and pulled down my knickers. All the time we were doing it he was keeping an eye on his parents through the kitchen window. The stool was wobbling all over the place and it was only the side of the cupboard that stopped me from falling off, it was hilarious.'

'I bet his mum and dad knew what you were up to,' Maggie giggled.

'No, I don't think so. I got up to go to the toilet as soon as we finished but Tom was still standing with my knickers in his hand and his trousers round his ankles when his mum tapped on the window and told him to put the kettle on. He had to lean against the sink and pretend he couldn't hear her so she couldn't see his lower half. All I could see was his bum as he leaned forward.' The girls collapse into hysterical laughter and for days afterwards someone saying 'put the kettle on' was enough to set them off again.

It doesn't seem so funny six weeks later, however, when Linda realises she is pregnant.

Of course, Maggie is the first to know, after Tom.

'How am I going to tell Mum and Dad, Mags? My dad will go mad and my mum will be so disappointed in me. I can't face them, I think I'll run away.'

'Don't be daft, where will you go? What did Tom say when you told him?'

'He just said we'll have to get married. He said we would probably have got engaged soon anyway so we'll just be bringing everything forward a bit. I think he's quite pleased now he's got used to the idea.'

'Well there you go then, it'll all work out fine,'

'But Tom doesn't know what Dad's like. He's always telling me to keep my legs crossed and Mum's always reminding me to keep myself nice. I really can't do it, Maggie, I can't face them'.

'You have to tell them. They'll find out soon enough anyway, but you can't leave it 'til then, you have to tell them now. I'll come with you if you like, I'm sure they'll be fine once they get used to the idea'. So Maggie goes round to Linda's house the next evening and holds her hand while Linda tells her parents that they're about to become grandparents. Maggie turns out to be right, they're unexpectedly calm when they hear the news. In fact, she can't help feeling they aren't even very surprised. Linda's parents agree to meet up with Tom later that evening to discuss 'his intentions', so Maggie, her job done, gets up to leave. As Linda walks her to the door, she bursts out:

'All that nagging about keeping my virginity, they made me feel so guilty, and it turns out they're not even that bothered. Why did they do it?'

'I don't know, but if your baby is a girl, just make sure you don't do the same thing to her.' As it happens, Maggie's 's advice will be unnecessary, because the birth of Linda's baby coincides with the advent of a readily available contraceptive pill.

CHAPTER 2

Linda and tom have been married for fourteen months now and are the proud parents of a beautiful little boy, Richard, known as Ritchie. Linda returned to work part-time when the baby was four months old, leaving Ritchie in the care of her mother, who adores him.

Meanwhile, Maggie has worked her way up to deputy office manager. She still hates her job but it's through her work that she meets Michael Johnson. Her employers are planning to upgrade their entire electrical installation, so they've arranged for a surveyor from the utility company to assess the job. When he arrives, he brings with him a trainee engineer, a good-looking young man who seems vaguely familiar to Maggie. The two of them start chatting while the surveyor borrows Maggie's desk to check over his notes. The boy has an easy, confident manner and a sly grin which reminds Maggie of an incident which took place several of years before.

'Oh, I remember where I saw you. It was at the beach. You went into the dunes with Sophie Tattler.'

'I don't think so. Why would I go off with her if you were there? It must have been someone else.' Maggie doesn't believe him, but she agrees to go out with him later in the week anyway. He's still very good-looking but it turns out that he's also great company, funny, charming and quite romantic so he quickly establishes himself as her boyfriend. Despite these attributes, she's never quite sure why Michael is the boy she finally gives in to. Maybe she's grown tired of being one of the few virgins left among her friends, or maybe it's just because he has his own car, an invaluable retreat for young lovers.

Whatever the reason, having slept with him once, she feels committed. After all, she isn't the kind of girl to sleep around, even though the fear of pregnancy has been removed by the availability of 'The Pill' as it's commonly known. Maggie tells her mother that her GP prescribed the pill to help with her painful periods and her mum doesn't question it. If she has any doubts about the real reason Maggie's now on the pill, she keeps them to herself.

Naturally, Maggie introduces Michael to her best friends, Linda and Tom,, and the two couples often share a night out together. They usually go for a drink or to a club and Linda's mum, who is besotted with her grandson, is always happy to baby-sit Ritchie. The foursome share the same sense of humour and the men support the same football team, so it's a friendship made in heaven. One evening, over a curry at their local Indian, Tom says he's planning to take Linda and the baby to Spain in the summer.

'Why don't you both come with us? We could stay at the same hotel, hire a car together and drive around a bit. It'd be a laugh.' Michael is immediately enthusiastic.

'It would be brilliant, Mags. It would be your first time abroad and we could spend the whole night together, every night.' Maggie blushes furiously and kicks him under the table, but Linda is equally keen on them tagging along.

'Go on, Maggie, come with us. Just think, we could all be sunning ourselves on the beach, eating ice-creams and drinking beers. Ritchie could play in the sand and these two can build him a sandcastle while we relax'. There are howls of protest from the men at this, before Tom says:

'Actually, Maggie if you both come, we could take it in turns to look after Ritchie in the evening. That way, Linda and I could go out on our own sometimes. You'd be doing us a favour.'

So the holiday is booked and the girls spend many happy Saturday afternoons shopping for beach clothes while their men watch the football on television. Maggie's dad isn't very happy about her going away with Michael. Her mum keeps her head down when she first broaches the subject, and Maggie knows her mother is waiting for Dad to explode. She tries to give the impression that Linda and Tom will in effect be her chaperones, but her dad isn't buying that.

'I don't know why you think I'll be happier, Margaret, knowing that you're going with that Linda. She's no better than she ought to be. She was only married a few months before that baby was born.'

'Oh Dad, don't be mean, you know they've been going out with each other ever since they were at school. Anyway, Michael and I are having separate rooms', she lies. For once, Maggie stands her ground, after all she's an adult now and can do whatever she likes. Still, she doesn't want to upset her parents, so she stresses that going with Linda and Tom makes the holiday 'respectable'. She would die if they knew how Michael keeps telling her that he can't wait to have her all to himself for the entire night, in a bed. The truth is that Maggie is looking forward to it too. She's tired of hurried and uncomfortable sex in the back of his car. The holiday will be almost like a honeymoon.

As it happens, Maggie and Michael don't have to do any babysitting while they're away. Ritchie is such a good little boy that he drops off to sleep in his push chair every evening as soon as darkness falls. All they have to do is put the push chair into the recline position and cover him with a blanket. Once he's asleep he's oblivious to the noise and lights around him so the four friends are able to go out together every night while they're in Sain.

There's one particular restaurant they like, it's right on the seafront, bordering the sand. The owner always makes a fuss of Ritchie and takes them to a corner table where he can be safely stowed away from the other customers. As it gets dark, they watch the moon reflected on the water far out to sea. A delightful, cooling breeze mingles with smoke from the barbeques which are grilling kebabs and fish all along the coast, and Maggie surrenders herself to the assault on her senses. She can't help wondering why her parents have never travelled further than the Isle of Wight. Since meals are included in the price of their holiday, they normally have dinner at their hotel then go to the restaurant for drinks afterwards. Maggie and Linda drink Babycham, while the men have a few beers, but during that holiday Linda also develops a taste for beer. Initially, she asks Tom for a sip of his drink because she's thirsty but by the end of the fortnight she's drinking half lagers.

Michael thinks it's unladylike for a woman to drink beer.

'I wouldn't like to see you downing a pint, Love', he tells Maggie when they're back in their hotel room.

'Don't worry, you won't, I hate the taste of the stuff. I can't understand how you men can down several pints of it in one night.' He's already pulling down the straps of her sundress and undoing her bra so he can kiss her back, all the way down. Now that they're together throughout the night Maggie understands for the first time the difference between a quick coupling and making love. Michael never hurries, he's very sensual but also tender. It's important to him that she enjoys the foreplay. He introduces her to the pleasures of her body, guiding her though the mysteries of eroticism. He's the perfect teacher and, naively, she never asks herself where his expertise comes from. She makes the mistake made by many other women and confuses sexual compatibility with love.

Sometimes they leave the beach to explore the countryside. One day they drive up the winding mountain roads to Ronda, where Michael pretends he's going to climb down into the gorge. He slips away leaving Maggie distraught as she leans over the old stone wall, trying to spot him. Like a parent playing hide and seek, he waits for a minute then he emerges from behind a crumbling old house, grinning.

'You idiot, you scared the life out of me', Maggie wallops him with her shoulder bag and is rewarded with a big hug.

'Why would I want to go down there when I've got my gorgeous girl up here?' and he pulls her in even tighter, squashing her boobs against his chest and dropping a kiss on her cleavage. 'Michael, stop it', but she loves it really, it isn't as if anyone knows them there.

The day before they leave, they drive to Gibraltar. High up above the town they laugh at the Barbary monkeys jumping around and swinging from car to car. At first Ritchie laughs excitedly too, gurgling 'bow wow' and pointing at them but when a particularly large and vicious-looking specimen starts to bang on their windscreen he turns his face into Linda's chest and wails. Michael leans forward and pats Ritchie gently on his back,

'Come on, Tom, they're scaring him. Let's go down and look around the town now. Maggie puts her hand on Michael's knee and gives it an affectionate squeeze. It's one of the things she likes about him, he's so kind-hearted.

They descend to the town and wander round, fascinated by the little Jewish shops which probably haven't changed for hundreds of years. Linda buys a couple of cute little outfits for Ritchie and Maggie gets him a toy monkey and a miniature sombrero.

Even though they've paid for half board they don't have dinner at the hotel on their last night. They want to try the food in a genuine Spanish restaurant, the kind the locals go to. When they get there Maggie and Linda are determined to dip into Spanish culture, so they order king prawns for starters, but screw up their faces when they see the huge prawns are still in their shells. Laughing, Tom calls a waiter over to shell them, then Maggie bites into the sweet flesh of the plump prawns, savouring every mouthful. Later, they all eat the freshest fish they have ever tasted, washed down by heady Spanish wine. When the bill comes, Michael takes it from the waiter.

'No, put your money away, Tom. I'm paying. It's a thank you for inviting us on this holiday. We've had a fabulous time, haven't we Mags? Maggie is light-headed from the unaccustomed wine.

'We absolutely have. Let's drink a toast to good friends, shall we?' So they all raise their glasses, rather self-consciously, and repeat 'To good friends.' The memory of that first overseas dinner stays with Maggie for years afterwards. Far out to sea, stars are winking as, one by one, they lose their battle with the bright lights stationed along the shore, and Michael's smile from across the table is as warm as the balmy air. For the first time she feels free, unfettered by outmoded rules, sophisticated and self-assured. For years afterwards she remembers it as the most romantic night of her life.

After the holiday Maggie finds it hard to step back onto the daily tread mill which is her life. Work seems even more humdrum than before, and every day seems endless. To make matters worse, Michael is away on a course for a month, so she has nothing to look forward to in the evening. The atmosphere at home is just as joyless and suffocating as ever and the house itself, once her comfy, welcoming sanctuary, now seems dark and dingy in comparison to the bright, modern hotel room she has just left. Also, the contrast between Michael's warm embraces and Dad's off hand welcome couldn't have been more pronounced. At home, he's just as autocratic and impossible to please as ever. Mum is always fluttering around, trying to placate him. Added to that, Maggie has caught him checking out her figure a couple of times, so she's convinced he's wondering if she came home pregnant. *He would probably be happy if she had,* then *he could say he was right all along,* she tells herself sourly.

She does feel sorry for Mum, though, she's always walking on eggshells, waiting for Dad to find fault with something. Maggie can't understand why her mother panders to him the way she does. Every evening after supper he goes out to inspect their miniscule garden before coming back indoors and settling into his armchair. Before he sits down on the sagging old brown chair, he always switches the TV to a different programme, even if Mum's already watching something. She never protests, she knows that's the signal for her to get up and put the kettle on for his cup of tea. Maggie can't bear it, so she pops round to Linda and Tom's to escape. When she gets there, Tom is upstairs bathing Ritchie, while Linda clears up in the kitchen and picks up the toys which are scattered all over the little house. Bath-time is clearly an excuse for a lot of shouting and splashing, followed by a couple of bangs so loud that Maggie is afraid Tom is going to burst through the ceiling. That's the cue for Linda to call up the stairs

'That's enough, Tom, don't get him too excited', before going back into the lounge and collapsing on the sofa.

'Phew, I'm shattered, I've been running after Ritchie all day. Since he started walking he never stops. Thank God I don't have to give him his bath every night, though out of the two of them, I think Tom enjoys it the most. He's still a big kid at heart.'

18

'Tom's gold and you know it, Linda. You're lucky to have him,' Maggie picks up some brightly- coloured building blocks from the sofa then sits down next to her, throwing the blocks in the toy box.

'Are you OK, Mags? You seem a bit down tonight.'

'Just a bit fed up, that's all. My dad's being his usual pain in the backside and I really miss Michael. I've hardly heard from him since he went away, just a couple of postcards and one call last Saturday afternoon. He says the course is really hard, there's a lot of reading to do in the evenings and then it's a long walk to a phone box. Most of the time he just goes back to his room and does homework.'

'Oh, didn't he take his car with him then?'

'Yes, he drove down there, but they've put him up in a pub in the middle of nowhere. He reckons he'd get lost if he tried to drive through the lanes, so he leaves his car at the training centre. They drop all the students off by bus at the end of the day.'

'Hm. So how are things going between you and Michael? You ought to tie him down quickly if you really like him.'

'What do you mean?'

'Well, he's a catch, isn't he? There aren't many girls who'd say "no" to him given half a chance.'

'Well, they won't get a chance. Michael's only interested in me.'

'If you say so. Come on, let's see if there's anything on the tele.' But Linda's words rankle so much that Maggie leaves soon after that. She keeps going over them in her mind as she walks home, getting more and more annoyed with her friend. *If she had something to say, why hadn't she just come out with it?* she asks herself. By the time she reaches home her eyes are beginning to well up and of course that makes Mum ask her if everything is all right. 'I'm fine, Mum, but I think I've got something in my eye. I'll just go upstairs and wash my face'.

Once in her bedroom Maggie picks up the postcards which take pride of place on her dressing table. One shows a picture of a large, grey two- story building with a huge sign proclaiming "Dewbury Technical College" across its frontage. If it wasn't for the sign, the building could be mistaken for a block of flats. She turns it over and reads the brief message again, "Missed you last night" followed by a row of kisses. The second card has a picture of a country village. It is very picturesque and appears to consist of a pub and a couple of shops which look like they used to be cottages. The message on the back reads "I'll take you here one day" followed by another row of kisses. Maggie wonders why he didn't give her the address of the pub so she can reply. *He probably doesn't want to be distracted from his work,* she thinks as she goes downstairs and pops her head into the sitting room to ask if either of her parents fancy a cup of cocoa.

Maggie can't be angry with anyone for long, especially Linda, so by the weekend the girls are friends again. They are planning to go shopping in town for an hour on Saturday morning before taking Ritchie to the park. Maggie arrives at the bus stop five minutes before the bus is due but there is no sign of Linda. She is clearly running late so Maggie begins walking up the road to meet her. She has not gone far when Linda appears round the corner, red-faced and pushing a push chair in front of her like a weapon. The bus sails past just as Linda catches up with her. 'I'm sorry I'm late, Mags, we were just leaving when Rich decided to throw up. I had to go back indoors and wash and change him then wipe down the push chair.'

'Oh no. We don't have to go if he isn't well, Linda.'

'Does he look ill to you? He just had too much breakfast. He ate his and then shared Tom's, he's a little pig.' Ritchie does indeed look the picture of health as he leans over the side of his push chair. His cheeks are rosy as he is tries to stick a toy into the wheels as they spin round. 'Well, we may as well walk otherwise we'll have to wait here for twenty- five minutes. Half the time the conductors won't let you on with a pushchair anyway. Come on.' Linda's progress is hampered by a large bag which keeps slipping off her shoulder. It makes it difficult to steer the push chair and slows her down, so Maggie takes it and slings it over her own shoulder as they walk down the street.

'What have you got in here, the kitchen sink?'

'Just nappies, wipes, his drinking cup, some toys and a change of clothes, the usual stuff. I don't know how our mums managed with terry nappies.'

'They had those big, high prams, didn't they? They probably stuffed everything in the bottom of them. Anyway, according to my mum they didn't have all this other stuff then'. The two girls walk on, chatting as they go. Linda, who now works part-time as a supervisor in a wholesale clothing company, seems constantly to be at logger heads with her manager. According to Linda, the manager picks on her out of spite. She says she is jealous because Linda is already married with a child while her manager is a dried- up old maid. Linda is always moaning about some grievance or other, but she stays in the job because the money is good and the hours suit her. Maggie is only half listening as Linda drones on about invoices which have not been correctly logged. She's heard it all before.

They reach the intersection where two main roads meet and wait on the corner for a gap in the traffic. A car exits from a side road, then pulls over and stops, so the girls hurry across. While they are manoeuvring the push chair up onto the opposite pavement, Maggie realises the driver is getting out of the car and waving to them.

'Hey, Maggie, Linda, hang on a minute.' She recognises the posh accent immediately: it's Sophie Tatler. The two girls wait as Sophie hurries towards them,

'Hello, you two, still thick as thieves I see. Wow, is that your little boy, Linda? He's gorgeous'. She bends down to stroke Ritchie's cheek and is rewarded with a toothy smile. Ritchie loves attention. 'How nice to see you both. Where are you off to?'

'Town. Ritchie needs some new clothes. How about you. You don't come back here very often, do you? Sophie giggles.

'No, that's why Daddy bought me a car. He thinks that I won't have an excuse for not coming home at weekends now. Come on, I'll give you both a lift.' Maggie protests that they don't want her to go out of her way, but she tells them she's heading for the central library anyway. She opens the boot and Linda takes Ritchie out, then struggles to collapse the handle of the heavy pushchair. It takes two of them to lift it, but they manage to manoeuvre it into the boot then they all pile into the little car and set off towards town. Maggie is the first to speak.

'So what's it like at university, Sophie?'

"Oh, it's great fun. You meet lots of new people and there is always a party at somebody's pad, you're spoiled for choice.' But I'm in my final year now so I have to knuckle down a bit. That's why I'm going to the library. I need to do some research for an essay which has to be handed in on Monday. But we could go for a coffee first if you have time?'

It would be rude to refuse and anyway Maggie wants to hear more about university, so they find a parking space near to the library. Sophie offers to hold the baby while the others get the pushchair out. 'Oh, he's so sweet, Linda. I can't wait to have children of my own. What a pet!' She nuzzles his neck before handing him back to his surprised mother.

'I thought you would be planning a high- flying career after university. ' Linda is gratified by the compliments to her son, but she does not have Sophie pegged as the motherly type. 'Oh, I am. I'm going to be a solicitor, so I'll have to do another course once I get my degree and then it's a two-year training period before you're fully qualified. I won't be able to even think about having children until I've got all that under my belt.'

'So, have you got someone special ear marked to have those children with, Sophie?'

'No, it could be one of many' she laughs. How about you, Maggie? I hear you and Micky Johnson are an item, you lucky thing.' Linda raises her eyebrows and gives Maggie an "I told you so" look.

'How do you know that?'

'Oh, I come home every so often, and when I do I usually meet up with the old crowd. You should come next time I'm back here, it would be fun.' Maggie doesn't respond, she is painfully aware that she was never a part of Sophie's old crowd, most of whom stayed on for A levels. The coffee bar is busy with Saturday shoppers but an elderly couple seated at one of the larger tables calls them over. 'We're just going, love, you can have our table. That's a handsome lad you've got there', the old lady smiles at Ritchie as they bustle out. Once they're settled, Sophie continues the conversation. 'Trust

Micky to get the most fancied girl in the school. He always had a way with women.'

'Me? I don't think anyone fancied me when I was at school.'

'Well, of course they did, you had the biggest boobs in the seniors. All the boys were panting after you, weren't they Linda? Linda nods her agreement, but Maggie is gob-smacked. *How could she not have realised?* She's speechless, so Linda tries to fill the awkward silence : 'Boys are such idiots.' Suddenly all three girls collapse into helpless laughter until Sophie manages to gasp 'Did you really not know all the boys fancied you?'

'No, I really didn't'. Maggie manages to get it out between giggles.

'Well, Maggie, I bet Micky leaves you in no doubt on the subject'. Maggie always blushes easily and now she's pink with embarrassment, so Sophie knows it's time to change the subject. 'So tell me, what are you both up to these days?' The conversation turns to general chat and Sophie chides Maggie for wasting her time in a dead-end job. 'You were always clever, much cleverer than me. It's not too late to go to university. You should look into it.'

'There's no point. What would I do for money?'

'You could get a grant and if you went somewhere away from home, you'd probably get a maintenance grant too.' Maggie enjoys a fleeting vision of herself leaving home. *She could hand in her notice, share a flat with other young people, throw house parties.* But sanity returns. 'Oh, I couldn't go away and leave Michael.'

'So it is serious then. Well, I hope it works out for you, I really do. And you're happily married to your childhood sweetheart then, Linda. Tom, isn't it?'

24

So the conversation moves away from Maggie, leaving her with no opportunity for more questions about university. Soon after that Sophie says she must dash, as the library closes early at weekends. Before she leaves, she hugs both girls and blows a kiss at Ritchie, who has fallen asleep. Hugging is a recent innovation amongst young people. Maggie and Linda aren't really comfortable with, it, they think it's too affected and American.

'Wow, she's really nice, isn't she Mags? I never really liked her at school, did you?'

'I did like her but there were all those stories about her being a tart, so I never really mixed with her outside of school'.

'Hm, didn't you hear what she said about "one of many?" Sounds like she hasn't changed much then, doesn't it?' Ritchie chooses that moment to wake up and demand 'Drink' so the two friends spring into action. Maggie fishes around in the bottom of the bag for his drinking cup while Linda gets out the sandwiches she's brought for him. Richie is not impressed, he's spied cake. Red-faced, he pushes the plate away and howls, kicking at the underside of the table. It takes both girls to pacify him, and Sophie is forgotten in the commotion.

Michael's course ends the following weekend, but Maggie doesn't hear from him until Sunday afternoon. He arrives just after lunch while she is washing up in the kitchen. When the doorbell rings, she's scrubbing the plates as if her life depends on it and giving the saucepans a right bashing. She had expected him to rush back on Friday evening. Mum goes to the door and by the time Maggie rinses her hands and joins them in the hallway he has worked his charm on her mother.

25

'Oh Michael, you should have come an hour earlier, you could have had Sunday roast with us. We had a lovely bit of beef.'

'I wish I could have been here for dinner, Mrs Jenkins, I'm sure it was delicious, but I've only just got back. I came straight round, I couldn't wait to see this girl here'. He puts out his arm and pulls Maggie to his side, placing a chaste kiss on top of her head.

'Well, she's been on tenterhooks all weekend, waiting for you, but you're here now, so come in and have a cup of tea with us.' They go into the lounge where Maggie's father is enjoying his Sunday afternoon nap. He grunts, wakes and yawns before realising that he has a visitor.

'Oh, it's you, Mick. Our Maggie's been expecting you all weekend. What kept you?'

'Some of the lecturers at the college organised a night out for us all on Saturday. Apparently, it's a tradition they have at the end of the intensive course, though I think they enjoyed it as much as the students. Anyway, I felt I should go, they were all really helpful and I thought I should at least buy them a drink. To be honest, Mrs Jenkins, I had one-too-many last night,, so I overslept today.'

'Oh, that's understandable, isn't it Maggie?

'I suppose.' Maggie is not ready to forgive him yet, even though he does look exhausted, with dark shadows under his eyes.

'I thought we could go and see 'Cleopatra,' Maggie. It's on at the Gaumont. What do you think? It's a really long film, so we'd need to go to the early show.' Maggie is surprised, she expected him to be desperate to get her alone so they could make love, but she does want to see that film. Dad has been following all the gossip about the stars in the "Mirror" and "News of the World", shaking his head at their goings on but lapping it up all the same.

'Oh, that's lovely, isn't it Brian? I really want to see it too,' she hints wistfully to her husband, who merely grunts and picks up his newspaper. At the cinema they head straight for the back row. As usual, Michael puts his arm round her and pulls her close but that is all. Normally, he would run his hand up her leg under her skirt or slip it under her waistband to stroke her tummy. More than once, they both got so excited that they had to leave the cinema and find somewhere quiet. Maggie wonders if he's going off her, and sneaks a glance at him, but he does seem to be totally engrossed in the film. Relieved, she thinks *Don't be daft, he's just tired, Sit back and enjoy the film.* It is just as spectacular as the newspapers predicted, especially the scene where Cleopatra enters Rome. Maggie turns to share her appreciation with Michael, but he is sound asleep.

She needn't have worried because Michael is back to normal the next time they meet. He is as ardent and passionate as ever but they both miss the intimacy of the long nights they shared together in Spain. Somehow, their love-making is not as satisfying as it was there. Things come to a head one evening when they are alone at Maggie's parents. Her dad has gone to his weekly skittles match and Mum has popped round to her neighbours with a bowl of tomatoes from their garden. As soon as the front door closes Michael grabs Maggie:

'Come on, quick, before she comes back'. He pulls up her skirt. Knowing her mum might walk in at any moment seems to fuel his passion but Maggie can't relax. Instead of whispering sweet nothings she keeps urging him to hurry up. This is a serious problem because Michael is used to women who enjoy having sex with him. Afterwards, while they are rearranging their clothing he says,

'This is useless, we'll have to get married.'

'Isn't that normally what people say when there's a baby on the way?'

'I'm serious Maggie. My boss promised me a rise if I pass my exams and I'm sure I've done well; if I have, we'll be able to afford a flat, so what are we waiting for?'

'All right, if you're sure it's what you want. When shall we tell my parents?'

As proposals go, it is not the most romantic, but when Maggie's dad comes back from the pub they break the news. Mum is delighted and gives them both a big kiss, while her father begins calculating how they can afford to pay for the wedding. Michael goes off to get some celebratory drinks from the off licence before it closes, leaving Maggie feeling a bit flat. She really loves Michael, she has no doubts on that score, but it all seems rather matter-of fact. He returns in record time carrying a bag full of bottles and assorted nuts and potato crisps.

'Right, I've bought beer for us blokes and champagne for the ladies. Come on Mrs Jenkins, shove the champers in your fridge while I give my fiancé a proper kiss'. He pulls Maggie into his arms and kisses her deeply.

'Now you're officially the future Mrs Johnson', he smiles down at her. As she looks up at her handsome husband to be, she chides herself for her silly schoolgirl, ideas. She is going to marry the sweetest, most loving boy in the world. What more could any girl ask?

The following Saturday Michael buys her an engagement ring. Within minutes of arriving at the jewellers he has charmed the assistant, who goes out of her way to help them find the right ring. Eventually they narrow it down to two. One of them, a small solitaire diamond surrounded by tiny diamond chips, is quite a bit more expensive than the other. Maggie, brought up to mind the pennies, is leaning towards the cheaper one but the assistant intervenes.

'I think the solitaire suits you better Miss. I could ask my manager if he can give you a discount, Sir,' she offers. It turns out that the manager can, so the deal is done.

Before they leave the shop, Michael tells the assistant.

'This ring is only temporary. Once we're on our feet I'll be back to buy her a bigger diamond.' The girl smiles politely but secretly she envies Maggie. She really wishes she could get a good-looking, dynamic boyfriend like Michael. Maggie, however, is having none of his blarney.

'No, it isn't temporary Michael, It's my engagement ring. I love it, why would I ever want to change it?'

'Because you deserve the best and I'm going to give it to you, you'll see.'

Maggie isn't listening, she keeps checking to make sure the ring is still there, turning her hand this way and that to admire it under the artificial light.

They start planning the wedding straight away. Maggie's dad stipulates that it must take place in church, even though no-one can remember the last time he set foot in one. Maggie doesn't mind, she's already picturing herself walking down the aisle in a long dress, fitted in the right places to flatter her curves. Her parents also take it for granted that the reception will take place in the local community centre, so Maggie books it as soon as the wedding date is fixed. Linda ropes in her friend Megan, who works in a primary school, to help decorate the hall. Megan is used to putting up classroom friezes and is a dab hand with balloons and banners, so the two friends spend the afternoon before the wedding working on the decorations. Linda is determined to transform the utilitarian space into a fairy tale wedding venue for Maggie.

'I'll have to come back tomorrow to take the decorations down and clean the room, ready for the playgroup on Monday, Linda tells Megan. 'Do you fancy coming round to help me again? Tom says he'll help but he's certain to have a hangover, so I don't expect he'll be much use." Everyone pitches in to help with the arrangements, so the wedding is organised so quickly that Maggie's dad starts worrying again that she might be pregnant.

After much discussion they decide not to go on honeymoon. Maggie's parents think it is clearly more sensible to concentrate on equipping their new home, and Michael's widowed mother agrees. Although Maggie has always had romantic fantasies about her honeymoon, she doesn't really mind because Michael whispers in her ear

'Never mind Love, we've had the honeymoon already, haven't we?' when he thinks Dad isn't listening.

Michael's boss makes good on his promise of a pay rise and they find a flat within their budget not too far from Maggie's office. It is on the ground floor of an old Victorian end of terrace house. Although it is advertised as having two bedrooms, the smaller one is unusable because there is damp running down the walls, and boxes of discarded books and toys take up the space beside the mouldy old bed. Behind the bedrooms is a tiny lounge with a gas fire which provides the only heating. Tacked on to the back of the lounge is a lean-to with a glass roof into which a kitchen and a bathroom have been squeezed. There's only room for a bath in the bathroom, so the toilet is outside in the yard. It doesn't have any lighting and after using it you have to return to the kitchen to wash your hands in the kitchen sink. Inexplicably, there is a grand piano in the front bedroom. Soon after they move in the landlady, who lives upstairs, waylays Maggie as she is leaving for work one morning.

'Hello Dear, off to work? I just wanted to let you know that you're welcome to play the piano any time you like. Feel free. It's worth a lot of money, though, so you will look after it and keep it polished for me, won't you?' Naturally, Maggie feels obliged to buy a tin of polish and use it on the piano every weekend, but Michael just laughs and tells her not to make it too slippery in case they ever want to make love on it.

They quickly fall into a weekend routine of waking up later than usual then making love, followed by a late breakfast. Maggie usually prepares it, although sometimes she longs for a romantic gesture from Michael, such as bringing her breakfast in bed for a change. But how can she resist when he tells her that 'No-one scrambles eggs like you do, Love' stroking her behind as she gets out of bed. There are no laundry facilities in the flat, so after breakfast Maggie gathers up all their washing and heads off for an afternoon at the launderette, leaving Michael to pursue his own plans. Sometimes she worries that she's in danger of turning into her mother.

CHAPTER 3

Maggie is pregnant the first time finds out that Michael is having an affair. They are living in their first house by then, a nice little semi-detached near to the bus station. Soon after the wedding Michael, who is never satisfied, set his sights on buying their own property. They start putting away every spare penny for the deposit, but despite their combined salaries they find it difficult to save while they are paying rent. Added to that, it soon becomes clear to Maggie that Michael finds it almost impossible to give up his creature comforts.

This is doubly annoying because she is quite willing to economise on clothes and other luxuries. When he first suggested that they should start saving, her response was

'I've got a wardrobe full of clothes, they'll do me for a while. Anyway, I won't need so many clothes because we won't be going out much, will we?' But then Michael sabotages her efforts by buying her a set of expensive underwear from the new Janet Reger shop on the High street. What makes it worse, he seems incapable of staying at home in the evening. If Maggie says she is too tired to go out, he simply goes on his own. Some instinct tells her not to let him go solo too often, so she feels compelled to accompany him. Even if they only pop round to Linda and Tom's, he insists on stopping at the off licence on the way.

'We don't want them to think we're cheapskates, do we Love?'

Fortunately, the restless energy he channels into everything he does makes him invaluable at work, so when the company's site assessor retires, the job is offered to Michael. He is so excited when he gets home that day.

'It means I'm being promoted over more experienced people, but my boss says he's giving me the job because of my excellent customer relations skills. He thinks my personality will be invaluable in generating new business. It'll be brilliant, Mags. On top of the new salary, I'll be getting commission, so we'll be able to buy a house at last'.

Maggie insists on taking control of the extra income, so it does not take her long to save the few hundred pounds necessary for a deposit on a property. They start house hunting straight away and soon agree to purchase the neat little house. On the day they move in, Michael throws her onto the bed as soon as they have finished putting it together. The bedroom is the first room to be fully furnished because Michael says it is where they will spend most time. Maggie can well believe it. It takes them all day to move, packing up their possessions and ferrying them from the flat in Michael's little car, so the following morning Michael brings an exhausted Maggie tea in bed. She is only halfway through her drink when he takes away the mug and places it on the bedside table before pulling back the bed linen. He murmurs

'We can do this whenever we want to now' as he pulls up her nighty and starts kissing her. He's referring to the fact that Maggie was always uptight when they had sex at the flat because she was petrified that they would be overheard. Although the exterior walls were of solid Victorian brick, most of the interior had been partitioned off, so they could hear the landlady and her husband moving about and talking upstairs. Maggie thought it followed that they would be able to hear them making love on the ground floor below.

Over the next few years, they "Christen" every room in the house by having sex on each new flat surface as they gradually furnish their home. When the last item of furniture, an Ercol dining table, is in situ it is duly "Christened" in a complicated session which involves Maggie bending over and stretching out her arms so she can hang on to the edge of the table, Michael tells her 'You know we'll have to do this all over again in a few years' time when we move to a detached house'.

As soon as they know there is a baby on the way they turn the spare bedroom into a nursery. Michael paints it pale yellow then puts up a patterned pastel-coloured frieze. If he had his way the frieze would feature Mutley, his favourite cartoon character, but Maggie insists on having something suited to either sex, so they settle for one of the pretty new Laura Ashley designs.

It is a difficult pregnancy almost from the start. Maggie's morning sickness continues long after the usual three months and often carries over into the afternoon, so she never achieves the glowing radiance which is generally said to accompany pregnancy. It is because of this debilitating sickness that she discovers Michael's infidelity.

Maggie is in the general manager's office, helping him to co-ordinate the office holiday roster with that of the warehouse staff. She has been feeling particularly nauseous all day and she is struggling to concentrate on what her colleagues are saying. Her head is spinning and she's afraid she's going to throw up over her manager's desk. Actually, it is only the desk which is keeping her on her feet. She is leaning heavily against it, so when her boss glances up he takes in the almost green tinge of her skin.

'Maggie, you look awful, why don't you go home? Go on, I insist and don't come in tomorrow if you still feel grotty.'

So Maggie gets her coat and walks slowly down the street to the bus stop, where for once a bus comes along almost immediately. She gets on and sits with her head leaning against the bus window, grateful for the coolness of the glass against her cheek. In her handbag is an open paper bag in readiness for the vomiting which has threatened to overwhelm her for the past hour. She manages to hold it off until she reaches her stop, then gets off the bus and trudges towards home. When she reaches her street she notices a woman walking briskly in the opposite direction towards the corner . She looks like Clare from Michael's office. *'That's odd'* she thinks, dragging herself the last few metres and staggering up the garden path.

All she wants to do is draw her bedroom curtains, collapse onto her bed and sleep, so when she gets upstairs she is relieved to find that the curtains are still closed. *'I must have felt bad this morning',* she thinks as she steps out of her skirt. Normally, the first thing she does when she wakes up is open the curtains. Her head is still spinning as she unbuttons her shirt, but the cuff fastenings are giving her trouble as usual. While she is struggling Michael enters the room with a towel wrapped round his waist, rubbing his hair with a smaller one. He stops in his tracks then, recovering, goes over to sit beside her on the bed.

'Maggie, what are you doing home? What's wrong? You look terrible.'

'I felt too sick to work. Why are you here?'

'I popped in to change my shirt, got a meeting with George later. I thought I might as well have a shower before I change.' George is his managing director. Maggie is just drifting off into blissful oblivion when she remembers.

'But George is on holiday, you told me he went on Monday'. Michael rubs her shoulder and smiles down at her.

'Did I say George? I meant Malcolm, he's acting manager while George is away.'

'Oh, so what was Clare doing here?'

'Clare? She came with me on a site visit. I sent her back to the office to type up the report.' The foul-tasting, incapacitating bile rises at last, burning her throat and causing her stomach to heave. She pushes past Michael and rushes into the bathroom where she collapses onto the floor. Hanging onto the sides of the toilet, she vomits into it until her body feels as damp and as wrung out as a length of old rope. Exhausted, she pulls herself onto her feet and stands, gazing at her face in the mirror. She looks dreadful. She can see the open nursery door reflected in the mirror and notices for the first time the two pillows lying on the floor next to the cot. Alongside them are Michael's discarded clothes. She knows him too well not to realise what that pile of clothing means.

Michael puts his hand out to steady her as she exits the bathroom. He is not sure if she realises that he has slept with Clare in the baby's room, but she knocks his hand away.

'Don't touch me' she warns as she staggers back to the bedroom. Maggie looks so pale and wan that he is torn between concern for her well-being and the desire to wriggle out of the mess he has landed himself in. He stands at the door, afraid to approach her. After a minute's dithering he tries:

'Can I get you anything, Mags?' Summoning all her remaining strength Maggie screeches

'Get out, you scumbag'. He goes into the nursery, picks up his clothes and starts putting them on at the top of the stairs. When he has finished dressing, he tries again. "Are you sure you're all right, Love?'

'I said get out. Leave me alone, can't you?' She sounds so weary that his guilty feet are leaden as he goes down the stairs and leaves the house.

Ironically, Maggie feels much better when she wakes up next morning. Michael has left for work early leaving a mug of tea and a couple of ginger biscuits beside her the nightstand. She resists the temptation to hurl the mug against the wall and walks, zombie-like, into the bathroom. She notices that the pillows are no longer on the nursery floor and makes a mental note to find them and throw them in the bin later. For the moment, she needs the support of her best friend, so she gets dressed then makes her way to the bus stop, heading for Linda's house. Maggie realises that removing the pillows amounts to destroying the evidence, but she can't bear to think of Michael having sex with his lover in their baby's room. He doesn't even have sex with her in there. She does not give in to tears until she reaches Linda's house but as soon as she's inside the flood gates open.

They talk all day, but Linda is careful to confine her criticism to the behaviour of men in general. She does not say anything too derogatory about Michael because she's afraid of losing her best friend. Almost from the minute she opens her front door that morning, she is pretty sure that Maggie will forgive him. By the time they go to collect Ritchie from nursery school she is certain of it. Despite her tears, anger and obvious disappointment, Maggie makes no mention of divorce or even of splitting up. Growing up with her father as her male role model has conditioned her to the acceptance of male selfishness and her compliant nature has done the rest.

When Tom arrives home, he's surprised to find Maggie there.

'Hello, Maggie. You've started your maternity leave already, have you?' He bends down to give her a kiss. Maggie smiles wanly and tells him she is just feeling a bit under the weather, so she has taken a couple of days off. After she leaves, Tom comes back from the kitchen where he has been hiding.

'What's wrong with Maggie then, she's been crying, hasn't she?'

'I'll give you three guesses and they all begin with M'.

CHAPTER 4

When Maggie goes for her next maternity check-up, her doctor says he wants to send her for an ultra- sound.

'What does that mean, Doctor? What's an ultra- sound? Is there something wrong with the baby?'

'No, don't panic, baby's fine. An ultra- sound is a fairly new piece of equipment. It allows us to take photos of the baby in the womb. We'll be doing it routinely for every expectant mother soon'. As he begins writing up her notes he asks,

'Do you happen to know if there are twins in either your family or your husbands?'

'Why, do you think I'm having twins?'

'I do think there is a strong possibility that you've got two babies in there, but an ultra- sound should tell us for sure. The hospital will probably send you an appointment in the next two weeks. If you don't receive one, phone the surgery and we'll chase it up for you.'

Stunned, Maggie walks home. *Two babies? How can I possibly cope with two babies?* She is only just re-building her relationship with Michael after that terrible day when she found out he was cheating on her. She doesn't know if she can ever trust him again, but he has gradually won her over with ashamed apologies and promises that it will never happen again. She has also been swayed by the way that he has taken full responsibility for his behaviour.

'I'm an idiot, Maggie. You're the best, most beautiful girl in the world and I've let you down. I don't even know why. And I've taken advantage of Clare, an innocent young girl', he adds.

'I deserve to be shot'.

Maggie does not share Michael's conviction that Clare is innocent. There aren't many of those around nowadays from what she's heard. She does not tell him that of course, she is not that compliant. *Let him stew. An innocent young girl indeed! She's a tart if ever I saw one,* she tells herself, thereby doing what Michael failed to do himself, which is make excuses for him.

Maggie's mum goes to the hospital with her when she attends for the scan. She is not happy about Maggie having the procedure and keeps expressing her fears that it might harm the baby.

'I thought X rays are supposed to be dangerous. Why do you need to know if you are having twins anyway? If you are it'll be a nice surprise'.

'My doctor says that the mid-wife will monitor me more closely and I'll get extra appointments if I'm having twins, Mum'.

'I don't know why you need to have all these appointments either. I never saw a doctor when I had you and I didn't even meet the midwife until I went into labour.'

Maggie is nervous about having the scan herself and her mother's moaning is not helping.

'Oh, stop it Mum. Things are different now. Anyway, if you had seen a doctor, they might have found out why you never got pregnant again.'

She has hit a raw nerve. Her mother purses her lips and decides that she is not going to say another word, even though it is she who will have to pick up the pieces if this scan hurts the baby. A nurse calls Maggie's name and she starts to rise clumsily from her seat.

'Is Nanny coming in too?' the nurse smiles encouragingly at her mum, so they both get up and enter the room where a technician is waiting.

At first Maggie cannot make sense of what she sees on the screen. It just looks like a photo negative. The technician studies it for a moment then says

'Look, there's baby's head and that's the heart.' Transfixed, both mother and daughter watch the pulsing of the baby's tiny heart.

'Oh Maggie look, it's breathing, bless it'. Mum breaks her vow of silence.

'No, baby's not breathing yet, Nanny, that's its heartbeat'. And here's the top of another head and an arm, can you see?' The technician's seen it all before but she is still enchanted. She adds:

'There are definitely two of them. One's lying partly in front of the other one. Do you get a lot of heart burn?'

'No, but I am sick a lot.' Maggie isn't really listening. As she gazes at the photo of the two little heads her entire body is flooded by a torrent of emotion. It is the first time that she really feels the power of her love for her babies. Michael's ecstatic when he hears the news.

'Wow, two babies Maggie. I hope we have a boy and a girl. We must be really fertile, don't you think?' Maggie knows he is equating fertility with virility. *You'd think fathering twins means he is exceptionally virile, some kind of Superman,* she tells herself. Although she is really trying hard to put thoughts of his infidelity behind her, aspects of his personality which she previously found endearing have started to irritate her. She still loves Michael but now she has taken off her rose-tinted glasses. Quite soon after she found out, Maggie told her mother about the affair. She had a vague idea that Mum would somehow intervene and give Michael a good talking to, but she is disappointed.

'Well, what do you expect, Maggie? You're always under the weather, you look awful most of the time and you've probably gone off of sex, haven't you?' Maggie is astonished, her mother has never referred to sex in such a personal way before. Mum continues,

'A lot of men look for sex elsewhere when their wives are pregnant, it's only natural, they still have needs. In a way they're doing their wives a favour by not bothering them.' Maggie has always found it difficult to visualise her staid mother and dour father having sex, but now she wonders if her father was one of those men who looked elsewhere. She could kick herself for not being more suspicious of Michael in the past, remembering those times when he had to be away overnight or stay very late at the office. Clearly, she is going to have to be more vigilant and less trusting in future.

Maggie gives birth to two little boys nearly four weeks early in an uncomplicated, straightforward delivery. After the first baby is born she gasps to the midwife:

'No, I can't do it again' but the contractions re-start almost immediately and the second twin arrives only minutes after the first. Once the babies are clean and dressed the midwife and a nurse bring them over to Maggie's bed.

'Here you are, Mrs Johnson, two bouncing boys. One weighs five and a half pounds and the other six pounds two ounces.' Maggie leans back on the pillows which are propped up behind her, too exhausted to move.

''That's a bit small isn't it, are they both OK?'

'They're fine, absolute hunks. Twins are usually on the small side, but they soon catch up. Shall we ask Dad to come in now?

Michael and Maggie's mum are waiting anxiously outside the delivery room. They come in and Mum makes straight for the cots while Michael sits on the edge of the bed and kisses Maggie.

'How are you feeling, Love? Nurse said you had a nice, easy labour'.

'Easy! She should try it. I'm never doing that again.' He strokes her hair back from her forehead and kisses her again then goes and picks up one of the twins.

'I think this one looks like me, do you? Is he Mathew?' They have only agreed on one boy's name because Michael was convinced that one of the babies would be a girl. Mum comes over to the bed carrying the other baby.

'If he's Mathew can this one be Joseph, after my father?' Michael brings the first baby to Maggie and places him in her arms.

'Mathew and Joseph, what do you think, Mags?' She lays both babies on her lap side by side then bends forward and kisses each tiny cheek.

'Hello Mathew and Joseph,' she smiles'.

CHAPTER 5

Maggie's worries about coping with two babies turn out to be justified and she feels as if she is constantly running on a treadmill which won't slow down. Every chore has to be duplicated. When she bathes the tiny twins, the first is crying for attention again by the time she's finished washing the second one. She is constantly exhausted and she feels as though one of them is always screaming. If Maggie picks up Mathew, Joseph starts crying, even if he is asleep at the time. Joseph seems to sense when his brother is being given attention and it is already clear that he's going to compete for his share.

Maggie had intended to return to work part-time when her baby was ten weeks old, leaving the infant in the care of her mother. Her father was not particularly happy at the prospect of having to fend for himself occasionally. Even before they knew Maggie was expecting twins, he had announced that, if his wife was planning to help out with her grandchild's care, . he would still expect his tea to be ready on time. Now, with two very demanding babies instead of one, it is clear that Maggie's mum would not be able to look after both of them, especially with the prospect of an irate husband waiting for her at home.

With no other child- care facilities available, returning to work is not an option for Maggie at present. She feels trapped. Despite her love for the twins, the thought of long days at home with two screaming babies fills her with dread. It is difficult enough to travel by bus with one small baby and all its paraphernalia; carrying two would be impossible. To make matters worse, now that she has been pronounced fit after her post-natal check-up, Michael is as sexually demanding as ever. Once the twins are safely asleep in the evening Maggie just wants to collapse on the sofa, but she knows that at any

44

minute Michael will be snuggling up beside her with only one thing on his mind. She enjoys the fore play as much as ever, but she just does not have the energy for anything more. Maggie knows that she should have a sensible discussion with Michael about limiting the frequency of their love making temporarily, but whenever she screws up her courage to discuss it, she remembers her mother's words:

"It's only natural that men look elsewhere".

So Maggie does what thousands of young mothers are doing all over the country – she puts up with the loneliness and frustration of long, tiring days and inadequate sleep and just gets on with it. Once a week, Mum spends the day with Maggie to help out with the boys and it's noticeable that Joseph doesn't cry so much when she's there. Linda also spends time with Maggie as often as possible and these visits are like an oasis in a desert of loneliness. Michael does not understand why Maggie feels lonely at home. 'You've got plenty to do all day, Mags, and you've got the boys with you. You should make the most of your time with them, they'll be off to school before you know it'.

Everything changes when the Maclaren buggy is introduced into the UK. They buy a double, and Maggie starts taking the boys for long walks every day. She feels much better now that she can get out in the fresh air and the twins are beginning to settle into a routine. The exercise brings colour to her cheeks and she begins to feel more positive. She has been trying to take advantage of her time at home to read more so she often takes the opportunity to pop into the library while she's out. One of the librarians, Maria, always makes a fuss of the boys, telling Maggie to leave the buggy by her desk while she chooses something new to read. The twins are becoming much more alert now, smiling toothless miles and gurgling back at admirers from their nest of blankets. It is while she is at the library that Maggie notices the poster advertising an open day for part-time classes at the local college. The librarian notices that she is reading the poster and comes over.

'Are you thinking of enrolling? You may as well, Mrs Johnson. You get through so many books, you could get some extra qualifications while you are at it. Do you have many certificates?'

'Only O levels. They were all A's or B's though'.

'Well have you thought about getting some A levels while you're at home with the boys?'

'I'd love to but who would look after them while I was at college?

'But you wouldn't be at college all day. They do all sorts of part time courses now,

O levels, A levels as well as subjects like languages or drawing. Part-time courses are usually intensive, one three- hour session a week. Surely you could find someone to look after them for three hours?'

Maria is very good at promoting the college and is a strong supporter of continuing education. She is so persuasive that Maggie goes to the open day, buggy in the vanguard, and signs up for A level classes in English Land History. She has calculated that she should only be out of the house for four hours, including travel time, for each class. English is in the morning and she is sure that her Mum will agree to look after the twins for a few hours, particularly if Linda comes over to help her. History is another matter because the class takes place in the evening, so Michael will have to take sole charge of them. It is not that he isn't good with the boys, he is a great dad. Now that they've become more alert, he spends ages playing with them. In the evening while she is busy at the kitchen sink Maggie often smiles at the chuckles of delight coming from the sitting room where she knows Michael is probably swinging one or other of them up into the air. He is already looking forward to the time when they will be old enough to go to football matches with him. Despite this, Maggie postpones telling him that she is going to college in September. She knows she is behaving like Mum, burying her head in the sand, but she can't help it.

When she does tell him, his response is even worse than she expected. 'What do you want to be studying for? Haven't you got enough to do looking after the boys? Forget it Mags, it's just a waste of time.'

'But it's not a waste of time, I could get qualifications which would help me get a better job when I go back to work.'

'And why would you want to go back to work? I earn enough for all of us now and if you're bored you could always get a little part-time job once the boys are in school. Like Linda did, what's wrong with that?'

'There's nothing wrong with it, but I'm not Linda. She's happy with her little part-time job but I want to do something more fulfilling, make something of myself. If I don't try to do that while I have the chance, I'll always regret it.'

'But you have made something of yourself. You are a married woman, mother of two beautiful boys and the best-looking wife of anyone I know. What more do you want?' Maggie has slimmed down thanks to her long walks with the children. They have transformed her from a pretty but rather dumpy girl into a very desirable woman. Clearly Michael has taken note of this, but she is not one bit flattered. She has been reading some feminist literature which has only served to confirm what she has long suspected, that the subjection of women at every level is inbuilt within our society and culture.

'Well, I've made up my mind, Michael, so just make sure you're home on time every Tuesday evening from the fifteenth of September. And don't make any arrangements to go out again, either'.

Michael does not give up that easily, however. First, he tries to get Maggie's dad on side.

'What do you think about Maggie signing up for evening classes then, Mr Jenkins? She didn't even consult me.'

'What, she wants to learn flower arranging or something, does she? I suppose there's no harm in it, but I'd get her to take cookery lessons if I were you. I wouldn't let my wife sign up to anything without asking me first, though. And so long as she doesn't expect her mother to baby sit for her,' he adds, warming to his theme. So Michael begins coming home from work later than usual on Tuesdays as September approaches.

'We have so much work piling up after the weekends that it's the only way I can catch up', he tells Maggie.

'Catch up on Mondays then. I'm going to that class whether you like it or not, even if I have to take the twins with me and leave them in the corridor outside. I mean it, Michael.' Maggie knows that she would never leave her precious babies unattended, but as it happens the threat worked because Michael comes home bright and early on Tuesday the fifteenth and waves goodbye to her from the front door with a twin on either arm.

From that first evening, Maggie is in her element. For a start the history tutor, Duncan, is totally different to any teacher she has previously known. He bounces into the room and looks around at his new students before saying,

'Welcome, everyone. My name is Duncan and my mission in life is to dispel the idea that history can ever be boring. If you're here to learn about kings and queens you're in the wrong room. I'm here to talk to you about ordinary people, society from the bottom up. Together we'll try to understand the historical forces which have made our country what it is today.

Now, first things first. Are there any smokers here?' When some of the class hesitantly raise their hands, he goes on, '

Good, then we'll take a short break half-way through the evening. Only ten minutes though, I know exactly how long a quick cigarette takes and I don't take kindly to malingering'. Despite his light-hearted manner, the class understands that he means it. At break time some of the students file out quickly, giving the others an opportunity to get to know each other. They are a mixed bag. Some, like Maggie, are there to 'better themselves' while several younger people want to improve their grades, with university in mind. The oldest people there, a couple named John and Steff, must be at least sixty.

'We like to take a couple of classes every year, don't we love?' John asks his wife affectionately. 'We're not bothered about passing exams, we just want to learn about all the stuff we missed out on at school'.

Maggie, in contrast, makes up her mind from the start that she is going to pass the exams with flying colours. It is not always easy to keep up with the work, especially when the boys start teething. She prefers to do her homework in the evening when they are asleep but as soon as she gets out her books Michael tries to distract her,

49

nuzzling her neck and trying to tempt her up to the bedroom. Despite this, since it became clear that the classes are important to Maggie, he has become unexpectedly supportive, though it does annoy her when he refers to them as "her little hobby". This is particularly irritating because Michael has become engrossed in his own job, often bringing home work to do in the evenings.

He has been trying to persuade his company directors to branch out into sales, arguing that no-one is better placed to supply electrical components than a company whose business is installing them. Moreover, it is clear to him that their installation profits would increase, since all the materials they used would be at cost price from their own stock. He has started poring over manufacturers' catalogues in the evening, trying to put together a convincing case. Now they frequently work at the dining table together until Michael tells Maggie it's time for bed, while the look in his eyes tells her that it's time for love.

CHAPTER 6

By the time college breaks up for the Easter holiday the boys are walking. Joseph, now known as JJ, is still slightly smaller than Matty but he is as determined as ever to get the better of his brother. He is always trying to push in front on his unsteady little legs in order to snatch a toy or get on the push-along first. Michael and Maggie's dad, who is now tremendously proud of his grandsons, find this hilarious but Maggie fears that their rivalry does not bode well for the future. She is astonished at how often her father manages to tear himself away from his armchair and slippers these days to accompany her mother on her visits, but she can't help wondering whether it would have been another story if she had given birth to girls.

Linda is also devoted to the twins. She is pregnant again and determined to have another boy so that her baby and the twins can be best friends, with Ritchie as their older brother and role model. Maggie really appreciates all the support she is receiving from her parents and Linda now that her exams are fast approaching. She worries constantly that she will fail them, even though she has received good grades for her course work, so Duncan offers to give her extra help. 'Why don't you come to college on Wednesday? I have a two- hour window free between one and three. If you can make it then I'll try to find an empty room where we won't be disturbed'. Maggie's mum, Mary, is quite happy to look after the boys for an extra afternoon. Actually, since she has been going to Maggie's to baby- sit she gets very bored when she is at home. She has not had to get up and leave the house early since she was married, so looking after her grandsons has given her a new sense of purpose. She calls it her part-time job.

On Wednesday afternoon the twins are already having their nap When Mary arrives at Maggie's house .

'You just get yourself off, they'll be fine. I'm quite capable of getting them something to eat when they wake up, Maggie.' With Maggie safely on her way, Mary takes out her paper-back and sits down to enjoy a quiet half hour, but it's no good good, she cannot concentrate. She puts down her book and creeps upstairs to check on the twins. Their cots are lined up against the wall head to tail, taking up the length of the tiny bedroom, and JJ has pushed his arm through the bars at the base of Matty's cot. It is as if he is trying to colonise his brother's space. *'We're going to have trouble with these two rascals'* Mary thinks, gently pulling JJ's arm back through the bars. She inhales, relishing the irresistible scent which is unique to young children, knowing that the twins won't retain it for much longer, then she goes back downstairs and picks up her book.

Meanwhile, Maggie has arrived at the college. She goes up to the staff room where she arranged to meet Duncan, carrying her heavy bag of books.

'Maggie, we have a slight problem. There isn't an empty room available this afternoon, so we have two options. We could go to the library to work, but the librarian will probably keep shushing us, or we could walk along to "The Poets' Corner " pub. Do you know it? They have booths there so we should be able to find a quiet corner. What do you think?' Maggie thinks that the pub sounds the best option if she is going to make the most of this extra tuition, so they set off together. Walking along in the balmy spring sunshine is exhilarating and Maggie feels quite daring to be going to the pub with a man, even if he is only her tutor. She knows her father would be horrified. Thank goodness Michael is not so old-fashioned.

The pub is not very busy when they get there, so Duncan asks her to find a quiet booth while he gets them both a drink. The only empty booth is the one closest to the bar so Maggie slides along the bench seat and uses her hanky to mop up the beer spilt on the table. The yeasty odour of beer permeates the walls of the booth, bringing back memories of rainy caravan holidays when her dad would have a drink in the van while Maggie and her mum curled up on the bunks, listening to the rain pattering on the roof. Duncan is chatting to the barman and reaching into his pocket for his wallet when a young woman comes in. She stands near to the door, clearly waiting for someone. She is very attractive, with sleek fair hair, stiletto-heeled shoes and a smart business suit. She is the embodiment of Maggie's aspirations, a successful professional. The door swings open again and this time it's Michael who enters. He places his arm lightly around the woman's back and steers her to a seat by the window, then looks around the room. . He spots Maggie straight away and responds to her hesitant little wave by coming over to the booth. He gets there just as Duncan comes back carrying two glasses., so they arrive at the booth together. They both hesitate, sizing each other up before Michael says, bunking off, Maggie? I thought you were going to college this afternoon'.

'I did go but there wasn't a free room we could use, so we came here to work. We thought it would be quieter.' She indicates her books piled on the table, irritated that she is flustered even though she has no reason to be. 'This is my history tutor, Duncan, by the way.' Michael turns on the charm immediately. 'It's nice to meet you, Duncan. It's very good of you to give up your time to help my wife. You're really going the extra mile for her'.

'Not at all. It's my job to help all my students but Maggie is exceptional, she's so determined to do well that it's a pleasure to work with her'.

'Well, I'd like to stay and chat with you, but I can see that my wife is keen to get on with her work and I must get back to my companion. I'm hoping she'll come in with my firm on a new business venture'. Maggie understands that this last is directed at her and she has also clocked his proprietorial use of 'my wife'. No doubt they'll have words later on, but she is determined not to waste time worrying about it now, so she takes a sip of her orange juice and opens her note-book.

When she gets home her mum is sitting on the floor with the twins, helping them to build with wooden blocks. JJ places his bricks carefully, creating a surprisingly uniform tower, while Matt slaps the blocks down in a haphazard pile which soon topples over. When his wobbly creation collapses, he lashes out, knocking down JJ's tower too. JJ, red-faced, lets out a yell which is fortunately cut short by the sight of his mother. Both twins push themselves to their feet, bottoms in the air, and toddle towards her, grabbing at her legs. She wraps an arm around each of their torsos and picks them both up, then sinks back onto the sofa, afraid of dropping one. 'Give me kisses' she orders, then places big smackers on each of their cheeks, receiving dribbly kisses in return. JJ tries to turn her face away from Matty so that Maggie focuses on him, so Mary takes JJ onto her lap and asks:

'Where's my kiss then?'' Maggie suspects that JJ is her mother's favourite, although she strenuously denies any preference, but Maggie loves them both equally, fanatically even. Every time she returns after leaving them, even after a very short absence, Maggie is struck by how adorable they are. They are not so sweet when their nappy needs changing, however, so the acrid, disgusting stink which suddenly rises from Matty's backside prompts her to go in search of the changing mat.

Maggie's dad is coming over straight from work that evening, so Michael is getting fish and chips for all of them on his way home. She is grateful for her parent's presence today because it gives her time to think about what she is going to say to Michael later on. She is not sure she believes that he had a business meeting with the blonde woman. There are plenty of places nearer to his office where they could meet. On the other hand, why choose a window seat where they would be in easy view of anyone passing along the road. If he wanted to avoid being seen? Backwards and forwards, she rehearses this argument in her head as they all eat their supper. Michael has brought beers and a bottle of wine with the food and Maggie knows her dad is unlikely to leave until all the beer has been drunk. This is so frustrating because Maggie has made up her mind. As soon as her parents leave, she is just going to come out with it and accuse Michael of having another affair.

It turns out that she does not have to wait that long because he pre-empts her. When Mary, sensing an atmosphere, asks 'You're very quiet, Maggie. Is everything all right?'

Michael jumps in. 'She's probably thinking about her sexy history teacher'.

'Don't be ridiculous, Michael. Anyway, I wouldn't call Duncan sexy.'

'Oh, you haven't noticed that he's a good-looking bloke then?'

'No. I've only noticed that he's a good teacher'. This is a lie. Duncan is very good-looking and she would have to be blind not to notice. He is also funny and charming. Several of the other students have a crush on him and the word around the college is that he has had a string of girlfriends. Even Maggie has wondered what it would be like to be one of those girls, though she would never do anything about it, of course. Her thoughts are interrupted by Michael, who is obviously determined to fight fire with fire. 'Well, just so you know, he's obviously queer.'

'If he is that's his business, but how do you know that, Michael?'

'I can tell. He's as queer as a nine- bob note, it's obvious'.

'Well, you know what they say, it takes one to know one. Anyway, while we're on the subject, what exactly do you expect that woman to do for your company?' Mary gets to her feet, anxious to avoid the coming argument.

'It's time for us to go, drink up Brian. I'll get my coat.' She goes out to the entrance hall and when she returns, she is already slipping her arms though the sleeves of her coat. After her parents have left, her father clutching a half empty bottle of beer, Maggie returns to the attack. 'Go on, who was that woman? And don't pretend you don't know who I'm talking about.'

'If you're talking about the lady I was with in the pub, she works for Jamison's, the builder's merchants. She's their buyer and she knows everything there is to know about building supplies. She has good contacts, so if we do go ahead and diversify, she could get us substantial discounts. That's if she accepts a job with us.'

'And why would she leave a good job at Jamisons' to work for a piddly little company like yours?'

'It won't be little. Why are you being so negative, Mags? I'm really excited about this venture.'

'I'm not being negative; I just want to be sure you're not sleeping with her.'

'And I want to be sure you don't fancy that Duncan. '

'Oh, so it's all right for you to go out with a business acquaintance, but I can't, is that what you're saying?'

'Of course I'm not saying that. It's just that I was shocked when I found you in a pub when you were supposed to be at college, and then it turned out you were with some toffee-nosed twit. All right, I admit I was jealous.'

'Michael, once I've finished my studies I'll be going back to work. I want a proper career, not a dead-end job, so I'll probably be having lunch or drinks with a male colleague or a client occasionally. If you can't handle that then we have a problem.'

'No, there's no problem, I'm an idiot. Actually, I'm proud of you for being so ambitious, haven't you realised that? Come here.' He pulls her against him and kisses her face, then her throat. He's trying to find her breast but the neck of her blouse is buttoned too tightly so he pulls it out of her skirt from the waist then slides his fingers under the waistband. He knows she cannot resist him when he strokes her belly like this. 'Come on, Love, let's go upstairs before one of the boys wakes up.' By the time they have finished making love it does not seem the right time to ask about the blond woman again and anyway, Maggie is not in the mood to start another row.

CHAPTER 7

The summer of 1966 is dull and wet, but nothing can dampen Michael's enthusiasm for the new business venture. His company has rented a neglected bomb site with the option to purchase later. Planning permission for a new housing estate nearby is in the pipeline and if it is granted the bomb site will be in prime position for a warehouse. Its proximity would enable the company to supply materials to the developers at short notice and also reduce delivery costs.. If the planning application is approved Michael will be given a directorship with responsibility for setting up and running the new department. 'I won't get a rise, Love, but I'll get commission on all sales, and a cut of the savings on materials we use for our own installations. If it's a success, we'll be laughing all the way to the bank' he tells Maggie excitedly.'

But Maggie is preoccupied with her up-coming exam results. She cannot concentrate on anything else and has pushed aside all thoughts about the blond woman. As it is so wet outside, the boys cannot play in their tiny garden, so she still takes them for long walks in the buggy. Today she has decided to walk down to the beach. If the rain gets too heavy, there are shops and cafes nearby to which they can retreat. When they reach the beach, the sea is the colour of gun metal, making the water appear sluggish despite the ease with which the wind which is tossing white- tipped splashes of water onto the pebbles. Maggie loves the salty, fishy smell of the wind coming off the water, even though she knows it must be tangling her hair and creating a frizzy mop which she will have to sort out later.

They are going for a meal with Linda and Tom tonight; it will probably be Linda's last outing before the new baby comes. *'I'll have to get out the iron and straighten it when I get home'* she plans. The wind suddenly rises, blowing a fine drizzle under the canopy of the buggy . It is met with howls from the boys so Maggie bends to adjust the waterproof apron covering them. They're both rosy-cheeked so she's not sure if they're howling with delight or fear, but when the next gust takes JJ's breath away she knows it is time to beat a retreat.

At the café it is clear that she is not the only person to run away from the weather because the tables are all taken. One of them is occupied by a lone woman who looks as if she is working, judging by a book and a pile of typed documents on the table in front of her. Maggie goes over and parks the buggy near to her table. 'Would you mind if I joined you, I promise we'll be quiet'. The woman, who is probably in her thirties, smiles 'Oh, you don't have to be quiet, I'd be glad of a break. What sweet children, are they yours?'

'Yes, but they're not always sweet. They can be little horrors.'

'I can believe that, I have two of my own. They're both in high school now and you can't tell them anything. They think they know it all.' As if on cue, Matty throws his drinking cup out of the buggy and it hits Maggie's leg. The top comes off and squash runs down her bare shin, so she takes a paper serviette from the table to wipe it off. 'See what I mean? Horrors' and both women smile. 'Are you sure we're not stopping you from working?'

'No, it's fine. I'm just going over my dissertation for the last time before I hand it in. I should have submitted it three weeks ago but I asked for an extension, they're more lenient with mature students.'

'Oh, I thought you must be a teacher or something'.

'I haven't decided what I want to do after I graduate, but teaching is one of the options. It would be good to have school holidays off so I can keep an eye on the kids. They're getting a bit too much for my mother-in-law.'

'I bet they are. So did you type your dissertation yourself?'

'Yes, everything has to be typed, you can't submit hand-written work. Actually, it's much better if you can type your own work, otherwise you have to pay someone else to do it.'

'Do students actually do that?'

'Oh yes, especially the younger ones. Mature students often know how to type because they've had office experience. It's a great advantage if you can type your own work, otherwise you have to check someone else's typing ad that takes extra time. You're not a graduate then?'

'No, I've just taken two A levels, though, and I don't really know what to do next if I pass'.

'Why don't you apply for a place at university? You'd probably get in with two A levels as a mature student, though I think it might be too late to apply for this September. Why don't you take another A level and apply for a place next year? You'd be sure to get in with three and your kids would be that much older then, too.' Maggie goes to the counter and orders drinks. When she comes back she asks 'So what's this dissertation about?'

'The romantic hero in Victorian Literature'. Don't look like that, it's a very serious subject. I've linked it to patriarchal Victorian society and its effect on women.'

'Wow, I'm impressed.' It is true, Maggie can't imagine that she will ever be able to write anything so intellectual'.

'Don't be. It's all recycled ideas from other academics. You're not expected to produce anything original when you're an undergraduate. Anyway, I've bored you enough. Tell me, what are your little horrors called?'

The "little horrors" are getting hungry and it will soon be time for their afternoon nap. Maggie will have to sort out her hair while they are asleep and her leg is starting to feel sticky and uncomfortable from its dousing of squash, so she says goodbye and leaves soon after that.

CHAPTER 8

Towards the end of July the weather brightens up, becoming warmer, drier and much less depressing. This improvement coincides with welcome, if somewhat scary, news. The planning application for the new housing development is approved, galvanising Michael into organising the construction of a pre-fabricated warehouse. He is so energetic and enthusiastic that Maggie is reminded of the young man she first met. *'Perhaps I've been a bit too hard on him since he had that affair. Everyone makes mistakes and apart from that one slip-up he's been the perfect husband'*. She knows that she has not shown much interest in his new project recently, she has been too preoccupied with college and exams, so now that they are behind her she is determined to pay him more attention.

A few days later Linda gives birth to a little girl. She is so perfect and sweet, with curly fair hair and plump, pink little cheeks, that no-one remembers that she wanted a boy. When Matty and JJ go with their mother to view the new arrival, the swaddled baby girl is something of a disappointment for them. They had been led to expect a friend and playmate. Matty, always anxious to please, stakes his claim anyway. 'Bubba fren' he states, extending his fore finger. The baby's tiny fingers immediately curl around it, making him smile in delight. Predictably, JJ challenges him. 'No, JJ' he shouts, scowling at his brother across the bassinette.

'The baby will be friends with both of you when she gets bigger', Maggie promises, picking up the fractious JJ and holding him over the cot so that he can plant a sloppy kiss on the tiny head.

A few days after that, Maggie receives her exam results. They are posted on the college notice board, but when she gets there a throng of other students is gathered in front of the board, blocking her view. Layla, one of her history classmates, arrives and they wait together for their turn in front of the results lists .pinned on the boards. Maggie is so nervous that she feels physically sick and it does not help that Duncan is among the lecturers who are gathered to congratulate, or commiserate, with their students. He will be so disappointed if she fails, he is always saying he has high hopes for her and he's been so helpful, she will feel awful if she lets him down.

Some of the students move away, leaving a space in front of the notices. 'Come on, Maggie, let's do this together.' Layla drags her to the front and it doesn't take long for Layla to find her results because her Surname is Ali. She lets out a loud, triumphant 'Yes' when she finds she has a B and a C, then runs her finger further down the list, looking for Maggie's results.

'I can't stand this, I can't look. You tell me how I did,' says Maggie, moving away from the board. Layla finds her name further down. When she has finished reading she comes over to Maggie and after a dramatic pause yells:

'You're a bloody genius, Maggie Johnson, you got two A's. Come on, see for yourself'. Maggie goes over and follows Layla's pointing finger. She is right, Maggie can hardly believe it, an A for both History and English. The two girls hug each other, laughing, and then Layla steps aside for Duncan, who also gives Maggie a hug.

'I knew you could do it, it's well deserved. Well done Maggie.' He kisses Maggie on the cheek, then after a pause kisses Layla as well.

'And well done you, Layla. I'm proud of you both'. Layla is a single mum whose parents will have nothing to do with her since she left her violent husband. She works full time in a bakery and leaves her three year-old daughter with a friend when she attends evening classes. Michael does not like her, he doesn't approve of single mothers, but she and Maggie have become good friends.

'Oh, I promised to phone Michael as soon as I get my results, he'll be waiting to hear from me. Where's the nearest phone box?' Duncan, who is busy speaking to other students, notices the two girls leaving and calls after them,

'I'll see you both on Friday then.' The history class have arranged to go for a drink together on Friday and Duncan has been invited to join them.

'Somebody fancies you', Layla sings in Maggie's ear as they go in search of a phone box.

'Don't be daft, he's got all those young girls gagging for him'. But Maggie does not need to ask who Layla is talking about.

Most of the class turn up for a drink on Friday and Maggie suspects that the people who didn't come probably didn't get the results they hoped for, because everyone there is in buoyant mood. Duncan arrives and insists on buying everyone a drink, then John buys several bottles of wine which they fall upon. Maggie is on a high from a combination of excitement and too much alcohol, so she decides to leave while she can still walk to the bus stop. She says her goodbyes and is looking for her umbrella when Duncan announces, 'I'd better get going too, I wouldn't want my students to see me drunk and disorderly'. They all laugh as he hurries outside into the rain and catches up with Maggie. 'Wait, Maggie, you'll get soaked. Let me give you a lift'.

'Well if it's not out of your way, could you drop me at the bus station please.' They go back to his car and get in. Maggie is a little unsteady on her feet and she is grateful to be out of the driving rain. She is feeling light-headed and knows she shouldn't have accepted that last glass of John's wine. It was the proverbial "one too many".

'I think I'm a little bit tipsy, Duncan', she giggles.

'I think you need some coffee, Maggie', he replies and starts the engine. He pulls over in front of a block of flats near to the pier. It is quite a walk from there to the bus station.

'Come on, let's get you that coffee.' He switches off the engine and looks at Maggie. 'That's my flat on the first floor. Do you want to come up?'

He walks round to her side of the car and takes her hand, helping her out. She stands up, still unsteady, and somehow his arms are around her and they are kissing. Desire stirs, then quickens, throbbing deep inside, consuming her, threatening to banish rational thought. But not quite. It is a familiar response, but one that she has only ever felt with Michael. Sanity returns.

'No, don't. I've got to go'. She pushes Duncan away, heading towards the bus station and he does not try to stop her. Maggie is shocked and ashamed of her feelings, but she also feels foolish. *'Did she kiss Duncan or did he kiss her? Did he realise that she was turned on?'* She has always assumed that she would only experience those feelings with Michael, so now she feels like a tart. She is so confused that she forgets to put up her umbrella so she is soaking wet when she arrives home. That turns out to be a good thing because Michael is so busy fussing over her that he does not notice anything's wrong. That night, they have the best sex they've had for ages and afterwards Michael murmurs. 'Wow, if going out with your friends makes you that pleased to see me, you'd better go out more often.'

CHAPTER 9

Maggie signs up for two classes due to begin in the autumn, Maths and Typing. The typing class is only for one term and takes place immediately after the morning maths class. Her parents miraculously find that they are both available to look after the boys for a few hours once a week and Michael is particularly enthusiastic about the typing. 'That's brilliant, Mags, you'll be able to do all our letters and invoices and run the office once the supply arm of the business takes off'. She says nothing but her real motive for learning to type is to enable her to type her own work once she embarks on a degree.

Once all this is organised, she is free to enjoy the summer, which promises to be warmer and drier than it was the previous year. The newspapers are full of the so-called 'Summer of Love' and the entire country is imbued with a feeling of freedom and liberation. Despite their status as staid married women, Maggie and Linda are going to take their children and go on holiday together. Michael has already said that he is too busy to take time off and easy-going Tom is far too confident in his relationship with Linda to have any misgivings about her going away without him. Linda's baby girl, Lily, is too young to be taken abroad so they book a week at a holiday camp in dorset..

At the camp there are plentiful activities available for children, so they hardly see Ritchie during the day and there is also a day nursery with qualified staff to look after the twins. Little Lily, who still sleeps most of the time, spends her days sheltered from the sun under a shady canopy screwed onto her pram, leaving the girls free to stretch out in their bikinis and relax in the sun. Linda is breast-feeding Lily, so she fills out the top of her bikini for once and Maggie has always had generous curves, so the pair of very attractive young women draw a lot of attention from the groups of young men staying there. At first, when they are chatted up, they explain that they are both married and on holiday with their children. Maggie should have known better because her own father had predicted quite emphatically that two married women going on holiday without their husbands would give rise to all sorts of expectations. From the lecherous comments they receive, it seems he was right: 'Oh yea, don't you get enough at home then, Love?' or

'Fancied a bit of a change in the bedroom, did you?' are typical so after the first two days they give up and just tell their admirers to piss off.

While they are alone and stretched out on loungers the girls chat about everything, revealing intimate details of their marriages for the first time. Maggie is surprised to hear that Linda and Tom, who used to be "always at it", have a lot less sex than her and Michael.

'But I thought everyone did it nearly every day' she tells a laughing Linda.

'Only when you're courting. It kind of tapers off a bit after you've been married for a while. The relationship becomes the important thing, the sex is just part of it. Don't look so sad, it gives you a chance to fantasise about all the other people you fancy doing it with.'

'Like who?'

'Oh, Donny Osmond, Hutch, the Bay City Rollers.'

'All of them?'

'Not all at once, you dummy. Anyway, don't tell me you've never wondered what it would be like to do it with someone else.'

'No, never' lies Maggie. 'But do you ever wonder what it would be like to do it with a real person, I mean someone you know?' Since the night when she and Duncan kissed, she has often wondered what would have happened if she had gone up to his flat and what it would have been like to sleep with him.

'Course I have, every time the bin men come round. They all look super fit, even the older ones, and they're always tanned from being outside all day, haven't you noticed?' They both collapse into giggles, waking up Lily so Linda takes her back to their chalet to be fed. Maggie gets up to go and check on the boys, glad the conversation ended before she said too much. She almost told Linda about the night when she imagined was having sex with Duncan while she was in bed with Michael.

The autumn term begins and Maggie quickly learns that she's never going to get an A for Maths; she finds it too hard. Luckily, she does not really need it because she can get into Teacher training college with her two 'A' levels, so long as she already has 'O' level maths. She does not tell Michael that because she enjoys her day at college and does not want to give it up. He is already disappointed that she is determined to pursue a separate career instead of going to work with him in the new sales department. It is already doing so well that the blonde woman, Julia, has given her employers notice that she is leaving at the end of the year. What she has not told them is that she is taking several of their customers with her.

The first time Michael invites Julia to have dinner with them they take her to an Italian restaurant where she eats hardly anything and drinks quite a lot of red wine before leaving as soon as she can. Michael is annoyed with Maggie and later accuses her of being anti-

68

social and unwilling to help him progress in his career. 'You could have made more effort, Maggie, instead of just interrogating her'.

'What do you mean? I only asked her if she has always worked in a builders' yard and whether she has ever been married.'

'Yes, but it's the way you asked. You came across as very condescending and you must have made her feel like an old maid, sounding so surprised that she isn't married. She's only twenty- nine, not ninety.'

'Well, I am surprised because she's so attractive. Anyway, we don't have anything in common, so I didn't know what else to talk to her about.' But Maggie knows that she does not normally have a problem making small talk; she gets on well with other students with whom she has nothing in common. She just could not relax and be herself with Julia and she suspects that she made the other woman feel the same. Maggie also knows that it is hypocritical to suspect Michael is having another affair when she came so close to being unfaithful with Duncan. So she makes up her mind to put suspicion aside once and for all and make the most of the life she shares with Michael. Since she is being honest with herself, Maggie also faces the realisation that, although she's done well academically, her lack of interest in the new sales division is not very clever. Michael is a hard-working, loving husband and father but he is also a good-looking charmer who loves attention, a magnet for other women.

Determined to make amends, she waits for an evening when the boys settle down in bed early, then makes two mugs of tea and plonks them on the kitchen table in front of Michael. He looks up from the inevitable pile of catalogues and smiles, squeezing her knee under the table.

'All right, Babe?' This is a new style of speech which he has adopted recently, picking it up unconsciously from the contractors he spends so much time with. Maggie rather likes it. 'Babe' is much sexier than the mundane 'Love' that he normally uses.

'Yes, Michael, but I've been thinking. I can probably get into teacher training without the A level Maths. I should know in January whether I have got a place for next year. In the meantime, I could give up the maths and come to work for you. I could do your typing and generally help out in the office. What do you think?'

'What's brought this on, Mags? I know you love your day at college, why would you want to give it up?'

'Because I realise that I've been selfish. You're slogging away every day, trying to build up a business and I could take some of the load off you. I know how to manage an office and I could free you and Julia up to concentrate on the sales.'

'But what about the boys? You wouldn't want to be away from them all the time, would you?'

'No, of course not, but now that they're getting older I wouldn't mind working three days a week. I'm sure Mum and Dad would jump at the chance to have them for an extra day and I was wondering if your mum would like to look after them for the other day?'

Michael's mother, Helen, is a widow, an odd woman who never seems to be very interested in Michael, her only child. She is quiet and reserved and always leaves it to Michael to initiate any contact between the two of them. Sadly, she does not even seem bothered, or surprised, that he doesn't do it very often. Maggie feels sorry for her mother-in-law and makes a point of inviting her round for

Sunday lunch from time to time. She invariably accepts these invitations but she never invites them back in return. Michael just shrugs and says that she has always been that way, but Maggie finds it hard to imagine how she ever managed to produce such an outgoing and friendly child as him.

However, since the twins were born, she has thawed slightly, especially since they started to talk. She is still quiet but she listens to them and they clearly enjoy that. Maggie thinks they like her because she is calm and unflappable, very different from her bluff, opinionated father and neurotic mother. So she invites her to tea on Sunday and broaches the subject as she is passing round the ham sandwiches. 'Helen, I'm going to start working with Michael soon and we're trying to arrange childcare for the boys. My mum and dad have agreed to help out and we wondered if you would have them for one day a week. We could drop them off to you on our way to the office.' Her fingers are crossed under the table because she knows Michael will be embarrassed if his mum says 'No'. She takes a deep breath, waiting for Helen's answer, willing her to agree but half expecting her not to.

'Actually, I would love to do that, so long as it's not on a Wednesday. I always go up to Southampton to visit my mothers' grave on a Wednesday. Thank you for asking me, Maggie.'

'Is it my imagination, or has she turned slightly pink? I think she's pleased to be asked'. Maggie realises, ashamed that she has not made more effort with Helen in the past. She jumps up and goes round the table to give her a hug and JJ, whose high-chair is standing next to where Helen is sitting, leans over and tries to hug her too. In the process, the mucus which is sliding down from his nose ends up on her cardigan. 'Well, if that doesn't put you off, Helen, nothing will.' Says Maggie's dad.

CHAPTER 10

The sales side of the company has been operating for nearly seven years now and it has proved very successful. Michael, Maggie and Julia have built up a close working relationship and are also good friends. Maggie doesn't even remember that she was once suspicious of Julia, who gives one hundred per cent commitment to the company and is the most loyal of colleagues.

One evening Maggie and Linda take Julia on a girly night out. She recently split up with her boyfriend and the outing is intended to numb the pain, although Julia doesn't seem particularly upset. After a few drinks, the conversation inevitably turns to men. Linda, forthright as ever, starts the ball rolling:

'So why did you dump him then, Jules, wasn't he any good in bed?'

'No, he was OK when he eventually came to bed, but he'd stay up half the night fiddling with his video player. Every evening he was either watching films or recording something from TV to watch later. I'd be sound asleep and wake up to find him pawing at me. At first it just annoyed me, then I realised it was actually insulting. He was treating me like some kind of Geisha. Well, one night I'd just had enough. You've heard the expression "I wouldn't kick him out of bed?" Well that night I literally did just that. The next morning, he packed up his stuff and left, taking his video player with him.

'Good for you, Jools, the cheek of it. He was punching above his weight anyway.'

'Well, I wish Tom would still wake me up for sex, I think it's romantic. Last time we did it in the morning Ritchie nearly caught us. Tom was on his hands and knees on top of me when Ritchie

72

walked in. Tom told him he was looking for his glasses, but they were sitting on top of his book on the night-stand. Luckily, Ritchie didn't notice them, he was just after his breakfast.'

'Sounds as though that's what Tom was after too' Maggie snorts and the girls erupt into raucous laughter. Once they had brought it under control, Linda reaches over the table to take Julia's hand.

'Never mind, Jools, I have a feeling your next man will turn out to be Mr Right.'

'I hope so, but somehow I don't think that will ever happen' and Julia looks sad for the first time since she became single again.

'At least you'll always have good friends around you. I'm so glad I decided to work with you and Michael. I can't believe I actually enjoy going to work now, and it's mostly thanks to you. And to think I used to be terrified of you', Maggie adds.

'But I was frightened of you. Michael was so proud of you and he'd told me so much about you, how clever you are and how well you were doing at college. Then when we met you turned out to be gorgeous too. I felt like a boring little mouse, especially since I've never had any qualifications. I went to work at Jamisons straight after school and I've worked full-time ever since.

'Well, that hasn't stopped you from having a successful career, you're a fantastic sales manager. Michael always says the department would never have taken off so quickly without you.'

'Well in that case I think you owe Julia another drink, and I'll have a Martini please, Maggie..' Linda drinks the last of her martini and hands Maggie her glass.

Maggie goes to the bar and orders more drinks, a White Russian for Julia and Martinis for herself and Linda. The barman puts the drinks on a tray with a bowl of peanuts but before she can pick it up a man waiting at the bar offers to carry it over to her table. He carefully places the drinks on the table, then addresses Maggie, 'You're Michael Johnson's wife aren't you? He's left you on your own tonight then?'

'Actually, I've left him alone. He's at home looking after our children. How do you know Michael?'

'Oh, we go way back. I worked with him at one time, and we did an intensive engineering course together one summer. I know all about Michael.'

'I doubt that, but t hanks for bringing our drinks over.' Maggie sits down with her back towards him and says: 'Come on, ladies, drink up, our lifts will be arriving soon'. Clearly brushed off, the man retreats to the bar.

'He was a bit weird, wasn't he? He obviously thought his luck was in', laughs Linda. Do you fancy a fling to celebrate your break-up, Jools?'

'Well if I did, it wouldn't be with him,' says Julia, screwing up her face at the idea, or possibly at the strength of the vodka in her drink.

'Right, then it's time to play 'Who would you like to have a fling with. You go first, Jools', orders Linda.

Later, Tom arrives to take Linda home while Maggie and Julia share a taxi. They are both tipsy now and Maggie is feeling quite drowsy, but she suddenly remembers something. 'What do you think that weirdo meant, he knows all about Michael?'

'Probably nothing important. Michael hasn't got any secrets, has he?' Julia studies Maggie's face, illuminated by the streetlights, but her eyes are closed. Julia has to wake her up when the taxi pulls up outside her house.

Quite soon after that, Maggie, Michael, Linda and Tom are taking their four children on holiday together. They have rented a villa in the South of France and plan to do some exploring while they are away. Ritchie, now twelve years old, has turned out to be rather a quiet boy but JJ and Matty are still as boisterous as ever. They are also still very competitive with each other, probably because JJ makes such a big thing of it whenever he manages to solve a puzzle, or score at a school football match. Whenever something like that happens, Matt merely shrugs it off philosophically.

One thing that unites them, however, is their unswerving devotion to little Lily. They both adore her and who can blame them? She has natural highlights in her long, tawny hair, dark lashes on eyes which seem to change from blue to green, depending on her mood, and a pert little nose. To complete the picture, her skin has kept its golden sheen ever since her first suntan. She is just one of those little girls who you know will be beautiful all her life.

Michael adores her too; he would love to have another child, preferably a girl, but Maggie steadfastly refuses to even consider it. She insists that two children are quite enough for any family, but secretly she has another reason: she has never forgotten what her mother said: 'You can't blame a man for looking elsewhere.'

They invited Julia to join them for at least part of the holiday, but she refused. She told them it would be stupid for all three of them to be away at the busiest time of their year. Now, on the evening before they leave, Maggie feels bad knowing that Julia will be on her own again now that the boyfriend has gone. 'I wish you would change your mind and come, Jools, at least for a long weekend. We'll have plenty of room at the villa, the boys can move in with Ritchie.'

'Don't keep on, Maggie, Julia knows what she's doing. She can hold the fort while we're away and then she can have a holiday later, when the summer rush dies down'. The blind on the window has been pulled down to keep out the evening sun so when Michael pulls Julia into a farewell hug, Maggie can see their reflection in the window. Julia's face is pressed against his upper arm and Maggie realises for the first time that Julia is in love with her husband.

CHAPTER 11

At the firm's Christmas party George Thomas, the founder of the company, announces that he plans to retire within the next year.

'My boy Malcolm will take over full management of the service side of the business. You all know he has been more or less running things for the past few years anyway, so nothing much will change.' There are sycophantic murmurs of regret from several of the staff then someone proposes a toast to wish George a happy retirement. Meanwhile, the three salesmen are exchanging anxious looks. One of them pipes up:

'What about the sales division, George? Will anything change there?'

'That is still under discussion at this time, but I can tell you that nobody will lose their job. Now come on everyone, drink up, it's Christmas!'

In fact, it is Michael who is having the discussions with George. His son Malcolm is an electrical engineer who is not interested in the sales side of the business, and Michael sees this as an opportunity not to be missed. He has already applied for a bank loan in order to buy the warehouse himself and, if that application is approved, he plans to take full control of the sales side, leaving the service business for Malcolm. Michael has already clocked up substantial shares in the sales division and is trying to negotiate a preferential price for the remaining shares. In exchange, he has offered to supply Malcolm with all future materials for his service business at a discounted price.

He will almost certainly need an additional loan in order to buy the extra shares and the prospect of all this debt terrifies Maggie. 'But how will we ever repay the loans, and what will we live on?'

'Don't worry, Mags, I've got it all worked out. If the repayments for the land are too high, I won't buy all the remaining shares straight away. I'll do a deal with George to keep the option to buy them a block at a time. I don't really want to do that because I'd have to pay him dividends in the interim period, but let's see what happens first.'

'But what if George refuses to sell the rest of the shares? He might need some extra income once he hands over to Malcolm.'

'Then he'd retain a share of the business, but I doubt that he'd want that. He wants to enjoy his retirement and the money he'll get from the sale of the warehouse site will be more than enough to live comfortably on. Don't worry, Babe, I've looked into all the problems which could arise from splitting up of the company. The whole thing will be done properly through solicitors, so both sides will be bound by the agreement.'

'Still, have so much debt. What if we can't make the repayments?'

'Well, you and Julia will have to make sure there's enough money coming in so that we can. You'll have to work your beautiful ass off, but it will be worth it, you'll see.' Michael puts his arms round her and grabs her bottom, pulling her against him. 'Hm, I think I'd better check this one out, see if it's up to the job. Come on,' and he turns her around, puts his hands on her bottom and guides her towards the stairs.

While they're waiting to hear if the bank loan will be approved, they visit a solicitor to discuss their plans. Unlike Michael, who is entirely confident in his ability to make the business succeed, Maggie is nervous, so she leaves him in the waiting room and goes in search of the ladies' toilet. She is washing her hands when another woman enters, brisk and business-like as she greets her. 'Afternoon. Are you my next appointment? I'm Sophie Stewart'. The surname has changed but Maggie would have recognised the voice anywhere. It still has the power to make her feel inarticulate, insignificant, common. 'I don't think so, our appointment is with a man. How are you Sophie?'

'Maggie! I'm sorry, I only saw the back of your head and you're so much slimmer than you used to be. I don't need to ask how you are, you look great.' They exchange air kisses, then Sophie ushers Maggie out. 'Come on, I'll walk you back. I'm guessing that your appointment is with Jeremy? Jeremy Nichols?' they walk back along the corridor and she continues, 'I'm so glad you're not here to see me, I handle all the family law. It can be very sad sometimes, especially when it involves children.' She knocks on the door at the end of the corridor then opens it and sticks her head in, 'Were you looking for Mrs Johnson? I'm afraid I kept her chatting, she's an old friend'. She pats Maggie on the arm and turns to leave, saying 'Let's keep in touch, I'll ring you.'

Jeremy advises them to set up a limited company. Michael will be the Chairman, Maggie the Company Secretary and Julia a salaried Director. Although it is an exciting time, Maggie also finds it quite scary because her confidence has ebbed since she started working with Michael. While she was attending college, she felt challenged, but confident that she could achieve anything she set her mind to. Now, no matter how much she enjoys working in the office, it's not really much different from the job she was so desperate to get away from. Sometimes she regrets giving up those ambitions, but then she reminds herself how well it has turned out for them all.

The truth is that, without the income from the sales division, they would never have been able to afford their beautiful, detached house. They moved into about a year before. It is perched high up on the hill with spectacular views over the city, particularly at night, and it is in the catchment area for an excellent high school where the boys are enrolled to start in the autumn term.

For the past year, Maggie and Michael have been renovating their new home and have just finished the last section to be upgraded, the granny annexe. It was unoccupied for several years before they purchased the house, so it needed a complete makeover. Now Maggie and Michael are inspecting the newly decorated annexe, which has been transformed into a lovely two-bedroom apartment. It has its own lounge which, like the main part of the house, has panoramic views of the city and a compact, well designed modern kitchen.

Now that all the work is finished Michael plans to rent it out, but while they're looking round the newly decorated apartment, Maggie has another idea. 'Why don't we ask Helen to move in here? It would be much nicer than having strangers going in and out of our driveway and I'm sure she would love to live next door to you and the boys.'

'Hmph, she's never shown any desire to live next door to me before, and we would lose out on the rent. I can't very well ask her to pay rent, can I?'

'Oh don't be such a grump, Michael, the possibility of living next door to your mum has never come up before. Anyway, if she did move into the flat, she would probably either sell her house or rent it out. Either way we could come to some agreement about money.' Maggie is warming to the idea by the minute, but Michael still does not have much time for his mother, so Maggie goes for his Achilles heel.

'Think about it. The boys are going to high school next year and they have already said they want to walk home after school. They are looking forward to it. If Helen moves into the annexe, she'll always be here to keep an eye on their comings and goings. I don't want them to be latch-key kids, do you?'

'You worry about them too much, I always walked myself to school, even when I was a Junior.'

'Things were different then. I walked myself to school too, but the roads weren't so busy and there weren't so many perverts hanging around.'

'For heaven's sake, Maggie, you'd turn them into a pair of pansies if you had your way. They're boys, they have to learn to stand on their own two feet.'

Despite his initial resistance, Michael changes his tune when Helen tells them she would love to move into the annexe, but only on condition that she pays the full market rent. She also insists on a proper tenancy agreement. Helen knows that students will rent her three-bedroom terrace for much more than a family can afford to pay, so everyone will be financially better off. Once the tenancy is properly set up, Helen insists on handing over an envelope containing the rent before she moves into her new home. 'There's three month's rent in there, Michael. Students pay termly as soon as they get their grant, so I'd rather give it to you now.' Michael is delighted and later chortles to Maggie 'I didn't know you get a much higher rental from students. My mum's got a good head for business, hasn't she?' She's a real dark horse'.

81

'Well, perhaps you would know that if you showed some interest in her. Who do you think you get your business flair from, anyway?' The truth is that he probably does get his work ethic from Helen, who was widowed when Michael was still a toddler. Determined to support them both, she agreed to a contract under which she made curtains and soft furnishings to order for a large department store. The work was well paid, but it entailed long hours bent over her sewing machine, leaving her little time for Michael. To make matters worse, the strain on her eyes had usually given her a headache by the time he came home from school, leaving her with little energy for after-school activities. Gradually, her solitary existence caused her to withdraw into herself, but she was determined to pay off her mortgage and ensure Michael always had a stable home, even if he did not appreciate the work she had to put in to provide it. It was not until the twins arrived that her apparently icy exterior began to thaw slightly, helped on by Maggie, who gently eased her into their lives. Now Helen and Maggie are close friends. She has become more like an older sister than a mother-in-law, so Maggie knows that she can rely on her to provide snacks, help with homework and generally keep the boys out of trouble when they arrive home from school.

There is another, unforeseen, benefit from Helen living at the house. It turns out that she loves gardening. Since they moved in Maggie and Michael have struggled to keep their large rear garden under control. There is an elderly man who mows the lawns of most of the neighbouring houses, but he can't cope with anything more strenuous. As Maggie puts it:

'He only does the easy jobs'. Consequently, keeping their garden tidy and free from weeds is a constant struggle. Michael is not really interested in it and the boys ruin the lawn playing football. They did help Maggie rake up the fallen leaves last autumn, a mammoth task, but then thy started throwing the heaped- up leaves around in a mock battle which left the garden looking just as untidy as before.

So generally, the person who does most to keep the garden in order is Maggie. She does not mind, in fact she quite enjoys it, but sometimes she wishes Michael would help out a bit more. She is out there now, pulling up weeds and wondering what to do about the dandelions dotted all over the lawn. There seem to be more of them every week. Her reverie is interrupted by Helen asking: 'Would you like me to help you with that, Maggie?'

'That's really kind, but I think it would be too much for you, Helen. You're welcome to get a chair and keep me company though.'

'You forget that I used to hump heavy bolts of furnishing fabric around when I was working. I'm probably stronger than you are. Anyway, I've always wanted a proper garden instead of a postage stamp lawn and a few bedraggled wall flowers. Have you got another kneeling pad?' From that day on their partnership was formed: They became the family's gardeners.

CHAPTER 12

It is the boys' first half-term holiday since they started at their new school and they have already made new friends. Matty has inherited his father's easy charm but sometimes Maggie suspects that JJ fits in simply because he is Matty's brother. Luckily, siblings are not put into the same class in their new school, so Maggie is hoping that being separated from Matty will give JJ the chance to assert himself and make friends in his own right. After one term at high school, she already senses that the boys are trying to shake off the parental apron strings and move towards adolescence, and though she knows it is inevitable, she can't help feeling sad.

She and Michael are throwing their first party in the new house and have given in to the boys' pleas to invite some of their friends to a party of their own. As it's a Halloween party, the basement, which is just a storage space at present, is the perfect venue for the young people's party, leaving the main part of the house uncluttered for the adults. The boys have already set up their music equipment in the basement and are going to move the garden furniture inside later that day. Now they are seated at the kitchen table, eating the lunch of fruit and sandwiches which Helen prepared for them and bickering over who should be invited to their party.

'Dad said we could ask six friends each, that makes fifteen with us and Lily.'

'But Lily can't very well be the only girl there. I think we should ask two girls each to make up the numbers', says Matty.

'No, she's younger than the girls in our year, she won't get on with them. She'll probably just want to hang around with us as usual. Anyway, you only want to have girls there so you can snog the one with the tits', accuses JJ.

'Don't you then?' The boys grin at each other across the table, prompting Helen to make a "tutting" sound and cuff Matty lightly round the head.

'You shouldn't talk about girls like that, have a little respect', but she can't repress a smile so she turns away to hide it. Matty is already showing an unashamed interest in girls, unlike JJ, who tends to keep his feelings to himself. Neither of them really wants Lily to come to the party. She is still totally unaware of her beauty and disdains girly things, but the twins have lost interest in the games they have always played together. Nowadays, she's reduced to an annoying hanger-on. Her parents have not realised this yet, so they take it for granted that Lily is invited.

Maggie and Michael have been so busy renovating the house that they have had little time for socialising, so they are looking forward to getting to know their neighbours. Naturally, old friends like Linda and Tom will be there too, although they will have to leave early to pick up Ritchie. He is going to a party at a friend's house and Linda insists on collecting him because she knows someone is bound to smuggle alcohol in, so she wants to make sure he gets home safely. Helen has promised to keep an eye on the youngsters in the basement, under the pretext of checking on the refreshments, leaving Maggie free to entertain her guests. Since Helen moved into the annexe, Maggie's father has been making snide remarks, hinting that Helen is taking advantage somehow, so Maggie feels obliged to invite her parents too. She is just hoping her father will be kept so busy with the buffet and free drinks that he won't come out with one of his sexist or racist comments, especially since she suspects that the people who live next door, David and Paula, are Jewish.

David is a dentist but Paula doesn't work. She is very glamorous and always wears a lot of Jewellery, even when she is dressed for the Gym. They also have two sons, one at university and the other in the sixth form of a private boarding school, but they rarely see either of them. Also, David plays golf every weekend so Maggie suspects that Paula must be quite lonely.

Soon after they arrive, Paula makes a bee line for Michael, hanging onto his every word and laughing too loudly whenever someone makes a slightly humorous comment. Maggie is used to the effect Michael has on women by now, so she tries to ignore Paula and concentrate on making sure the party is a success. She does feel sorry for David, though he hardly seems to notice that his wife is making a fool of herself, he is too busy drinking and practising his golf swings. Quite a few of their neighbours play golf and Michael has been thinking of taking it up himself. He thinks it would be a good way to meet the right people, people who might help advance the business, but he is also worried that he has put on a little weight recently, so it would be killing two birds with one stone.

Now Barry, owner of a builders' yard and a near neighbour, offers:

'I'd be happy to sponsor you for membership at Petersfield. It's the best course in the area and the pros are good. You could take lessons with them while you're waiting for your membership to come through.'

'Oh Maggie, don't let him take up golf, you'll be all alone every weekend like me. And on summer evenings too', adds Paula, putting on a little girl pout. Maggie excuses herself with a polite smile and goes to greet Linda and Tom, who have just arrived.

Tom hugs her with one arm while trying to hand over the bottle bag he is carrying. 'Don't give me that bottle now Tom, I might use it to as a weapon.' As she kisses Linda Maggie tilts her head towards the little group gathered round her husband. They are all laughing, and Paula has her hand on Michael's shirt front now, just above the his belt.

'Right, Batman to the rescue, come on Linda'. Tom takes Linda's hand and pulls her towards Michael, squeezing Paula out as they both say their "hellos".

Meanwhile, down in the basement, JJ is also struggling to control his jealousy. He and Matty may not have noticed Lily's burgeoning appeal but some of the other boys have. They are homing in on her, challenging her to games of fooze ball or ping pong and teasing her mercilessly in the way that young boys do when they fancy someone. Lily is innocently basking in all the attention she is receiving, but JJ, who has never experienced jealousy like this before, does not know how to handle it. He looks towards Matty for help, but he is busy chatting up some girls himself, so he waits at the end of the ping pong table until Lily's match is over. When she loses he snatches the bat from the boy at the other end of the table and announces, 'I'm playing next.'

Lily has other ideas, though. She throws her bat down on the table and says, 'Phew, I'm thirsty. Come on, let's go and get something to drink.' She walks away, followed by her opponent, leaving JJ standing, bat in hand, with nobody to play against.

Upstairs, the party is in full swing, so Maggie is kept busy, and it is not until she returns to the lounge after checking the refreshments that she realises that Michael has disappeared. Irritated, She is doing the rounds on her own, urging their guests to help themselves to the buffet laid out on the dining room table. They are starting to drift in that direction when Michael reappears with Paula tottering behind in her ridiculously high heels.

'Oh Maggie', Mikey's been giving me a guided tour of your beautiful home. I love what you've done with it', she gushes. 'And you must give me the details of the people who made the drapes in your bedroom, they're so stylish.' Actually, Helen made all their curtains and accessories, but Maggie has no intention of telling her that, so she smiles through gritted teeth and offers Paula a plate.

'I would have smashed that plate over her head', murmurs Linda from behind her. 'The cheek of it, going into your bedroom. You'd better make sure that your bed hasn't been slept in too'. Maggie knows that Linda is not serious, but she is still rattled. She can never entirely ignore the suspicion that lurks under the surface, nibbling at her self- esteem, whenever Michael is talking to another woman.

By the time the other guests polish off the refreshments Paula, who eats hardly anything, has clearly had too much to drink so David takes her home. Once she is gone Maggie feels free to relax and enjoy the party. She tries not to be embarrassed by her dad's loud and disparaging comments about women who can't hold their drink and is rather surprised when Barry agrees with him. Maggie likes Barry, he is direct and down to earth but he's got a great sense of humour, so she hopes Michael will take him up on his offer to sponsor him at his golf club. She certainly does not want him playing golf with David.

CHAPTER 13

By the time the boys are fourteen the family routine is well-established. Michael travels a fair amount on business, leaving Maggie in charge of the office. With Julia sharing the workload and Helen doing the same at home she is not particularly challenged. In fact she is often bored. Still, she is not complaining because this way she has plenty of time to keep tabs on the boys. Also, it is usually Maggie who has to ferry them to rugby matches and other activities, although it is more likely to be JJ who needs transport to a match nowadays.

Quite unexpectedly, Matty has lost interest in sports. Instead, he has become very involved in the school's drama productions. He appears to have a talent for both acting and working backstage, where he helps to design sets and tweak scripts. For some reason, Michael finds this funny and is always teasing Matty about it. Luckily, Matty is supremely confident and just grins at his father's gentle ribbing but Maggie knows that it would be a very different story if JJ was the artistic one.

This evening, Maggie is walking the hill track overlooking the city with Helen and Hetty, their springer spaniel. The wind sweeping in from the sea can be ferocious, but today there is only a gentle breeze rippling through the long grass, so the two women are taking their time, strolling along, and chatting about the coming weekend. Michael is away in Germany and will not be back until late on Saturday morning, so Maggie is taking both boys to watch the sixth form girls' team compete in a hockey tournament in Northampton.

'The twins are not over- joyed at being roped in, but the school likes all pupils and parents to support the school teams whenever possible, and this is an inter-county event. Anyway, Layla's daughter,

Jasmin, is playing and she does not have any relatives to cheer her on, so Maggie has told them that they're going whether they like it or not'.

'Oh, they could have stayed with me, but I've promised to go shopping with Kate. We were going to go to the pictures afterwards, but I'll see if I can cancel'. Helen has made a few friends in the area and now has quite a busy social life.

'No, Helen, why should you change your plans? The boys need to learn that not everything is about them'.

So Maggie gets up at her usual time on Saturday, then showers and dresses before going to drag the boys out of bed. Gone are the days when they would be awake at six on weekends and invariably demanding pancakes. The twins always mixed the batter, under Maggie's supervision, then ran upstairs to wake Michael, leaving Maggie to clean up the resultant chaos in the kitchen. Michael is adept at tossing pancakes so the boys would stand, plate in hand, shouting "Hoop la' every time he tossed a pancake onto one of their plates. Nowadays, only the aroma of bacon grilling gets them out of bed at weekends.

'Do we really have to go to the stupid tournament?' groans Matty from under his duvet. Maggie grabs it and pulls it off him before going to the room next door where JJ is already awake. She goes over to pull back the curtains.

'Get up, JJ, it's going to be a lovely day, look'. She is relieved because it has been raining heavily for the past three days and she was not really looking forward to standing in the rain all afternoon.

'Come on, breakfast will be ready in ten' she calls as she heads down the stairs. In the hallway the answer phone is pinging. It is a message from the school to say that the match has been cancelled because the grounds of the host school are flooded and there isn't an alternative available.

She goes back upstairs and calls

'Ok guys, there's a change of plan. The match is cancelled so you can have an extra hour in bed. We'll be able to meet your dad at the airport instead'. She goes back downstairs, puts the kettle on and opens her book. Two hours later the boys have finished their breakfast and are now wide awake. They love meeting Michael at the airport, partly because he usually arrives with surprise presents stowed in his hand luggage. Maggie is backing the car out of the garage when Helen's friend, Kate, drives in. Helen comes out but goes over to Maggie and sticks her head through the open car window.

'Hi Maggie, I thought you were leaving early for the tournament. What happened?'

'Oh, it was cancelled so we're going to collect Michael from the airport instead.'

'Good, he'll like that. Well, Kate and I will probably get something to eat while we're out and don't forget we're going to the pictures, so I might be back quite late.

'Ok, have a good time then. Come round tomorrow for lunch, I'll do a roast.

The arrivals lounge at Southampton airport is not very large, so they see Michael immediately he emerges and makes his makes his way towards the exit. The boys saunter towards him, living up to their resolve to be cool at all times, but Michael is looking back at a young woman walking a step or two behind him. She looks like a page three girl, with tight jeans and a top cut low enough to show off her ample boobs beneath a fitted leather jacket. She flicks back her long, blonde hair and Michael says something to her.

'Trust him', Maggie thinks, amused, but then everything changes. Michael grabs the girl's butt and pulls her against him, squashing her boobs as he kisses her, a long, lingering kiss. She tilts her head back and smiles up at him, but he is looking at the boys, who are now standing in front of him. Red heat floods Maggie's body, so sudden and fierce that for a moment she can hardly stand. Michael, flanked by his sons, is looking at her now but she turns her back on them and walks briskly out to the car park. By the time they emerge from the building she is in the car and heading towards the exit.

She drives home, fast, and goes straight up to their bedroom where she begins to pull Michael's clothes out of the wardrobe. Fueled by adrenaline, she slings shirts, underwear and shoes over the bannister, then goes back for more. When she hears the front door open and his voice speaking to the boys, she literally sees red, but when he ascends the stairs and stands on the landing and the fire in Maggie's veins turns to ice,

. 'Are you crazy Mags, you left the boys on their own at an airport. Anything could have happened to them.'

'They weren't alone, they were with you and your floozy. Take your stuff and get out, Michael.'

'What? You are crazy. You don't really want me to go.'

'Don't flatter yourself, I meant what I said. Get out. I gave you another chance once before but not this time. Now go'

'Maggie, you don't mean that. You know I love you. Other women don't mean anything to me, it's just sex. They're not important'.

'Other women? How many have there been, Michael? No, don't answer that, I don't want to know.' Suddenly the fire inside her flares up again

, 'I gave up my dreams for you, Michael. I wanted a career, but I gave it all up to help you build up your business, not so you could sleep around with little sluts'. She is beside herself now. Her voice is strained, rasping, but she goes on shouting and she goes on throwing his clothes over the banister. Acutely conscious that his sons are lurking downstairs, Michael picks up his hand luggage and walks out of the house.

CHAPTER 14

Over the next few months, every conversation Maggie has with Michael is fuelled by anger. Through all the recriminations, pleas for forgiveness and tears her resolve does not weaken: ~Their marriage is over. In many ways, Michael has been a good, loving husband and he has never been boring, but he has also never been faithful. She can see it now in the eyes of her closest friends, Linda, Julia, even Helen and she is angry that she did not see it herself. None of them seem surprised that their marriage is ending. Sometimes she thinks they are surprised that it lasted so long.

One of the things that hurts the most is the jealousy. She gave herself to Michael totally and unreservedly, both in and out of bed, and she thought he had done the same. Now, painful as it is, she can no longer ignore the fact that, for him, their union was not exclusive. Clearly, he can share his deepest feelings with other women as easily as he sets up a business deal.

Since the dramatic scene at the airport, Maggie has been going through each day on auto pilot as she tries to make sense of this tumult of emotions, but now it is time to move on. She is going to see Sophie Stewart this afternoon to set the wheels of a divorce in motion.

Sophie turns out to be another friend who is not surprised by Maggie's predicament. They have a preliminary chat during which they both agree that infidelity is the only possible grounds that Maggie can cite if she applies for a divorce. Once this is decided, Sophie sits back in her chair, gazes across the desk and tells her,

'Maggie, before we go any further, there's something I feel I must say. Every day I sit here and listen to sad stories from brokenhearted wives or husbands, and one thing I've learned is that some people simply cannot be faithful to one partner for the rest of their lives. It's nothing to do with love, I'm not sure what the reason is, but some people just can't do it. Now, are you absolutely certain that you can't live with Michael and accept that he just can't help himself? Can't you look the other way? Is a divorce really what you want?'

'I've made up my mind, Sophie. I can't live with Michael anymore. I'd always be wondering if he's with another woman and the thought of him with someone else makes me feel physically sick.' Maggie is in tears now, so Sophie comes round the desk to give her a sympathetic hug.

'Ok then, let's get down to business.'

The initial forms are completed and sent out, and the divorce goes through in record time. Now that Maggie has convinced him that she is not going to change her mind, a devastated Michael agrees to every demand she makes without hesitating. His share of the house is signed over to Maggie and she will continue to live there with the boys. Her part of the mortgage will be paid off by her shares in the company, a complex transaction for which the expertise of Jeremy Nichols is required. Michael wants her to retain some shares Maggie is adamant that she wants to cut all ties with the company and, by implication, with him.

Clearly this is not possible because of their children but, since neither of them wishes to get involved in a tug of war for their affections, they soon reach an amicable agreement on that too. The boys will stay with their father every other weekend and he can also take them on outings during the week, so long as he brings them home at a reasonable time. Michael will continue to contribute a generous amount of money for their upkeep, and since Maggie is now the sole owner of the house, she is entitled to collect Helen's rent, so she will be financially secure.

As for the boys, apart from that first day when they met Michael at the airport, both parents have been careful to avoid any discussion in their presence, nor has either of them resorted to rowing or bitching about the other, so the effect on them has been minimised. Of course, they are both sad that their parents no longer live together, but there are compensations. Michael now lives in a spacious flat near the sea, affording them access to the promenade and all those other attractions which young teenaged boys love. In addition, when they are with Michael they can escape from the over-anxious attention of their mother and make the most of his 'boys will be boys' parenting style.

When Michael arrives to collect the boys, Helen usually comes out for a chat with him. Sometimes he even goes indoors with her for a cup of tea, but he never comes to the house specifically to pay her a visit. Maggie knows that Michael still sees Tom and Linda occasionally, as does she, and on these occasions they all make a point of avoiding any subject which might be embarrassing. They do not want to seem to be taking sides. On the surface it is a very civilised divorce, but Maggie is still deeply hurt and unhappy and so is Michael. She assumes that he is seeing other women and that thought still has the power to make her wretched. Sometimes she thinks that she will never overcome this feeling unless she sleeps with someone else herself, but she has no idea of how to go about it. She has never slept with anyone but Michael. And then she bumps into Duncan.

She is walking out of the new college building, where she has been picking up information about courses, when he walks in. 'Maggie, what are you doing here? I thought you'd given up the idea of a degree.'

'Well, circumstances have changed. Anyway, I could ask you the same question. This is not your usual stamping ground, is it?'

'No, but I teach a couple of classes here. You look well, Maggie, still as beautiful as ever.'

'And you're still as full of bullshit as ever.' They both laugh and then they agree to meet for a drink later that week. They are going to the pub where they celebrated her A level results. When Linda hears that Maggie is meeting Duncan for a drink, she gets quite excited.

'It's about time you went on a date, Maggie. You've got to get out there before you turn into a dried- up old maid. There are plenty of younger women on the market.' Linda has been telling Maggie this for a while now.

'It's not a date, I'm just meeting an old friend for a drink. And I'm not 'on the market' as you so charmingly put it.'

'Yea, yea, if you say so.'

Now that Maggie is usually the person who drives the boys to school, she cannot afford to lose her driving licence, so she takes a taxi to the pub. She is looking forward to having a couple of drinks, something she rarely does nowadays, and Duncan was always good company. At the pub she feels awkward and ill at ease at first, but by the time she is on her second drink she relaxes. For the first time in months her mind is not preoccupied with thoughts of Michael, so she is startled when the landlord starts to call 'time'.

'Is that really the time? I must go. I'll ask him to ring for a taxi for me'.

'Do you have to go so soon? It's till early. Come back to mine for a coffee, then I can call for a cab from my fla.t.' Actually. Maggie is not in a hurry to go home, she is enjoying herself and she hasn't thought about Michael all evening.

'OK, good idea.' They leave the pub and stroll down towards Duncan's car. 'I live down in the bay now, is that all right?'

'Oh, my ex has an apartment down here somewhere. It would be funny if you two turn out to be neighbours.' Duncan grimaces and says:

'Really, what's his address?'

'I don't know, I only know it's somewhere near the water.'

'The posh end, then.'

'Yes, that sounds like Michael.' Maggie banishes all thoughts of her ex, she is determined to enjoy this rare evening out. It is a cold, bright night with a chilly wind which tugs at her hair, reminding her of evenings when she walked home as a teenager. She fee's the same exhilaration that she felt then, knowing that she is an independent single woman. The wind carries with it the tang of the kebab shops on Commercial Road, she can almost taste them, a promise of things unknown and unexplored. She revels in the thought that she is free to do whatever she chooses When her heel catches on the uneven pavement, almost tripping her up, she grabs Duncan's arm to steady herself. The warmth of his arm against her side is delightful, like hot chocolate on a snowy night, so she hangs on, leaning against him until they reach his car.

When they get to his flat, he helps her off with her coat and throws it across the back of an ancient leather armchair. 'Would you like a coffee, or I can offer you some brandy?'

'Not on its own. Have you got anything to mix with it?'

'A splash of orange juice?'

'Perfect'. Maggie takes the glass and tilts it, gently swirling the liquid inside until the colour of the brandy is intensified by the orange juice, then takes a sip, inhaling the rich, fruity aroma of the brandy. As its warmth pervades her body, trickling down her limbs, they become limp, languorous. She leans back and turns toward Duncan, who has joined her on the settee. She knows she has had too much to drink but she doesn't care, although she is careful not to spill any brandy as she places her glass on the coffee table. She smiles up at Duncan and they both know what is coming next.

Afterwards, in the taxi on the way home, Maggie's head is spinning, full of images of what she did with Duncan, and the alcohol she drank does not help. When she was with Michael her entire body iwas consumed by passion, her parts could not ot be divided into separate entities, and even though she enjoyed the sex with Duncan, it was not the same. Despite their divorce, sleeping with someone else is an enormous step for Maggie and having taken it she is left feeling very confused. She needs to think about it and then talk about it with her best friend Linda.

CHAPTER 15

The next morning, after she drops the boys off at school, she heads straight for home. She is not surprised to hear the telephone ringing as she walks through the front door, .so she picks up the hand- set, smiles and says

'Hello Linda'.

'Well, how did it go? Or should I say 'How far did you go?'

'You sound like a teenager "How far did you go". I'm not exactly a virgin, am I? OK, OK, I'll tell you but not over the phone. What are you doing today?'

'I'm meeting you for a coffee, obviously.'

'Let's make it lunch, shall we? If we go to the Poets corner we can get a booth and talk in private. I'll tell you all about I then.' So they meet at the same pub where Maggie first saw Julia. She arrives first and while she is waiting for Linda, Maggie thinks about how insecure she was then. *Strange how Julia turned out to be one of my best friends. I don't think I'll tell her about last night, though,* Maggie muses. Linda rushes in, hair flying as usual. She draws admiring glances from the men standing at the bar, which she ignores. She is still as slim as ever, unlike Maggie who has to watch what she eats nowadays. Maggie has already bought her a drink, pineapple juice with lemonade. so Linda picks up her glass and taps it against Maggie's.. While she takes the first sip, she studies her friend across the table.. 'You slept with him, didn't you? Come on, I want to hear every detail'. So Maggie gives her a brief but factual account of her fling with Duncan.

'We went back to his flat for a drink, started kissing then moved to his bedroom where we had sex on the bed.'

'But what was it like? Was he any good? Come on,, give me details'.

'We took off all our clothes first.'

'Maggie!'

'I don't know if he was any good. He was different from Michael, but it was quite pleasant.'

'Quite pleasant? Well, did it make you feel better? Did you get your own back?'

'No, if we're talking about revenge, it probably made me feel worse. At first, I just thought *if this is sleeping around, I don't know why Michael bothers'*. Then I went back to thinking that there must be something wrong with me which caused him to turn to other women.'

'No, you must never think that, you've moved on from that, Maggie. Maybe you should try someone else?' Maggie contemplates her best friend; judging from her expression whether she is serious. She can't help seeing the funny side of this suggestion coming from Linda, long time faithful wife that she is, and she snorts through her drink, then collapses with laughter which she cannot hold back. One of Linda's admirers, on his way to the door stops and asks' What's so funny, love?' and Linda starts laughing too.

It is not until the following Christmas that Maggie truly feels that she is over Michael. The previous year the boys had Christmas dinner with her then went to Michael's where they stayed over until boxing day. Maggie spent the evening with Helen getting quietly drunk and Michael really missed being with the boys when they opened their presents on Christmas morning. As for the boys, they hated being shuttled between their parents at Christmas time too, so it was rather a sad day for all of them.

Maggie is determined that this Christmas will be a happier one, so she has invited her parents, Michael and Helen to spend the day with them. She has also suggested that Michael stay the night, then he can take the boys out the next day. She has prepared the guest room, laying out the best towels and she has even bought him Christmas pyjamas to match those she bought for the twins.

They all have a lovely time. After lunch Michael, Helen and the boys take Hetty for a walk, leaving Maggie and her mum to clear up the kitchen. Maggie's dad stays behind, dozing in front of the TV with a can of beer at his side, under the pretext of waiting to hear the Queen's speech. Later, after the guests have all left, the boys disappear upstairs to play on their new computerised games, leaving their parents to have a quiet drink together. They start to watch a film, but Maggie dozes off and is wakened by Michael saying, 'Come on Mags, you're shattered, let's get you up to bed.' He pulls her to her feet and they make their way upstairs. Maggie is still half asleep so Michael places his hand on her back to steady her.

Outside her bedroom door hey stop and Michael says

'Thank you for a wonderful day, Maggie, I really appreciate it. Sweet dreams Babe' He kisses her and the kiss deepens. It's all so familiar, now they're entwined together and then they're stumbling into the bedroom. Michael pushes her onto the bed, pulling at her clothes and they make love. Afterwards, Maggie lays back on her pillows and thinks *Actually, that wasn't so different from doing it with Duncan.* Michael smiles down at her.

'I'm so happy Mags. When shall we tell the boys?'

'Tell them what?'

'That we're getting back together. Shall I see if they're still awake?'

'Whatever makes you think that we are getting back together, Michael? That was just sex.' Michael gets up from the bed slowly, dumbfounded. Crushed, he starts to say something, then stops and silently leaves her room. Maggie knows she has been cruel, but she doesn't care, He deserves it. She has wanted to say that to Michael ever since the incident at the airport and now it is done. As Linda would say, she has got her own back.

Over the coming years, Michael occasionally makes a half-hearted pass at Maggie, but he never makes the same mistake again. Their relationship is clearly defined after that Christmas: they're just ex-lovers who have shared responsibility for their offspring.

CHAPTER 16

Maggie is about to start the final year of a law degree. She originally planned to apply for a place on a history course but changed her mind on the advice of Sophie Stewart.

'Why History, Maggie? History degrees are ten a penny and what would you do with it afterwards? If I were you, I'd think about applying for law.'

'But it would take me years to become a solicitor. I've already spent the last nine months on that "Return to education" course so now I want to get on the career ladder as soon as I can.'

'You don't have to become a solicitor. A degree in law would open so many doors for you, look it up in the university brochure.' So Maggie looks it up and finds that Sophie's right, a law degree can lead to a surprisingly wide variety of careers. Once convinced, she applies for a place to study law as a mature student at Southampton University. She'll have plenty of time to drop the boys off at school before lectures and they usually return home on the bus nowadays anyway. Maggie does not regret choosing the law; she enjoys its black and whiteness, the fact that it sets such precise boundaries.

It will also be a tough year for the he boys. They are due to take their O level exams next summer while Maggie will be working hard to get through her finals, so she is planning to take them on a special holiday this year. They are already very reluctant to go anywhere with her and she knows that this might be the last time that they have a family holiday together.

Linda's son, Ritchie, is going off to Kos with his friends in the summer and the twins are green with envy. Linda is not very happy about it, but Ritchie is at university now and all his friends are going, so Tom tells her she needs to loosen the apron strings and let him grow up.

'Don't you think so, Maggie?' Maggie assents half-heartedly. She knows that he is right but her heart clenches at the thought of JJ and Matty travelling abroad without her, so she comes up with an idea.

'Why don't you both go to Greece at the same time as Ritchie? You could stay on the mainland, then you wouldn't be too far away if he gets himself into trouble', she suggests. Ritchie has grown into a quiet, sensible young man so it is unlikely that he will get into any kind of trouble, but Linda jumps at the idea.

. 'Yes, that's a brilliant, idea, Maggie. We could have a holiday and Ritchie needn't even know we were there. It would just make me feel better to be on hand in case he needs us.

'And how do you think Ritchie would feel if his friends found out that we'd followed him when he was on holiday in case he needed his mum? The whole point of Ritchie going away with his friends is so that he can learn to stand on his own two feet. The last thing he needs is to have you just around the corner, making him look ridiculous in front of his mates. Forget it, Linda, we're not going.'

'Speak for yourself, Tom. Maggie, you said you wanted a holiday, how do you fancy Greece?'

So Linda and Maggie are taking Lily and the twins to a very plush hotel in the beautiful area of Pellepponese. It has the most fantastic beaches, ancient villages, and is only a short drive to several important archaeological ruins. The idea is the trip will be a "something for everyone" experience. However, for Linda the main attraction of that part of Greece is its plethora of transport options from there to Kos. The island can be reached by car, ferry, train or even plane from Pellepomese. Now she can wave Ritchie off content in the knowledge that, once she arrives in Greece, she will be on hand if some unanticipated disaster befalls him. Neither Linda or Maggie realise that it is the other kids who they about. be worrying about. They cannot imagine that the relations between Lily and the twins could cause a rift in their friendship.

They have hired a car and intend to explore the immediate area, then spend a couple of nights in Athens. At the hotel, the two dark-haired, handsome twins accompanied by flaxen-haired Lily provoke a lot of attention and they are soon at the centre of a noisy group of youngsters. Every day after breakfast, the teenagers all met up to confer over whether it's going to be a pool day or a beach day. If they decide on the beach, their parents have no option but to follow them because the beaches, although beautiful, are also completely unspoiled. They are as nature intended them so there are no lifeguards or safety equipment. There aren't even any toilets, so if Lily needs the loo she has to be accompanied up a rocky path to get back to the hotel.

After a few days spent lying in the sun, Maggie and Linda want to go exploring. They warn the kids that they will be going out in the car the next day, provoking scowls and moans.

'Why do we have to go? We can stay here on our own, Stavros' mum and dad left him and went out for the day, why can't you?'

'He's older than you and he can speak Greek. Anyway, I want you to see the ancient theatre at Mycaena, they still hold concerts there.'

'Booooring', drawls JJ, elongating the word for emphasis, but Matty perks up at the sound of the word "concert". His interests always tend towards the cultural, unlike his brother who is hooked on sports and sciences. The following day they set off after breakfast. JJ has the map on his knees and is navigating, leaving the other youngsters to carry on a desultory conversation, They had been driving for about forty minutes when they saw the first road signs for Mycaena. Linda was driving so Maggie turned round to tell the passengers in the back;

'Nearly there' then adds 'Well done, JJ, ;brilliant navigation.'. Matt and Lily are both fast asleep.

The sun is high up in the sky by the time they arrive, but both boys perk up once they see the huge amphitheatre and they rush off to explore, with Lily tagging along behind. Linda doesn't like Lily, to get too far ahead so she calls them back..

'Kids, why don't we go and get a drink before we look around. You can have something to eat, too. Aren't you hungry?' Naturally they say that they are, the boys are always hungry, so they go to the café where they all order cold drinks and the youngsters eat huge wraps bursting with fresh vegetables and goat's cheese. When he has finished eating JJ asks

'Mum, I want to know more about how the theatre was built and where they got the marble for the columns from, but all the signs seem to be in Greek. Can we see if there any books for sale here?'

So they go in search of the gift shop, where they find an impressive range of guide books, but they are all in Greek too.

. 'Why don't you go and join the queue at the cash desk, maybe you can hire one of those recorded guides' Maggie suggests, moving back into the shade and fanning herself. A man politely moves to one side to make way for Linda under the canopy and she smiles her thanks. Judging by the grey streaks in his thick, dark hair he is probably approaching forty, but he is very slim and looks fit. Maggie takes this opportunity to ask

'Excuse me, do you speak English? Can you tell me whether there is anywhere nearby where I can buy a guidebook in English? My son is eager to learn about the construction of the theatre.' The man takes off his sunglasses before saying in heavily accented English,

'Good afternoon Madame, I don't believe you will find such a book nearby, but I can give you a guided tour if you wish? I can tell you everything you would like to know about this antiquity. Here is my information'. He offers flyers to Maggie and Linda, then continues,

'As you could see, I am very qualified and in addition I am knowledgeable about everything this antiquity. My tour will last for one and one half hours and then we will go to the café for coffee and questions.'

Maggie gestures to JJ to leave the queue and join them,

'What do you think, JJ, shall we book a tour with this gentleman?'

'That would be great Mum. Are you up for it, Linda?' Linda is, so they set off with the guide, whose name is Alex. Matt and Lily tag along for a while, until Matt says, I'm going up to the top of the hill to look at the view; anyone else coming?'

Lily is also bored so the two of them set off, using the ancient stone seats like steps to get to the top. Linda calls out to them,

'Be careful Lily. Matt, let her go in front of you in case she slips.' He waves his acquiescence then turns and follows behind Lily. As they scramble upwards, Lily's long, tanned legs are tantalisingly close to Matt and he notices for the first time that she has blond body hair. *It's the hair which makes her look as if her skin glows. It's a pity she's not a*

108

bit older. Does that make me a paedophile? He wonders. Like a butterfly, Lily is evolving before his eyes from the little girl who always tags along into something so beautiful it hurts.

Down below, Alex turns out to be telling the truth. He does know everything about this antiquity, and several others, because he teaches history at the university in Athens. He explains how the huge amphitheatre was constructed without the benefit of modern equipment and he also describes the means used to transport the building materials across the unforgiving terrain. He shares all this information in a light-hearted way, interspersing it with amusing anecdotes about the historic characters associated with the theatre. He is a natural raconteur and JJ, Maggie and Linda are fascinated. At the end of the tour, he reminds them that his price includes a coffee in the café.

'We'd love to have a coffee with you, Alex, but we'll have to round up the other kids first', says Linda.

'Of course, Madame, I will find a table and wait for you.'

The three of them set out along the winding pathway leading to the top of the theatre and meet Matt and Lily heading downwards. Matt is in front again and Lily, who is almost as tall as him now, has her hand on his shoulder for balance. She says something and he turns, laughing, so their faces are on the same level as she steps down. Even at that distance Maggie can feel the chemistry between them, and so can JJ. His face gives him away as he turns abruptly and starts back down the track, but Maggie sees it and thinks '*Oh no, they can't both be stuck on Lily*'.

At the Cafe Alexander is waiting for them, as promised. He has managed to reserve a large table even though the café is crowded, presumably because he has some clout with the proprietor. He orders coffee and cold drinks then invites them to ask further questions Both Maggie and Linda are curious to learn about the lives of the average Greek and Alex paints a vivid picture. He makes it sound as if life is much harder here than in the UK.

'In the summer I give guided tours because it is difficult to live on my salary from the university. I grew up quite near to your hotel and my brother still lives in that village. It is very beautiful, there, every house has a lovely garden, I would like to show it to you' he tells them. 'Actually, it has a very nice little restaurant, too. I can take you there tomorrow night if you wish'.

'That's very kind of you but I think it would be too late for the kids. They're always starving by six o'clock, so we usually have dinner in the hotel' Linda says quickly. 'But Maggie could go. Perhaps you could show the rest of us your village during the daytime.'

'Perfect. I shall collect you from your hotel because the roads are a little bit dangerous at night. Shall I find you in reception at seven o'clock?' Maggie is furious with Linda but she feels it would be churlish to refuse. Alex is so enthusiastic about everything in his country.

As soon as they are in the car she vents her annoyance

'Why did you do that Linda? You put us both in an awkward position. He probably gets commission when he takes a party to that restaurant, now it will be awkward. He might think he's obliged to pay for me.'

'Don't be ridiculous, you can go Dutch. Anyway, it's obvious he fancies you like mad. I did you both a favour, but if he's really only interested in his commission, he may not turn up.'

'I hope he doesn't'.

Linda puts out her hand to squeeze Maggie's knee.

'Sorry Mags, I thought you liked him. If you really don't want to go with him on your own, take the boys with you. At least he'll get his commission then.'

'No, I've agreed to go now. Anyway, it will only be for one night because he said he's going to Athens to see his PHD students the next day, didn't he?'

'Oh, why don't you come to my village, and I will give you a private tour of my leetle house ', JJ mimics from the back seat and the other two collapse with laughter.

'No, I will show you my marrow in the beautiful garden' counters Matty. More laughter. The boys continue in this vein, their jokes getting bluer and bluer until Maggie snaps:

'Cut it out now, I need to concentrate on driving. I can see what Alex meant about the roads being dangerous at night, though. You can hardly see the road ahead, it's pitch black out there.'

111

CHAPTER 17

Despite her apparent reluctance, Maggie is freshly showered, perfumed and ready to go at five minutes to seven the next day. She makes her way down to the reception area where Alex is waiting, looking very dapper, freshly shaved and wearing a carefully ironed shirt and chinos.

'Good evening, Madame, you are looking very beautiful tonight', he takes her elbow and gestures towards the door

Please, call me Maggie, otherwise I'll have to call you 'Sir'.

'Thank you, Maggie. I would like that greatly'. She smiles to herself at his quaint use of English.

It turns out that his pride in the local restaurant is justified. It has crisp white cloths on the he table, excellent service and good food. She chooses a sea food starter followed by dolmades while Alex opts for fish, freshly caught that morning.

'I will choose the wine, if you do not object, because I know about Greek wines. Maggie' and is happy to leave it to him. *Michael always chose the wine when I was with him,* she remembers, then wonders whatever made her think of that tonight. Before they leave the restaurant, he insists on paying the bill, just as she feared. 'Please, do not insult me, it is my invitation. He pushes her hand away and gets out his wallet, an ancient leather affair. It is hard to tell what its original might have been and the stitching is coming apart in places. 'He notices she's staring at it and explains,

112

'It was my father's. He left his house to my younger brother and his wallet to me. He said he knew I would always look after my money, but my brother would never be able to buy his own house.'

'That seems very unfair.'

'Possibly it was but my brother is a gambler. I think my father wanted to make sure that he always had a roof over his head. Unfortunately, a few years after my father died my brother had to sell the house to pay off his debts'.

'Oh, what a waste. You must have been very angry with him.'

'Not really, my brother can't help it: gambling is an disease you see. Anyway, I bought the house. He can't sell it again because I own it now, so my father knew what he was doing.

Now, would you like to walk down to the beach? The sea always looks so beautiful in the moonlight'. They walk down a sandy lane which widens into a beach and Maggie takes off her sandals. The air is balmy, infused with the scent of bougainvillea from the restaurant garden and Alex is right, the sea does look beautiful in the moonlight. When they reach the spot where the water laps gently onto the sand, Maggie picks up the bottom of her skirt and ventures a few steps into the icy cold sea. A wave rolls in, threatening to soak her dress, so she steps back and Alex puts out his hands to steady her. They stand like that for a moment, Alex holding Maggie's arms just above the elbow, then then he pulls her back against him. When she doesn't move away, he wraps his arms lightly around her body. 'Maggie, you have such a soft skin', he whispers against her neck. She turns, smiling, and touches his cheek.

'And you have such a rough one.' It is true, his stubble is already re-appearing. He traps her hand and kisses her wrist, a question in his eyes. There is no need for words, her answer is in the way she pulls his head down so that his mouth meets hers.

The first thing she does when she arrives back at the hotel is stop and listen outside the boys' room. Music is playing softly but there is no other sound. They are obviously sound asleep, so she goes next door to the family room she is sharing with Linda and Lily. It has two large, double beds, one of which is occupied by Lily, who is also asleep. Linda is in her pyjamas with a magazine in her lap on the other bed. Although it is after midnight, she is wide awake.

'Hi Mags, did you have a good time? Sit down and tell me all about it.' She pats the cover beside her.

'Shove over, Linda, that's my bed. I'll tell you in a minute, I need to have a shower first. I've got sand in my knickers.'

Alex has promised to meet them for breakfast at their hotel next morning before he leaves for Athens, where he teaches history. They are already in the dining room when he arrives, so he takes a seat at the table between the twins. He has a seemingly endless fund of stories about Alexander the Great which Matty can't get enough of, but JJ moves his chair closer to Alex so that he's fenced in. JJ always tries to put a space between his mother and other men; he still hopes that his parents will get back together. Maggie usually finds this endearing but today she wants Alex next to her. All she can think of is the way he ran his hand slowly up her leg and into her pants then followed it with his mouth.

Because of this, she's finding it difficult to follow the conversation: Linda is nagging Lily to eat something else because she has this bee in her bonnet since she watched a programme about anorexic teenagers and Matty is saying something about night clubs in Athens.

'I think you are a leetle young to go to night clubs, but I will be happy to show you the Acropolis when you are there' Alex says, glancing at Maggie for support.

'Who's going to a night club? Not you or JJ, Matty, you can forget it'. Matty gives JJ a "well I tried" look and says 'I'm going to get some more pancakes, coming JJ?' They both get up and Lily grabs her plate and follows them to the buffet.

The previous night, Maggie gave Linda a detailed account of what happened on the beach. Linda has heard of Alex' sexual techniques before but never experienced them. Neither has Maggie. Now both women are studying him from under their eye lashes, but Alex is concentrating on his breakfast, approaching the food in a business-like manner which Maggie suspects he brings to everything he does. He definitely did that last night on the beach. Linda is wondering if all Greek men make love like that. She is also wondering if she can persuade Tom to have a go.

Alex finishes his breakfast and gestures to the waiter for more coffee.

'So, shall I take you to the Acropolis when you are in Athens, Ladies?'

'Definitely, it's one of the places on our list, isn't it Maggie? She pokes Maggie's thigh under the tablecloth and Maggie agrees, looking Alex in the eye for the first time since he sat down.

. 'Well, sadly I must leave you'. He stands and turns to bid goodbye to the youngsters, who have returned with plates piled high with pancakes

'I go now to Athens, My students are awaiting me', he says, kissing Maggie's hand, then Linda's. 'I bet they are' croons Linda under her breath.

CHAPTER 18

With 0nly three days of their holiday left they check out of their hotel and drive to Athens. It's a long, hot drive and it takes them ages to find their hotel, so when they ado find it they are all reluctant to et back in the car to explore the city. After thcy have all showered and changed, Linda and Maggie sit outside on the terrace while the kids go to check out the facilities at the hotel.

'You order drinks, Maggie. I'm just going to phone Tom to check everything's Ok at home'. Maggie understands that she is really checking that Tom has heard from Ritchie. She has done this nearly every day since they came away and Maggie knows she will do the same thing herself when the time comes for the twins to spread their wings. That's assuming they are not already driven apart by this love triangle with Lily.

While she's waiting for Linda, she orders a chilled bottle of the crisp white wine from Peloponnese and thinks about Alex.

'Tom said that Ritchie's probably on his way to the airport now. I can't wait to get home and see him, says Linda, sitting down.

'And I can't wait to see Alex', thinks Maggie. Tomorrow he is going to join them at their hotel after breakfast so they can drive to the Acropolis in two cars. Maggie knows that the kids will have had their fill of ancient monuments after that, even JJ, so the last day of their holiday will be spent looking round the shops. While they are waiting for the wine , Linda remembers they haven't agreed a price for this tour.

'Or is he doing it for love?' she smiles at her friend across the table.

'Of course not, I imagine he'll expect to be paid. We'll just offer him the same amount as we gave him last time. It will probably take about the same amount of time'. Alex arrives and the boys pile into his car, eager for some male company. 'Wait one moment boys, I must speak to your mother'. He gets out and walks over to Linda and Maggie.

Good morning, ladies. If you like I can direct you to a place where we can park which is not too far for walking. Would you like to follow me?' So they get into their hire car with Lily in the back and follow him up to the Acropolis. Even this early in the season there are long queues for tickets, so they are relieved when Alex says

'It is not necessary that you queue, I will get tickets quickly because I am tour guide. Children do not have to pay, so please give me thirty- three thousand, four hundred drachmas each for the ladies. They hand over the notes and Alex goes inside to get their tickets. When he returns they realise that they still have to queue at the entrance gates. Luckily Alex manages to bypass much of the queue by calling out 'Excuse me please, tour coming through' in an official- sounding voice before shepherding them past the waiting tourists.

The view from the top is fantastic. Alex follows the kids up the rocky slope and begins pointing out places of interest in the city below. There is so much to see that Maggie and Linda wish they could spend several days there.

'Never mind', says Linda, 'maybe you can come back for a long weekend and stay with Alex'. They walk along to the Parthenon, hoping in vain that its pillars will offer some shade. Matt and JJ, impervious to the heat, rush off excitedly, followed by Lily. 'I'd better go and see what they're up to, Maggie. You stay here with Alex in case we get lost.'

Linda has only gone a few steps away when Alex runs his hand up her bare arm, brushing the side of her breast with his fingers. Slowly and deliberately, he slides them back down until they reach her wrist. She knows her pulse must be racing, he can probably feel it, but she doesn't care.

'You have very nice kids, Maggie'. His hand is on her breast now, his thumb gently circling round her nipple beneath the flimsy fabric

'Thank you, I think so too' She is finding it hard to control her breathing but manages ' Did you never want children, Alex?'

'Unfortunately, my wife and I are unable to have children.'

'Your wife? You didn't tell me you have a wife.'

'Of course I have a wife. All Greek men have a wife'.

'But you slept with me, on the beach'.

'I did, and it was wonderful. You are so beautiful and so passionate.'

'And does your wife know?'

'She doesn't ask me about such matters.'

'And you don't tell her.'

'Exactly. You are angry, Maggie. What did you think?'

'I think I'm stupid Alex. Stupid and selfish. Stay here, I'm going to find Linda.' Linda notices something is wrong straight away, so Maggie tells her she has a headache. 'You've had too much sun. Look, your shoulders are burning too. Do you want to leave?'

'No Linda, I'll be fine. I'll just sit here in the shade and wait for you all. Look, there's Alex with the kids. Go on, go and enjoy yourself.'

Later, Linda insists she will drive them back and much to Maggie's relief it is dark by the time they arrive at the hotel. She gets out of the car quickly and asks,

'Can you settle up with Alex? I just want to go up to our room and lie down for a while.'

'Of course, but are you sure you're OK, Maggie?'

'I'm fine, I just need to take some aspirin and get rid of this headache.'

'All right, then I may as well take the kids straight in to dinner and give you some peace.'

Later, Maggie is sitting up in bed in front of the television when Linda comes into the room.

'HI, Mags, how are you feeling?'

'Much better, thanks. Where are the kids?'

'They've gone next door. I said they can rent a movie so long as it isn't porn. What happened with Alex?'

'What do you mean?'

'Well, it was obvious he upset you. What did he do?'

'He told me he's married. Oh Linda, I'm so ashamed.'

'Why are you ashamed? You're not married.'

'No, but I never thought I'd sleep with someone who is. I can't stop thinking about his wife, and the way I felt when Michael did the same to me. And I was so horrible to Michael at the time, but now I'm just as bad as he is'.

'You're confusing me now. Are you upset about Alex, his wife, or Michael? He refused to accept any payment, by the way.'

'Who did?'

'Alex, of course. He said he spent a very pleasant afternoon with good friends, not clients. He has to be at the university tomorrow, so he won't be able to come and say goodbye, but he gave me his card.' Maggie waves away the card so Linda places it on the bedside table.

'Well, it's there if you want it. Alex said that he hopes we will correspond with him, by which he meant that he hopes you will, obviously.'

Just then Lily comes into the room, followed by the twins.

'How's your headache now, Aunty Maggie?' Maggie pats the bed beside her, Lily sits down and is pulled into a hug.

'It's nearly gone, Sweetheart, I'm sure I'll be fine by tomorrow. I've got to be, haven't I, because we're going shoooopping.' She emphasises the last word and the kids let out an extended "Yaaaay" in unison. The twins do not normally like shopping, but they have been eying up the erotic souvenirs which can be seen on sale everywhere and Maggie knows they plan to take some home with them, presumably to amuse their friends. As for Lily, like most young girls she is always up for a spot of shopping.

CHAPTER 19

Maggie gets her degree, a very respectable 2.1, and applies for a job in the local Polytechnic's admissions department. In the interim Linda has completed a course in data processing and now works for a large medical supplies company. It turns out that she has unexpected an aptitude for technology and as a result she is earning a good salary for the first time in her life.

It has been a hectic year for Maggie. She has had to juggle her own course work and prepare for her finals while making sure the twins are up to speed with their school work. Also, she did quite a lot of soul-searching after she returned from Greece, especially about her relationship with Michael. Although he continues to be a good and loving father and is punctilious about keeping to their agreement over custody, his manner towards her has been guarded, even frosty since the night they slept together. Maggie has come to realise that she was spiteful and unnecessarily cruel that night and she wants to make amends.

Michael usually celebrates his birthday in a restaurant, previously surrounded by family and friends. Sadly, since his relations with Maggie became strained, the party last year was limited to JJ, Matty and Helen. This year, Maggie wants to make the occasion a proper celebration again, so she invites Linda, Tom and Julia, who is bringing her latest man with her, to the dinner. Helen is delighted that Maggie plans to attend and insists on booking the table herself.

'I'll let Michael know, Maggie, it will be my treat. It's not fair that he always pays for dinner on his birthday.' Michael usually turns up early when he takes the boys out, so Maggie asks all the guests to arrive at the restaurant fifteen minutes before him. That way there will be no awkwardness when he sees her.

When Michael arrives, Maggie is touched by the way his face lights up when he sees his friends waiting for him.

'Well, this is just like old times. Move over, you two, I want to sit by my mate.' His hands rest briefly on his sons' shoulders before they change chairs to make room for him next to Tom.

'Linda, you look exceptionally stunning tonight. In fact, all the ladies do.' His eyes linger on Maggie as he looks round the table, the tension eases and everyone relaxes.

It turns out to be a good evening. The food is good and the company even better. Julia's boyfriend is intelligent, with an easy manner and the knack of making small talk. After chatting for a while with the adults he turns his attention to JJ and Matty.

'I hear you' both took your O levels last summer. I remember it as being a very tough year. What's it like at college, are you enjoying it?'

'It's OK, but it's a bit annoying that we're not allowed out on week nights, apart from Fridays', says JJ.

'Yea, we're only here tonight because it's Dad's birthday. If it had been one of our friends, Mum wouldn't have let us come,' Matty chimes in before they poop on the party with their teenage " hard done by " routine.

'That reminds me, you haven't given your Dad his present yet.' She knows the boys have bought Michael an expensive polo shirt which they seem to have forgotten. JJ gets up and hands Michael the shirt; still in the plastic store bag.

'Happy birthday, Dad, this is from both of us.

.' Michael pulls out the shirt and holds it up so that everyone can see it.

'Look at this, it's just what I needed. Thanks, Guys, I'll wear it every time I play golf.'

Now it'is Matt's turn to get up. He has another plastic bag in his hand as he makes his way round the table to his father.

'We brought you something from Greece, too, Dad, but we forgot to give it to you.' He plonks the bag on the table and Michael takes out a small white statue. It appears to be of a Greek God, naked from the waist up but with graceful folds of fabric covering the lower part of the body. The adults pass it round the table, not saying anything, until it reaches Helen.

'Oh, it's beautiful, boys, so graceful. I'm sure your dad will give it pride of place in his sitting room'. Tom snorts and Michael says,

'Look at it again, Mum.' All the adults are looking down at the table now, trying to hold back their laughter. Poor Helen, the long years of sewing have taken their toll on her eyesight. Even with her glasses on, she cannot see that what appears at first glance to be a wide pleat in the fabric is in fact an enormous penis. Helen runs her fingers up and down the little figure. It is as smooth as real marble.

'What made you choose this one, Matty?' she asks. Was it something that you learned about in Art?'

'Not really, Gran, it just reminded me of Dad', answers Matty and everyone at the table gives in to their suppressed laughter.

A few days later Michael phones and asks Maggie to meet him for lunch. He tells her

'Don't worry, I'm not going to try to get you into bed again, I just thought it would be nice for us to have a chat, clear the air'. Maggie thinks so too, so they agree to meet in a local restaurant. She is waiting at the bar when Michael arrives, wearing a suit and tie. C*learly he's come straight from the office*, she thinks. He leans forward and gives her a chaste kiss on the cheek, then asks:

'Do you mind if we go straight to our table, I have an appointment later this afternoon.' When they are seated, they regard each other warily over the table decoration until Maggie breaks the silence.

'Michael, I'm sorry I was such a bitch to you that Christmas. What I said was unforgivable'.

'You mean when you said 'It was just sex? No need to apologise, I deserved it. I know I hurt you'

'You did hurt me, but you were never deliberately cruel. I was. I can see that now but at the time I was so angry and jealous.'

'Jealous? Of me?'

'Not of you. I was jealous of all the women you slept with.' He grins.

'There weren't that many.' The waiter brings their order, a salad for her, a steak for Michael, so they wait until he moves away then Michael continues:

'So, why the change of heart now? You've met someone, haven't you?'

'Not exactly. But I have had a couple of dates.' He studies her across the table. Her face is burning because she is thinking about Alex. She wishes now that she had not accepted that glass of red, it always makes her skin blotchy.

. 'I'm not going to ask, it's not my business anymore. Just promise me you'll be careful.'

'You're sounding like my dad now,' Maggie smiles. 'Why can't we just be friends? You always were my best friend, you know.'

'I thought Linda is your best friend?' She chuckles:

'OK, so you're my second- best friend, after Linda.' They eat in a companionable silence until Maggie asks,

'So was there anything in particular you wanted to talk to me about?'

'No, I told you, I just think it would be nice if we could meet for a chat sometimes. The boys would like it, too.'

'I doubt they'd notice. All they think about is girls these days.' Michael grins and takes her hand.

. 'We've done well with those two though, haven't we?'

'We have, and I'm so grateful to you for not changing towards them or trying to use them to get at me.'

'You know I'd never do that. So, what do you think of Julia's new man? He seems like a nice bloke, doesn't he?'

'He does', Maggie replies.

'Maybe she'll settle down with this one. I can't understand why she's still single. She deserves to be happy.'

'Yes, she's such a lovely person,' Maggie says, but she's thinking *'He still doesn't realise.'*

'So how about you, Michael. Are you seeing anybody?'

126

'On and off. I don't seem to meet the right type of girl for a serious relationship. Most of the women I meet are either dolly birds or businesswomen looking for a fling while they're away from home. That's not what I want.'

'What do you want then?'

'I want what we had. Something permanent. I know, there's no going back, but I miss being married, Mags.' Maggie places her hand over his and says:

'Maybe you're not looking in the right places. The woman who is right for you could be right under your nose.'

They leave the restaurant and Michael walks her towards her car. When they reach it she clicks the lock open then, on impulse, turns and hugs him, squeezing him tight. He whispers into her hair 'You know I'll always love you, Maggie'

'And I'll always love you, Michael.'

She watches him in the rear- view mirror as she drives off. He looks so forlorn as he turns away, then he straightens up and walks towards his car with his usual confident stride. Over the years Michael has aroused a variety of emotions in Magggie, but this is the first time that she has ever felt sorry for him.

CHAPTER 20

Maggie is the deputy head of Admin by the time JJ and Matt sit their A level exams. She has been fast-tracked to that position, partly because of her years of office experience but also because her analytical skills were enhanced by studying law. She has the ability to scrutinise tasks and problems in a clear-cut, practical way which some of her colleagues lack. Most of them have worked in the department for years and are simply treading water until retirement.

In addition, she has been pro-active in implementing policies which encourage women to return to education. Thanks to Maggie, the polytechnic now offers crèche facilities and is also considering setting up a 'Return to Education course' for mature students as an alternative to A level entry. She knows from experience that individuals who have been out of education for a while often lack the confidence to take on the milestone that is Advanced level.

The twins have both been offered places at university, Matt on a Theatre Studies course in London and JJ to study architecture at Cambridge. They wanted to go travelling for a year when they finish their exams, but Michael put his foot down. He agrees to fund them until September but insists that they must take up their university places after that, provided they get the right grades.

'What if you have to re-sit one of your subjects, you can't do that if you're travelling round Africa, can you?' he tells them. The boys do not give up that easily, however. 'Thanks Dad, it's nice to know that you have confidence in us', JJ tries, but Michael is not going to change his mind.

'You need to get a degree under your belts first so you can get started on a career as soon as you can. Do you think I'd be where I am today if I had wasted a year when I was your age?' Matt rolls his eyes and starts to speak but Michael cuts him short. He cannot shrug off his working- class approach to life, or the value placed on independence and self- sufficiency, and neither can Maggie. She is also grateful that Michael has imposed a time limit on their travels. JJ and Matty will now only have time to visit Australia, New Zealand and possibly North America, countries : she considers to be relatively safe. On the whole she agrees with Michael that the boys should get jobs and earn enough money to support themselves if they want to go away for a whole year.

Over the coming weeks the twins keep trying to get Maggie on their side but she is adamant

. 'What makes you think that your dad should be willing to keep working hard so that you can both travel the world and live the high life? He has never been able to do it himself, so why should he pay for you to do it? Get yourself part-time jobs, you'll have plenty of spare time at university, and save the money to go travelling after you graduate' she suggests.

Both boys have finished their' exams are by mid-May, so they begin their preparations to be gone. They are constantly on the phone to their friends, discussing which boots, shorts and other necessaries will be most useful, and they have already had three sessions with their travelling companions to plan the journey. Five of them are going in total. The twins and one other boy are due to return home at the end of August, leaving the remaining two to set off for the Far East.

The boys have never been away without one or other of their parents, apart from school trips and the like, and Maggie is dreading it. Actually, she is not sure which she's dreading most, their extended holiday abroad or the likelihood that they will be leaving to go to university when they return. Knowing that their absence will create a huge gap in her life, despite her busy work schedule, she has taken up running. She has never been much of a fitness addict so initially she struggled but now she is quite a proficient runner. Part of the reason she persevered was because she wanted to lose weight, but as running got easier she found herself enjoying it more and more. Nowadays she looks forward to her evening runs.

She is often accompanied by her neighbour, Barry, who is a keen runner as well as a golfer. He still plays golf with Michael occasionally and they also have some kind of business connection, although Maggie doesn't ask him about that. When she first took up running, she went to a nearby park where the level pathways are much favoured by walkers and parents with children, as well as joggers. Now, at weekends or when the evenings are light enough, she avoids the crowds and takes the winding road up the hill. Even super-fit Barry works up a sweat going up-hill but near the top a lane branches off which has a much less steep gradient. The surface is also softer, making it kinder on the knees so Maggie prefers to run there. The lanes are so peaceful, there is hardly any traffic up there and in summer the branches of the trees meet overhead, dappling the ground with sunlight. In good weather, Barry and Maggie often stop for a breather along the lane. Sitting on a style at the end of the day, civilisation seems far away, even though they can see the houses and traffic down below.

On the day that the twins set off on their travels, Maggie, Helen and Michael drive them up to Heathrow. Later, in the evening, Maggie feels restless. Helen is going out to her book club, which suits Maggie because she's not in the mood to socialise. The house feels empty, She goes from room to room, picking up items of clothing the boys have discarded she cannot concentrate on anything. In the end she decides to go for a run. She changes into her running gear then starts up the hill but there are road works ahead and traffic is being filtered through one side of the street. She stops by a builder who is holding up a ""Stop" sign. and starts jogging on the spot, but she is not in the mood to be patient. *Oh, sod this,* she thinks, *I might as well go home and soak in a hot bath.* She runs back down the hill and is nearly at the turning leading to her house when Barry dives up in the truck he uses for work. He turns the corner then slows down.

'Hi, Maggie, did you have a good run?'

'No, couldn't get past the roadworks so I gave up. I've only been out for ten minutes.'

'It's not like you to give up. Is everything OK?'

'Yes, I'm just in a bad mood: The boys left today on their travels.'

'Well, don't stay at home moping. Maureen and I are going out for a meal, so why don't you go and get changed and come with us. Go on.'

'That's nice of you Barry, but I don't think I'd be very good company tonight.'

'Just go and get ready. You're coming with us, no arguments. We'll pick you up in half an hour.' Maggie does not have the energy to argue and anyway Barry has already driven off towards his own house. She goes indoors and finds Hetty waiting to greet her. The old dog spends most of her time sleeping nowadays but she is always ready and hovering near her bowl at mealtimes. Maggie goes into the kitchen and feeds her, then opens the back door to let her out into the garden before going upstairs. By the time she has showered, washed her hair and applied a little make-up the doorbell is ringing. There is no time to dry her hair properly now so she knows it will probably go mad and end up being unfashionably curly. Well, there is nothing she can do about it and anyway she does not really care, Maureen won't notice.

Maggie likes Barry's wife, Maureen, but even her best friend would not call her a style icon. She is plump and her clothes, though of good quality, are always frumpy. She speaks with a broad Yorkshire accent which somehow adds to the 'Mumsy' effect, although this is deceiving. She keeps a sharp eye on Barry's business accounts and is involved in several charities, as well as baby sitting her grandchildren. She also plays bridge and Maggie knows from experience that Maureen is as sharp as a tack, having played against her when she was trying to learn bridge. Like Barry, Maureen also has a great sense of humour, so the couple are always good company. They can liven up even the dullest party so Maggie feels better already.as she runs down the stairs and out of the front door,

Outside, Barry has exchanged his truck for their family saloon, a large BMW with impressive chrome headlights and tinted windows. Because of the windows, she has opened the door and put one leg inside the car before she realises there is someone else sitting in the back.

'Oh, Hello' she offers as she eases herself into the car. Barry twists round and looks over the back of the seat

' Have you two met before? Maggie, this is our friend Jonathan,' before engaging the gear and zooming off.

CHAPTER 21

Jonathan looks a little older than Maggie, late fourties or early fifties, she guesses. He is lean and looks fit, not exactly good-looking but with regular features and a pleasant expression. When he speaks his voice has undertones of a transatlantic drawl

. 'Hi Maggie, it's nice to meet you. Barry tells me you've just waved your kids off on their travels. That's tough, isn't it?'

'It is. It sounds as though you've gone through it yourself.'

'Yes, my son took a gap year and went travelling with his friends. He had a great time and grew up a lot while he was away, but I don't think I had a good night's sleep until he got back.'

Maureen turns in her seat and joins in the conversation.,

'We thought we'd go to Porto's if you're all right with that, Maggie?
'

'Of course, that will be lovely. If we're going to Porto's I already know what I'm going to order.'

'You've obviously been there before then' Jonathan observes.

'Yes, Michael and I have had some great meals there with Maureen and Barry.'

'And great times too', chuckles Barry. 'We were always the last to leave'. He is concentrating on driving so Maureen explains:

'Michael is Maggie's ex-husband.'

'Oh, I see. I'm sorry to hear that.'

'No need. We get on better since we split up, we've become good friends. So where is your son now?'

'He's studying medicine in London and his sister's doing law at LSE'.

'They're both high- fliers then.'

Yes, I'm very proud of them'.

'And did your daughter take a gap year too?'

'No, she started hinting that she wanted to take a year off to go travelling when she was in the sixth form, but I couldn't bring myself to let her go. In the end we agreed a compromise. She spent that summer going around Europe by train then last summer she went to New York as a nanny.'

'And was she satisfied with that?'

'She was. To be honest, I don't think she really wanted to go away for a year, she just thought it was the cool thing to do. And her brother told her some scary stories to put her off. He's very protective of her.'

'I can understand that, I would have liked to have a daughter. My best friend's girl, Lily, is like a daughter to me but it's not quite the same thing.'

'You only have the twins, then?'

'Yes. I don't think our families are very fertile. I'm an only child and so is Michael. We were lucky that we had twins, I suppose.'

'Be grateful you've only got boys, Maggie, daughters are hell. When our girls were teenagers I used to go out every night to get away from them.'

'Get away with you, Barry, you know you dote on them really', says Maureen.'

'I do, but it was hard to put up with all the drama and door-slamming when they lived at home. And the knickers all over the bathroom floor. Not to mention all their lotions and potions cluttering up the washstand. Some mornings I could hardly see in the mirror to shave.'

'They weren't that bad.. Anyway, they had their own bathroom.'

'Yes, but they didn't stay in it, did they? Our Sally is the only female I know who can occupy two bathrooms at the same time. One evening we were getting ready to go out but couldn't get into our bathroom because she was colouring her hair in it while doing something else in the other one. Do you remember that, Maureen?'

'I do. She had the conditioner laid out in our bathroom, ready to use when she washed off the hair colourant, so she went into the other one to put fake tan on her legs while she was waiting. ' Maureen answers, laughing.

'What's your Zoe like when she comes home, Jonathan?'

Actually, Zoe won't be home much this summer because she's got herself a job in a family centre. She's thinking of specialising in family law, so the idea is to experience first- hand the kind of problems she would have to deal with. I know it'll be an eye-opener for her, but I'll probably spoil her rotten when she does come down. I'm hoping that working in a family centre will make her realise how lucky she is.'

When they arrive at the restaurant they are greeted effusively by the head waiter. 'Mrs Johnson, how nice to see you again. No need to ask how you are, you're looking wonderful, as usual.' Maggie notices that he does not ask after Michael, so assumes he must know that they split up. She wonders whether Michael has been there with other women, then dismisses the thought. It's not her business any longer.

Once they are all seated at the table the conversation becomes more general. Barry and Maureen have the gift of putting people at their ease but Maggie suspects that Jonathan is equally comfortable in any company. He is relaxed and unassuming, with a dry sense of humour which contrasts nicely with Barry's more blunt observations, so the group soon gels. By the time the waiter brings their main course they are laughing and joking, just like old times.

A couple seated in a corner on the other side of the restaurant are obviously friends of Barry and Maureen, because they exchanged waves when they came in. On their way to the door, the couple stop for a chat. While they are talking, Jonathan leans towards Maggie and wispers,

'Do you get the feeling that we've been set up?'

'Yes, I do. I'm sorry, it wasn't my idea, I thought only the three of us were going out.'

'Don't apologise, I'm glad they did it. Are you?'

'I am actually'. And Maggie realises that it's true.

Maggie and Jonathan see a lot of each other that summer. The first time they go out for a meal together, he tells her about his marriage.

'We met at university. Her family have a ranch in Arizona, and she was over here on a student exchange. When we fell in love and got married; both of us thought we would be happy forever so long as we were together. I suppose we were too young to think things through. Anyway, we were happy at first, although she missed the open spaces of Arizona. She said riding just isn't the same here. She hated the idea of keeping to bridle paths and rarely getting above a trot.

After our daughter Zoe was born my wife was lethargic and depressed, so I suggested she take the children on an extended visit to her family. I thought it was the ideal time, because once Jonathan junior started infant school we would only be able to take them away during school holidays. So she went, provisionally for six weeks, but she kept delaying her return, telling me how much Jon was enjoying himself. By the time she had been there for nine months I had some accrued holiday entitlement, so I went over to join them. The plan was that she and the children would all return to the UK with me. We spent a happy ten days together but just before we were due to travel back to London, she told me she wasn't coming. She said she could never be happy away from the ranch.'

'Oh, that's terrible. Didn't she give you any indication that she wasn't coming back with you before that?'

'Well, I suppose the signs were all there, but I was too busy with my new career to read them.'

'So, what happened about the children?'

'They stayed with her. In the beginning I tried to get a job there. I took six months sabbatical and stayed with her folks while I applied for work, but they lived much too far away from the world of publishing. I couldn't see any point in moving to New York on my own when they were all happy in Arizona, so I came back here. I used to go over there to see the kids once or twice a year and they spent a couple of summers here with me when they were old enough. I should tell you now that we never divorced, Maggie. Officially, I'm still a married man.'

'And unofficially?'

'Oh, our marriage was over years ago. She has an on-going relationship with someone else, but doesn't seem in any hurry to marry him, so we've never really discussed divorce.'

'So how come your children are over here now?'

'They each came to live with me when they reached high school, one after the other. They prefer living here, where everything is virtually on tap, compared to the wide- open spaces. I brought them both up from age eleven. And what about you, Maggie? Why did you get divorced?'

'I divorced Michael because he was a serial two-timer and I couldn't live with that. He was a good husband in every other way though.'

Every time they meet, they talk and talk: Over dinner, walking along the sea front on a cool evening, or looking down over the city from his car'. They even go to an open- air performance of "Tosca" in the castle. It turns out to be a chilly evening and Maggie is soon shivering beneath the jacket she thought would be warm enough, so Jonathan takes off his pullover and insists she puts it on underneath her jacket.

They are sitting on the ground on a picnic blanket, so he puts his arm round her and pulls her close for additional warmth.

'Come on, you can share my body heat, too.' It's a friendly, gentleman-like gesture and Maggie receives it as such because, although she enjoys his company, they've never exchanged more than a chaste peck on the cheek at the end of their dates.

She leans in against him and it is only natural in that position that her head should fit comfortably onto his shoulder. Tosca has just promised to sleep with Scarpia if he lets her lover, Cavaradossi, go free, so there is a brief interlude in the singing while the sets are adjusted. Moved by the passion and emotion of the opera, Maggie blurts out

'How come you've never tried to sleep with me, Jonathan?' Jonathan smiles his enigmatic smile and says

: 'I'm waiting for the right time and place and I don't think that's here, do you?'

'If you'd asked me that question twenty years ago, I would probably have disagreed with you, Jonathan', she laughs.

A few days later, Maggie and Helen are pottering in the garden. They more or less took charge of the gardening after Helen moved into the annexe and they enjoy working on it together. If there is a job which is too much for them, they call in a local handyman, and Barry is always ready to send one of his workers if he notices something needs doing. He'll phone and say,

'I noticed your hedge needs cutting again, Maggie. I'll send one of my lads round with the hedge-cutters. He can do it on his way home. No need to pay him, just slip him a couple of quid as a tip'. Now Helen is dead-heading the roses while Maggie is pulling off withered geranium shoots and giving the remains a last feed before the autumn. They are both absorbed in what they are doing and do not hear the doorbell ring, until they are alerted by Hetty's barking. She still takes her position as a guard dog seriously, despite her advancing age. Helen, who is nearest to the side gate, says

'I'll go'. When she returns a little later, she is followed by Jonathan.

'I hope I'm not intruding, I just called in on the off chance that I'd find you here. But I can see that you're both busy.'

'No, not at all, I was just going inside, I've done enough for today', says Helen. This is the first time she has met Jonathan and she is giving Maggie an approving thumbs up behind his back.

'Are you staying for supper?'

'Oh, I wouldn't want to be any trouble, Mrs Johnson'.

'It's no trouble at all. I made a Bolognese sauce earlier, so I'll only have to cook some extra pasta. We'd love you to stay, wouldn't we Maggie?' Helen goes inside and Jonathan moves nearer to Maggie. She is flushed from her exertions and her hair has been blown about in the wind.

'You look exactly the way you did on the night we met. I like your hair when you let it curl like that.' Maggie laughs,

'I didn't let it, the wind did it.'

'Well, I like it. I imagine this is how you look when you're making love.' He's suddenly serious, looking straight into her eyes and Maggie returns his gaze without flinching, refusing to look away as she says

'Well, there's only one way to find out, isn't there? Come on, let's go in and make the salad'

After supper, Helen leaves them alone.

'Do you mind if I leave the dishes for you to sort out, Maggie, I feel a bit tired now'.

Then she turns to Jonathan

'It was nice meeting you, I hope you'll come again.' He walks Helen to the door then comes back and starts scraping the plates, putting them in the dishwasher while Maggie tidies the kitchen and wipes down the kitchen table. She gets out a second bottle of wine.

'Come on, let's go and sit in the lounge. Bring your glass with you.' When they are comfortably seated on the sofa Jonathan asks,

'Are you sure you don't mind my dropping in like this? It must be awkward for you with your mother- in- law living so near.'

'Not at all, Helen's one of my best friends. I'm as close to her as I am to my own mother.'

'But doesn't she mind you having men friends here at the house?' Maggie laughs.

'If you're asking whether she minds me having men staying the night here, the answer is, it's never happened. I wouldn't dream of sleeping with anyone here if my sons were at home, either.'

'Well, your sons aren't here now, so come here.' He pulls Maggie towards him and kisses her, a long, deep kiss, taking his time. But Maggie doesn't want to wait any longer so she moves away and says,

'Come on, let's go upstairs.'

A few evenings later, Maggie goes round to Helen's with a takeaway. She rings the doorbell before using her key to open the front door, then calls out

'Meals on wheels delivery service, where are you?' as she heads towards the kitchen. When Helen comes into the kitchen she looks as if she has just woken up and Maggie knows she often dozes off in front of the TV these days.

'Is it Chinese? Oh super. I only had a light lunch today, I was saving myself for the takeaway.'

'Well, tuck in then. I got you prawns in chili sauce and chicken chow mein. Is that OK?'

'Perfect'. They chat while they're eating until Helen opens the subject which Maggie has been dying to talk to her about.

'Your Jonathan seems very nice, Maggie'.

'He's not my Jonathan.'

'Well, he could be, he's obviously very taken with you.'

'Do you think so? He's a difficult one to read. I know we get on really well together, we always have a good time when we go out.'

'Then perhaps you should stay in with him sometimes, see how things develop.'

'Mrs Johnson, are you suggesting I should have carnal knowledge of him?

Maggie laughs.

'Yes, I am. Maggie, you do know that I wouldn't mind if Jonathan stayed here overnight, don't you?'

'Really? You wouldn't mind? What about Michael?'

'It would be nothing to do with Michael. Though I'm sure he would be upset if you took up with a wrong 'un, which Jonathan clearly isn't, because he still cares about you.'

'I know. So, you really liked Jonathan, did you? He is funny, isn't he?'

'I think he's funny, and charming and polite. He's also very attractive. Not handsome like Michael and the boys, obviously, but there's something about him which draws you to him, I can't quite explain it.'

'I can see I might have some competition then if things get serious,' Maggie smiles.

'You might. I may be old but I'm not dead, as they say.'

CHAPTER 22

Maggie does not miss the twins as much as she expected she would, mostly because she is spending so much time with Jonathan. Since his first meeting with Helen, he has become a regular caller at the house. Sometimes he just pops in for a short visit or to pick up Maggie if they are going out, sometimes he stays the night. Helen says she likes him more and more every time she sees him, which gives Maggie enough confidence to introduce him to the person who has the potential to be his biggest critic – namely Linda. Linda has been dying to meet him but has been working longer hours than usual recently. She is involved in developing software for selling online and has already spoken to Michael about the potential benefit to his business of installing the software.

Now Michael, never one to miss out on a business opportunity, is trying to get Linda to give up her job and go to work for him. He wants her to set up and manage an IT section, but so far she has refused his offers. She is afraid that it would put them both in a difficult position if the current amicable relations between him and Maggie ever break down. Now, despite her heavy workload, she has ring-fenced this evening for a dinner date with Tom, Maggie and Jonathan, announcing to her colleagues at the office,

'I don't care if we're running out of time. Tonight I'm going to meet my best friend's new man.'

Unaware of the magnitude of the event for Maggie, Jonathan offers to do the driving this evening. They have not gone far before he senses that Maggie is nervous. He asks whether she is OK and she says she is fine, but she keeps fidgeting, opening and closing her handbag and adjusting her skirt as though she was going to a job interview. While they are parking the car outside the restaurant Jonathan reaches over and takes her hand,

'Relax, Sweetheart. Your friend will love me simply because you do. You do love me, don't you?' This is the first time either of them has mentioned the word love. It is so typical of Jonathan, matter of fact, no drama. Surprised, Maggie says

'Yes, I suppose I do.' He pulls up the hand brake and turns to face her,

'Good, because I'm nuts about you.'

Inevitably, Maggie must get together with Linda as soon as possible to hear her verdict on Jonathan, so she arranges to go round to Linda's the following Saturday evening.

'Good, we'll send Tom down the pub then we can have a good gossip', Linda tells her.

Tom already has his coat on when Maggie arrives, but he stops to kiss her and say, 'Nice bloke, that Jonathan, Maggie.'

'He is, isn't he Tom? I'm so glad you liked him.'

'Go on, Tom', Linda urges, impatient for her gossip session with Maggie.

'OK, I'm going, though I don't know why I can't stay. We all know what you're going to be talking about this evening.'

'Well, if you know what we'll be talking about there's no point in your staying, is there? And don't forget you might have to pick up Lily tonight, so you can't have more than one pint.'

Lily has just turned seventeen so she can now get into the night clubs frequented by students. She has promised her parents that she will never come home on her own late at night. She usually shares a taxi with a friend, but sometimes that isn't possible. When that does happen, she telephones to ask her parents for a lift. Because of this, neither of them can relax until Lily is safely home at night.

Once Tom has left Maggie and Linda settle down in the lounge. 'Do you fancy wine or a G and T, Maggie?'

'It had better be a G and T I think. If you open a bottle of wine, I'll keep drinking and I have to drive home'.

'You could always stay here, or phone for a taxi. Why don't you leave your car here and get the lovely Jonathan to drop you back to collect it tomorrow. '

'He is lovely isn't he?'

'OK, I can see this is going to be a long conversation. I'll open a bottle of wine'. Linda knows Maggie so well that she can tell that Jonathan makes her happy. He is not the best-looking guy she has ever been out with, and he definitely can't hold a candle to Michael in the looks department, but he is just so nice. As soon as they met Linda felt he was genuine: honest and direct and clearly very witty. At dinner the other night he had them in stitches with his dry comments. In some ways, Jonathan's gentle, unassuming manner reminds Linda of Tom.

The two women settle down, each with a glass of wine in her hand, and inevitably the conversation turns to sex. 'So come on, Mags, tell me, what's he like in bed?'

'What makes you think I know?'

'It's written all over you, in fact all over both of you. Anyone can see you're sleeping together. So tell me'.

'All right, he's lovely. Sweet, gentle, takes his time.'

'No acrobatics then?'

'No, and I don't want any. Sex with Jonathan is very satisfying, that's the only way to describe it.'

'Well, you can't get better than satisfaction, can you? Come on, I want details.' Later in the evening, tipsy from the wine, they start reminiscing. 'I can't remember a time when you and Tom weren't together, Maggie tells Linda.

'Haven't you ever wondered what it would be like to sleep with someone else?

'Of course I have. I wonder what it would be like to sleep with Leonardo de Caprio all the time.'

'No, seriously.'

'Well, when you meet a good-looking guy you can't help wondering what it would be like, but I've never been tempted to find out. I love Tom and in bed it's just like it is for you with Jonathan – satisfying'.

'But you weren't always that easily satisfied, the pair of you were always at it. Do you remember the time you did it on a stool in his mother's kitchen? You were like a pair of stray cats.' Linda giggles.

When Tom arrives home Maggie and Linda are in the kitchen. Maggie is putting crackers and crisps onto plates and Linda is taking cheese out of the fridge.

'Ah, a midnight feast. Good idea, girls,' says Tom. 'Put the kettle on, Love.'

Tom cannot understand what he said to make both women double up with laughter.

CHAPTER 23

The boys return home, sun-tanned but scruffy in clothes that have not seen an iron for ages. They have obviously had a great time but now their focus is on preparing for university. Actually, all they really seem interested in is stocking up on new clothes, the trendier the better, so inevitably Maggie is left to shop for the boring stuff, mostly kitchen equipment and bedding. She has just returned home after an exhausting trip to the shops when she gets a telephone call from Michael.

Hi Mags, I bet you're glad to have the terrible twins back. I'm really phoning to ask for your help. It's Mum's seventieth birthday in two weeks' time so I want to give her a surprise party.'

'Oh, Michael, that's a lovely idea. She'll be so pleased. How can I help?'

'Well, I've provisionally booked the function room at the golf club. Obviously, I'll invite the usual crowd, Tom and Linda, Barry and Maureen and a few others, but I don't really know any of Mum's friends. Can you get hold of their contact details and invite as many as you can? Then let me know how many of them can come.'

'That's easy, I'll pinch her phone book and get in touch with all of them. Shall I invite my parents too?'

'Yes, of course. And we need to get her there without her suspecting anything. I thought we could tell her that we're going to the club for dinner, just the four of us.'

'The four of us?'

'Yea, I thought you might want to bring lover boy.'

Well, your mother does like Jonathan, so I'm sure she'd be happy to see him there. I'll see if he's available. What about the boys?'

'They found their way all over Australia so they can make their own way there. Anyway, seeing them waiting for her will be part of the surprise. Just make sure that they get there, no excuses.'

'I will, leave it to me. Is there anything else I can do, organise menus, decorate the room?'

'No thanks, everything's sorted. I've got a friend helping with all of that.' Maggie knows that the friend will be a woman. She wonders if this one is likely to be serious, he has never involved one of his women in family events before. Still, she is glad that he is doing something special for Helen, even if he has left it until the last minute. Typically, he just assumes that everyone else will be available to fit in with his plans.

The boys are upstairs, ostensibly sorting through their clothes and bagging those destined for the charity shop, but Maggie knows they are probably lying on a bed and talking in that shorthand that only twins can share. They have come home with dozens of photos taken on their travels; most of them with girls prominently featured.. She guesses that they are now sexually active, assuming they weren't before they went away, and worries that one of them will get some nice girl pregnant, or even contract AIDS. She will have to ask Michael to talk to them again about behaving responsibly. She always gets embarrassed whenever she tries to talk to the twins about sex.

Now she forces herself off of the couch and goes upstairs to tell them about the party. They are instantly enthusiastic, which pleases Maggie because they are at that age when family get- togethers are something to be avoided. The twins are fond of all their grandparents, Maggie's mother because she still fusses over them and her father because his sexist comments make them laugh, but Helen is their favourite. Now all Maggie has left to do is tell Jonathan, who has not met Michael yet.

'Jon, will you be available on the Saturday after next for Helen's seventieth birthday bash? It's a surprise party.'

'Of course, I'll look forward to it.'

'The thing is, Michael is organising it and he wants us to pretend that we're just taking her out to dinner. She'll think it strange if Michael doesn't come, so he wants the four of us to leave together.'

'So, you want me to pretend that Helen, you and I are going out to dinner with your ex?'

'Basically, yes.'

'Well, I guess that should make it interesting. So what's the plan?'

'Michael will collect the three of us and drive us to the golf club where everybody else will be waiting. If you like, I'll make sure Helen sits in the front seat so you and Michael won't really have to talk to each other much. It's only a twenty- minute drive from my house.'

'Well, now I'm really looking forward to it.'

But Maggie isn't. Michael has never shown any desire to meet Jonathan before and she suspects that, since she has helped organise it, Michael's new woman will be at the party. She thinks he probably wants to show her off and, although Jonathan is definitely not someone to be ashamed of, she is worried that the evening will turn into a "who has the best new partner" competition. She knows she is being ridiculous, but she can't help it so, instead of looking forward to Helen's party, she is beginning to dread it.

Nevertheless, that does not stop her from making sure she looks the best she possibly can, so she buys an expensive new dress and has her hair and nails done on the morning of the party. Matt and JJ are still junior members at the golf club, so they are going to play a round of golf then shower and change there. Now she is nervously waiting for Jonathan to arrive. She almost wishes he will be late so they will have to leave without him, but he arrives ten minutes early and parks his car in front of the garage. He is normally right on time, so Maggie wonders whether he has come early to establish possession before Michael arrives, then dismisses the thought. Jonathan is just not like that.

. 'I know I'm a bit early', he says. 'I wanted to make sure that everything went off as planned. Do you think Helen guesses there's something up?'

'No, I don't think she has a clue. Careful, here she is now'. Helen comes out of her front door and Jonathan goes over to wish her a happy birthday, handing her a carefully wrapped little parcel. Soon after that Michael arrives, driving too fast as usual. Michael is always exceptionally polite when he feels uncomfortable and tonight it shows as the introductions are made. He insists that Jonathan takes the front seat, saying

'No, my mother will be more comfortable in the back with Maggie, she doesn't like the way I drive', before helping Helen into the back of the car. He then goes round to the other side and says

'Maggie, you look beautiful tonight, as always', before opening the door and ensuring her skirts are safely tucked inside before he slams it shut.

Helen is moved to tears at the number of people who have come to celebrate her birthday. She cannot stop hugging everyone, first Michael, then Maggie and Jonathan, she literally hugs her way round the room. When she reaches the spot where Matt and JJ are standing, delighted smiles on their faces, Maggie notices for the first time the woman standing next to them.

She is tallish, thirtyish with longish hair - *everything about her is "ish". I wonder if she's Michael's new friend. She seems to be quite familiar with the twins and she's got her hand on JJ's arm.* JJ notices his mother watching them and moves back slightly, forcing the woman to take her hand away. *That clinches it, she's Michael's new girlfriend, JJ doesn't want to upset me. He and Matty must have met her before they went away, so she's been with Michael for at least three months. Perhaps he's going to settle down a last, she thinks. Poor Julia'.*

Michael has decided on a buffet meal because it will be more informal, so there is plenty of time to mingle with the other guests while the food is being set out. Maggie has not met some of Helen's friends before, so now she wants to thank them for coming at such short notice. She is chatting to a charming white-haired old lady when Linda appears at her side.

'I'm sorry to interrupt, Maggie, but the caterer wants a word'. As soon as they are out of earshot Linda hisses,

'See the dark-haired woman over there talking to Jonathan? I think she's Michael's girlfriend'.

'Well, let's go over and find out, shall we?' Jonathan senses their approach and turns.

'Ah, here she is now. Maggie, have you met Michelle? She's responsible for organising this party. I was just saying how beautiful the room looks.' Maggie looks around the room at the soft swathes of muslin which have replaced the usual heavy brocade window hangings. There are also vases of rose buds and gypsophilia scattered around the room, all decorated with pale pink ribbons. On one end of the buffet table there is a bank of pink flowers with "Happy birthday Mum" spelled out in white. It is all blatantly sentimental, not at all Helen's style so Maggie mentally adds "mawkish" to her list of adjectives.

'Yes, it's lovely. It must have taken you ages to organise all this.'

'Not really, I do it for a living. I'm an events manager'. She holds out her hand, forcing Maggie to take it. She is outwardly forceful and assertive, but Maggie senses that her apparent confidence probably masks insecurity. She almost feels sorry for her as asks

'Nice to meet you, Michelle. So tell me, how did you meet Michael?'

Later in the evening there is dancing. The DJ gets the ball rolling with a sedate waltz and Michael escorts Helen on to the floor for this first dance. After a few turns other couples join in and Jonathan cuts in on Michael,

'Sorry, Mike, your mother promised me a dance' before whisking her away. Michael has never been particularly fond of dancing, but seeing Maggie standing nearby he he pulls her onto the dance floor.

'Come on Mags, let's show 'em how it's done.'

'It's not like you to take to the floor willingly, Michael. What's the occasion?'

'I don't know, I just had the urge to dance with you again. You're not really serious about that lefty bloke, are you?'

'I am and he's not a lefty. What makes you think he is?'

'He's in publishing isn't he? They're all lefties.'

'Oh Michael, can't you just be happy for me?'

'No, I can't. I will never be happy to see you with somebody else.'

'Well, that's the difference between you and me, isn't it Michael?'

Maggie leaves him in the middle of the dance floor and goes over to where her parents are talking to the twins. She hopes her dad is not saying anything inappropriate to them, but she suspects he is because the boys are laughing but her mother isn't. Recently her father has started treating the twins as if they are drinking buddies with whom he swaps racy stories. He goes into a huddle with them, often not bothering to lower his voice, then asks them "what they get up to" with girlfriends. The boys find it funny but Maggie finds it disgusting. Not only is he encouraging bad behaviour but he is fostering a disrespect for women which she finds totally unacceptable. She knows there is only one way to stop him, so she goes over to him and says

, 'Dad, I haven't bought you a drink yet. Come on, come to the bar with me then we can get a drink for Mum too.'

The party is due to end at midnight, so Maggie starts to gather up her flock at a quarter to twelve. She has booked a taxi to take her, Helen and Jonathan back to her house and does not want to keep the driver waiting. Before she leaves the club, she just wants to remind the boys that Michael asked them to spend the weekend with him. She can see JJ across the room. He is chatting to Jonathan and Tom, no doubt telling them about his travels, but there is no sign of Matty. She spots Linda and goes towards her, meeting her halfway.

'Have you seen Matty anywhere?' at the same time as Linda says,

' Do you know where Lily went?' They both turn and survey the room. There is only one entrance apart from a wired- up fire exit. Maggie is thinking *'If he's done anything he shouldn't with Lily I'm going to kill him.'* She does not know what Linda is thinking, she is afraid to look at her.

'They probably went out for some fresh air, or maybe Matty is showing her round the club, Linda. Come on, let's go and look for them.' They go into the adjacent bar which opens onto the terrace. In the daytime it is usually busy with people having a drink after golf, but now it is deserted. Linda goes over to the stone balustrade and looks out at the deserted golf course.

'I can't see anyone, can you Maggie?' Maggie knows she will not see them on the course because she has spotted someone lurking in the shadows, away from the light.

'No, theymust have walked round to the front. You go and look from the inside and I'll walk round on the grass. That way, we're bound to bump into them.' As soon as Linda goes inside Maggie turns and calls,

'Matt, is that you?'

'Hi, Mum, what's up? I was just telling Lily about Australia. She wants to go there next year.' He comes towards her, Lily following slightly behind him, pulling at the hem of her ra-ra skirt. It is very clear to Maggie that, whatever he was telling her, it was not about Australia.

'Lily, your mum's looking for you. Go back through the bar and wait with your dad.' Lily retreats inside, her head down to mask her sheepish smile.

'Matt, you do realise that Lily's parents are my oldest friends. How could you? And don't say you were telling her about Australia. I'm really disappointed with you. And how do you think your brother would feel if he knew?'

'What do you mean?'

'You must know that JJ's been in love with Lily for years.'

'What, JJ?'

'Yes, JJ. Your twin brother. Don't tell me you haven't noticed. How long have you been out here, anyway?'

'Not long, about ten minutes. We were only messing around, Mum. Nothing happened.'

'Well, something happened to her skirt. Tell the truth, Matt. Did you do anything with Lily?'

'If you mean, did we have sex, the answer is "No".

'But you would have if we hadn't come out, wouldn't you?'

'Maybe. I don't know. Look Mum, I'm sorry. I didn't realise she's off limit'.

'Well, you should have realised. I can't believe I need to tell you that.'

'What about JJ? You won't say anything to him, will you?'

'I don't know, I'm too angry to think at the moment. Go and find your father. You're going home with him tonight, remember?'

157

Maggie goes back to the function room. Most of the guests have already left, leaving Jonathan, JJ and Helen waiting there with Michael.

'Come on, Maggie, where were you? These guys want to go home.' Michael indicates the waiters, who are already at work tidying the room.

'Sorry everyone. Let's go then, shall we?'

They all troop outside to where a lone taxi driver is waiting.

'How are you getting home then, Michael?'

'Michelle's offered us a lift. She's gone to fetch her car from the car park. She won't be long.'

'Well, we'd better go. Your mum must be tired and our driver will be fed up by now.' The truth is Maggie does not want to linger. She is still angry with her son but she can't say anything in front of JJ. What is more, she does not want to watch Michael and the twins drive off with Michelle At the house they see Helen safely into her flat, before Jonathan asks 'What's wrong, Hon?'

'Nothing's wrong. I'm tired, that's all'. He gazes at her for a moment.

: 'OK, I'll just go then, shall I?'

'No, don't go. Come in, I'll make us some tea.' In the kitchen Maggie switches on the kettle, then blurts out:

'I found Lily and Matt snogging outside.' Jonathan waits for her to continue. When she doesn't he asks: 'And?'

'I 'm just so disappointed. Lily's like a sister to Matt and he hadn't even realised that JJ's in love with her'. She is tearful now, so Jonathan moves nearer and puts his arms round her.

'You're not making sense, Maggie. Was Matt forcing her or something?'

'No, of course he wasn't, but I didn't expect to find them snogging.'

'Well eighteen year- old boys do snog girls, you know. It happens all the time.' He smiles.

'Yes, but not Lily. I told you, she's like their sister.'

'So how can JJ be in love with her then?'

'I don't know, he just is. He always has loved her. I've been worrying about it for ages. If JJ finds out what they were doing he'll be furious, the boys might even fall out over her. And Lily encourages Matt. I think I'm going to speak to Linda about it.'

'I wouldn't. Matt and JJ are going away in a few days. They'll meet other girls, lots of them. Lily isn't the only pretty girl in the world, you know. Why drag Linda into it?'

'Oh, I don't know. JJ is so sensitive, and I don't want anyone to get hurt.'

'So let it be, you'd only complicate matters by interfering. Now, where is that tea you promised me?'

CHAPTER 24

But Maggie cannot let it go. The next couple of days are busy ones for her and Michael because they drive Matt to his university halls on Monday, then take JJ to his halls the following day. JJ comes with them when they drop off Matty, so she does not have the chance to bring up the subject of Lily. On both journeys she is quiet and distracted, her mind filled with the problem of what to do about the teenaged love triangle. Luckily, Michael and the boys assume she is quiet because they are going away, so they try to jolly her along.

'Cheer up, Maggie, you should be proud and happy that our kids have done so well.'

'I am proud of them, but I'm allowed to be a bit sad that they're leaving home for good, aren't I?'

JJ leans forward and puts his hands over the seat, resting them on her shoulders. 'It's not for good, Mum. We'll be home for reading week before you know it.' Maggie cannot help noticing that Matt is not as considerate as his brother. His mind is already focused on the fun he is expecting to have on Freshers' week. On Wednesday she rings Linda and suggests that they meet for a drink after work.

'I can make it on Friday but I can't stay too long, Maggie. I've still got people to feed when I get home, don't forget, and I've promised to drop Lily off to a party.'

'Can't Tom do that?'

'He could, but I don't want to ask him. He's always shattered on Friday evenings. I think he's feeling his age.'

'Don't be daft, he's the same age as Michael. He's probably just stuck in a rut. He needs to try something new. Why doesn't he take up golf, or try an evening class?'

'You're probably right. Anyway, shall we meet in the bar of the Angel hotel, say six o'clock?'

Linda gets to the hotel at exactly two minutes past six because her office is just down the street from the hotel. When Maggie arrives a few minutes later Linda is at the bar and paying for two gin and tonics.

'Hi Maggie, go and bag that table over there, I'm just waiting for my change. Maggie slides into one of the chairs under the vacant table. She has been rehearsing the conversation she plans to have with Linda all day, but she still feels nervous. 'Thanks, Linda, I needed that. I had piles of work to catch up with today, I was worried that I wouldn't make it here.'

'You should have cancelled. We could have met up next week instead. I'm glad you didn't though, we never seem to have a chance to really talk these days. Did the boys get off all right?'

'Yes, fine. We helped them take their stuff up to their rooms and made up their beds. By the time we'd done that, other kids were knocking on the door to say "hello" so we more or less left them to it. We were all a bit tearful when we said goodbye though, but the boys managed to hide it.'

'I know what you mean. When Ritchie first went to university, I cried all the way home. Tom got annoyed with me in the end. I expect I'll be the same when Lily goes. '

'Actually, I wanted to have a word with you about Lily'. ' Linda looks concerned. she waits for Magge to go on.

'I don't know if you're aware of the way she behaves when she goes out.' Linda's still waiting.

'At Helen's party I found her out on the balcony snogging Matt. It looked pretty heated. Her skirt was practically round her ears.'

'The little Shit. I hope you gave him a bollocking. That boy gets more like his father every day.'

'I did, but I don't think it was entirely his fault. Lily was clearly enjoying herself, in fact I think it might have gone a lot further if I hadn't interrupted them. She's a flirt'.

'No, Maggie, she's a child. Matt's nearly nineteen and Lily's only just seventeen, Two years make a huge difference at their age. He should have known better'

'That's not entirely fair, Linda. Lily is always throwing herself at Matt, you must have noticed.'

'All I've noticed is that your sons think of nothing but girls. That may be normal, but they should stick to girls of their own age.'

"Oh, come on, Linda. Lily's not backward in coming forward. She'll do anything for attention.'

'What exactly do you mean, she'll do anything: are you saying my daughter is a tart?'

'Of course not. I just wish she would leave Matt alone.'

'Oh do you? She's not good enough for your precious boy, is that it?'

'Of course not, Linda, stop twisting things. I just thought you could talk to her, tell her to stay away from him'. Maggie is struggling to find a way to explain without mentioning JJ, but it's too late, Linda is really angry now.

'I'll do that with pleasure. Don't worry, Lily won't be bothering you or your precious sons again. Linda storms out, pushing past a group of men gathered round the bar. One of them spills his drink and calls after her,

'Excuse me, an apology would be nice.'

'Don't worry, her majesty over there will buy you another one.'

Maggie is nearly in tears as she drives home. Jonathan was right, she should have listened to him. At least he is not around to say "I told you so", he's away on business and will not be back for another week. She decides to go for a run, that always cheers her up, so when she arrives home she goes straight upstairs to change. She sends Barry a text while she's running back down the stairs, then jogs up and down the drive, warming up, until he comes out.

"Hey, Maggie, this is nice. We hardly ever run together these days,' he pants as they jog up the hill side by side.

'I know, I've been so busy with one thing and another, but I'll have more time now that the boys are settled.'

'It's not Jonathan who's keeping you busy then?'

'Well if it is, you've only got yourself to blame. You set us up, didn't you? He grins and they run on. They are on flat ground now, going along the lane which runs between fields. Some of the trees are already changing colour, orange and tan leaves clustering among the green. When they turn into a track leading only to fields they stop for a breather. There's a style half hidden by thick brambles. These are now drooping under the weight of ripe blackberries. Maggie plucks some, holding out her palm so Barry can share with her.

'I wonder why no-one picks these anymore. My friend Linda and I loved going blackberrying. My mum used to make blackberry and apple pies which we would eat still warm from the oven. Mum smothered them in custard. Not the stuff out of tins, she made her own custard.'

Maggie has always loved this time of year. From fields being ploughed ready for sowing to the sound of excited children at starting a new school year, they all bear witness to nature's cycle of renewal. Normally those sounds never fail to lift her spirits and make her smile.

But this year autumn is tinged with sadness because the new term has taken her boys away from her. To make things worse, she's afraid she has driven away her best friend too.

'You're quiet tonight, Maggie. Missing your kids already, are you? Don't worry, they'll be back before you know it, bringing their dirty washing with them'. Maggie smiles and moves over to make room for Barry on the style. Once seated he asks, 'So what do you think about me and Michael going into business together?'

'Well, I don't really know what you're planning. I am surprised he is considering a partnership though; usually he likes to keep tight control of everything he's involved in. One thing I can say, he may be a womaniser but he's straight as a die when it comes to business. I worked with him when he first started Johnson's Electrics and I know his word is his bond. He's fair, too. I've never known him try to con anyone.'

'Yes, that's pretty much what I've heard through the grapevine. It's my own assessment of him too.'

'So what is it you're planning?'

'We're going to build a new housing estate. We've bought some land over towards Bedhampton and we've got an architect drawing up plans to submit to the planning department. We're hoping to get permission to put three hundred homes there.'

'Wow, that's impressive. So whose Idea was that?'

'Actually, it was Michael's. He had his eye on that piece of land so he asked me if I could recommend a builder. I said, 'Yes, me. I've built houses before, Maggie, but never that many at the same time. Anyway, the numbers don't matter. So long as you get your costings right, you've just got to find good, reliable tradesmen. That's really where I come in, I've got the contacts.'

'So why do you need Michael?'

'He found the land. And it's always good to share the risk in a project of that size.'

'What is the risk?'

'Our planning application could be turned down, for a start.'

'Is that likely?'

No, but they might limit the number of houses we can build there.'

'I see. Well, good luck with it, I hope it works out for you both. Come on, let's head back before Maureen sends out a search party'.

CHAPTER 25

But Maggie just cannot conjure up the optimism which normally inspires her in autumn. Her spirits lift a little when Jonathan returns but her buoyant mood is short-lived when she tells him about the conversation which led to her row with Linda. He does not say "I told you so", he asks instead why she doesn't just phone her

'I've tried, but she never answers the phone. She's obviously told Tom and Lily to say she's out too.'

'Well, why don't you go round to her house?'

'I just can't. I'm afraid she'll say something about me being stuck up in front of Tom or Lily, then they'll hate me too,' she wails.

Underlying Maggie's despondency is the feeling that everybody she knows is moving forward with their lives, while hers is static. She is pleased that the twins are excited about going to university and she thinks Michael's new business venture sounds great. She is also delighted that her old friend Layla has found happiness at last with a very nice guy named Andrew. It is not even that she is not happy with Jonathan, she is, but she has always wanted more from life than merely a relationship. Being in a strong relationship has always given her the springboard to meet new challenges, but somehow that is not happening at the moment.

Later Maggie is sitting up in her bed with Jonathan. She is nestled into his side, his hand threaded round her back so that he can stroke the soft flesh of her upper arm. She normally finds this erotic, a prelude to foreplay, but tonight it is simply irritating. She shrugs her shoulder and moves away, then relents.

'Sorry, Jon, I don't know what's wrong with me lately, I'm such a grump'. She tries to explain to Jonathan how she feels, not very rationally because she is confused herself. He is quiet for a moment, then he asks,

'Have you ever felt like this before?'

'Only when I split up with Michael.'

'And what did you do about it then?'

'Nothing. I was so angry and hurt I couldn't really think straight. And the boys were younger then, so I had to worry about their feelings. I was probably horrible to everyone else, though.'

'Well maybe you need to explore new interests. Have you thought of taking up knitting? Belly dancing? Train spotting?' She picks up the spare pillow from the floor and hits him with it, then straddles him.

'I thought at first you were being serious'. She pushes him back against the headboard, laughing.

'I am. At this moment I'm very serious. Are you going to twitch again if I start stroking your bum?' he smiles up at her.

'No, you can stroke it,' she replies.

Afterwards, they sit up again and talk properly. Jonathan tells Maggie that she has obviously come to a crossroads in her life.

'Or, more accurately, a roundabout. 'Matt and JJ were the centre to which all the other aspects your life connected. Now that centre has been taken away, those links have been cut adrift. They probably all seem pointless. It's known as "flying the nest syndrome".

'But I am happy for them, and so proud of how well they've done. Do you think I'm being selfish then?'

'Not at all. Something which was central to your life is no longer there, and you haven't worked out how you're going to fill the space yet. Why don't you write down how you're feeling? You might find it helps.'

'I wouldn't know where to start. I've never done any writing before.'

'Just write about how you're feeling. And don't say you can't write. You write reports and stuff for the university all the time'.

'Yes, but that's all factual stuff.'

'Well if you write about how you're really feeling it will be factual, won't it?'

So the following evening Maggie sits down and begins to write. She starts off by describing how she felt when she and Michael left Matty outside the university halls and drove away. She describes the dread she felt on the second morning, knowing she had to do it all over again with JJ. After a few lines she stops to read it through and realises it needs reorganising. She draws a line through the script and re-writes it before continuing, adding and crossing out words as she goes. She's struggling to express her feelings coherently and somehow these triggers memories of earlier times. The boys' funny little ways when they were toddlers, and events which she had long forgotten, come rushing back, making her smile as she writes. After a while she sits back and stretches, decides it is time for a cup of coffee. When she goes to the kitchen and looks at the clock she is surprised to see that she has been writing for nearly two hours.

CHAPTER 26

A few days later Maggie and Jonathan go to see the latest Bond film, "A View to a Kill". Afterwards they go to a pub for a drink before Jonathan drives her home. In the car, Jonathan says,

'You seem more yourself tonight, Hon. I'm glad.'

'Yes, it must be all that writing', she answers archly. He looks at her, puzzled, for a moment before he realises what she means.

"Oh, did you try my suggestion?'

'I did and I've been writing every bloody evening. I can't seem to stop.'

'Can I read what you've written? Or you can read it out to me if you prefer.'

'That's Ok, you can read it, so long as you promise not to laugh.' They go into the house and Maggie brings her note pad from the dining room, clutching it against her stomach protectively.

'Promise?'

'I promise I won't laugh. Now hand it over.' Maggie gives him the note pad and says she is going to make them some tea. In the kitchen she takes her time, placing the mugs on a tray then getting out biscuits and fussing over laying them out on a plate. Her heart is racing, she feels like a schoolgirl who has just handed in a completed exam paper.

'Maggie, this is really good, you should try to get it published as a short story.' Jonathan has come into the kitchen.

'You're joking.'

'I'm not joking. You've obviously got the knack of conveying your emotions when you write and that's not easy to do. It does need a little tweaking to turn it into a story, but I could help you with that. And I'm pretty sure I can find you a publisher. Women's magazines just love this kind of thing.' True to his word, Jonathan spends a couple of hours giving her pointers on short story writing and suggests ways she could give her work more impact. After that, she works on it every evening, re-writing and reorganising until she is satisfied that she has transformed her memories into an interesting story. Once she is finally happy with it, she sends samples to several women's magazines. She is still waiting for a response when the boys come home for reading week.

Matty's train is due to arrive first, just fifteen minutes ahead of JJ's, so Maggie picks them up at the station together. When JJ alights from his train he greets his brother with a laconic 'All right, Bro?' and a Rapper-style handshake, but Maggie can tell that they are really happy to be together again. Both boys are hauling large hold-alls full of dirty washing, just as Barry predicted. When they arrive home, Helen is watching from her front window, almost as excited as Maggie. She rushes out to envelop them in hugs. Michael is coming round to see them shortly, so Maggie has prepared supper for them all. When they gather round the table the boys attack their meal as though they haven't seen food for weeks. Michael smiles benignly at them from his seat at the head of the table and for a short while it feels as if they are a proper family again.

The boys sleep late the next morning so Maggie, who has taken the day off of work, joins them for a late breakfast. Since leaving home Matt has become a vegetarian, so he declines the bacon in exchange for extra eggs. His hair, which yesterday was carefully styled in imitation of the boys from Wham, has collapsed. It keeps flopping over his face, making him look like a little boy again. In contrast, JJ's hair is cut short at the sides but with a much longer fringe which he flicks back a la Duran Duran. They are not fully awake yet, so they hardly speak while they are eating. Their faces, still puffy from sleep, are so reminiscent of when they were of little boys that Maggie's heart clenches with love: She wishes they could stay that way forever.

After they finish eating Matt, a recent convert to coffee drinking, gets up switch on the electric percolator. The eggs have done their work and he is wide awake now. 'Did I tell you, Mum, Ritchie and I have met up a couple of times', he tells her.

'That's nice. How is he?'

'Yea, he's fine, earning a lot of money in the city.' Maggie hopes Matt will not be infected by the current obsession with wealth which is especially prevalent among young people. It seems to have permeated all levels of society under Thatcher, creating an 'I'm all right Jack' mentality which she hates.

'He's even got a girlfriend who's a model; not a famous one, though'. Matt adds.

'Will we see Aunty Linda while we're here, Mum?'

'I don't know, JJ. We're both so busy nowadays. We'll see.' Maggie meets Matt's eyes and he looks away. '*He knows we've fallen out. Ritchie must have said something*' thinks Maggie and abruptly changes the subject.

'Have I told you that I've taken up writing? I'm trying to get a story published.'

Naturally, the twins want to read her story, so Maggie gets it out, neatly typed, and hands it over, then goes back to the kitchen to clear up the breakfast dishes. Her heart is thudding. They will be the first people to read it apart from Jonathan, so she will be devastated if they do;t like it. She is wiping down the table when they return. JJ puts his arm round her and says

' I think it's good Mum. It's sweet and funny, I really liked it.'

'It is good Mum, but do you really want to spend your time writing "sweet" stories? You might as well write for Mills and Boon. Why don't you write articles on serious subjects? You're always going on about homelessness and social inequality'.

'What do you know about Mills and Boon, Matty?'

'I know a girl who is writing her dissertation on Mills and Boon. She says their books are all filled with unrealistic romantic nonsense; they're pure escapism.' Initially, Maggie's only thought is about this girl. When she was younger, friendships between girls and boys were quite rare. Their relationships were primarily romantic, or sexual, or both. So now she is thinking: *She must be in her final year if she's writing a dissertation. He's going out with a much older girl?.*

She does not think about what Matt actually said about her writing until later when she realises he is right. She enjoyed writing her story because it was based around the twins when they were younger, but she does not want to spend any more time churning out similar stuff. She is already planning what she is going to write next.

CHAPTER 27

The twins go back to their respective universities, heads filled with thoughts of Halloween parties and "after parties, whatever they are. She tells Jonathan that she wants to start writing non-fiction, so he suggests she begins by sending a written response to editors of newspapers whenever she disagrees with an editorial item.

'It will be good practice for you, and you never know, you might be asked to expand one of your letters into an article. Don't be disheartened if only one in ten gets printed though. Writers have to get used to rejection, a bit like actors'. Jonathan is alluding to Matt, who recently announced his intention of going into acting as the first step towards a career in directing and script writing.

The following Saturday morning Maggie is sitting in the lounge reading 'The Times'. On the table beside her is a copy of 'The Guardian', which has published an article with opposing views on the future of North Sea Oil. Maggie wants to write a piece discussing their differing opinions and is planning to start it this weekend while Jonathan's away. He and Barry have gone to Twickenham to watch a rugby match and they do not expect to be back until the following day. Apparently, rugby matches are two-day affairs, according to Barry, mainly because everyone goes out and gets drunk after the game, win or lose, so they need the next day to recover.

Maggie is just starting to jot down some notes when the phone rings. The voice on the other end is muffled and croaky. I initially she thinks it is a heavy breather so she answers impatiently. 'Who is this?

'It's me, Linda'.

'Linda?'

'Maggie, I need you. Can you come round?'

'Linda, of course I'll come. Shall I pop in later this afternoon?'

'No, now. I need to speak to you now, Maggie. Please'.

'I'm on my way.' On her way to Linda's house Maggie's mind is buzzing. She goes over all the things which might conceivably make Linda cry like that. *One of her parents must have died, or maybe something bad has happened to Ritchie; or Lily. Oh God, I hope nothing's happened to Lily.* The only question which does not occur to her is why Linda, who has not spoken to her for weeks, chose to phone her rather than somebody else.

Linda is waiting at the open front door when Maggie pulls up outside her house. They meet halfway on the garden path where Linda literally throws herself into Maggie's arms, and they both stagger under the weight of her body. Maggie regains her balance and gently steers Linda towards the door, supporting her with one arm.

'Come inside Lin, then you can tell me what's happened.' Once indoors, Maggie tries to ease Linda sit onto the sofa, but her body is rigid, seemingly fixed in the upright position.

'No, I can't sit down. I don't know what to do.' Linda's trying to say something, but it is hard for Maggie to understand because she is sobbing, huge, gulping sobs from deep within her.

'Shush now', Maggie tries to calm her, holding her close and gently rubbing her back. Gradually she becomes calmer and slightly more coherent until at last Maggie understands what Linda is trying to tell her.

. 'It's Tom. Maggie. He's dying.'

Tom has felt tired and slightly under the weather for months now. He has also ignored the symptoms of bowel cancer, shrugging them off as a stomach upset or too much spicy food. Unfortunately, Linda has been so busy that she has not really noticed that he is not well. She has simply put his complaints of tiredness down to his age, despite the fact that he is only one year older than she is. Now that he has at last consulted his doctor it turns out that he has left it too late. He has undergone tests which show that he has bowel cancer which has metastasised. His body is now riddled with cancer.

Linda stops sobbing at last and Maggie, stunned, goes into the kitchen and makes two strong mugs of tea. She is trying to think of the right words, but she can'.t

'So, tell me again, why can't they operate?'

'Apparently it's gone too far. He's got an appointment at the hospital to see an Oncologist next week. He will probably recommend chemo- therapy, but it will only slow down the cancer, it won't stop it spreading.'

'How long has he known?'

'Well, he knew he was being tested for cancer, but he didn't say anything. He got the results yesterday, but he didn't want to tell me while Lily was here.'

'So where is he now?'

'He's gone to the care home to tell his mother. I doubt she'll understand, but he said she had the right to be informed. I think he wanted to get away from me, give me a chance to cry properly.' The tears are streaming down Linda's face again, but only an occasional sob escapes now. This was so like Tom: so considerate, so anxious to avoid any fuss. Maggie knows she must appear to be cold and unfeeling, but she is trying to control her own emotions. She does not want to break down like Linda, that wouldn't help anyone. The best thing she can do is to focus on practicalities. She can cry for Tom later.

'What about Lily? Where is she?'

'She's at work..' Lily has a Saturday job at one of the stores in town.

'She's going out somewhere in town tonight, so she's staying over at a friend's house.'

'Good, but you will have to tell her, and Ritchie. They have a right to know, Linda.'

'Can't you do it?' Linda is crying again.

'I'll try to get them both together and prepare them, but I think you and Tom should be the ones to tell them. What's Ritchie's number?'

When Ritchie hears there is a family emergency, he says he will drive down from London immediately, but Maggie manages to persuade him to leave it until the next day.

'Will you stop at my house and pick me up on your way? I can tell you all about it then.' Maggie plans to pick up Lily too, then take them both somewhere quiet and prepare them for this terrible news. This sorted, she turns her attention back to Linda.

'Right, we need something stronger than tea, where's your booze cupboard?'

She takes out a bottle of brandy and two glasses and has just started pouring when Tom returns. Wordless, she goes over and puts her arms around him. She can feel his ribs against her chest and wonders why no-one noticed how thin he has grown. He has been part of

Maggie's life since she was fourteen and she cannot imagine the world without Tom in it. Bereft of words, she finally lets her tears flow.

The oncologist tells Tom he has only a few months to live, but chemotherapy will give him a fighting chance of holding the cancer at bay. He says it could extend his life for as much as nine months. However, he warns him that he will feel extremely tired while he is having the treatments and there will be other side effects, such as nausea and hair loss. Also, because the chemicals will destroy his immune system, he must isolate himself from most social activities.

'Luckily, because surgery is not appropriate in your case, we can start the chemo straight away. I'll contact the oncology department today and they will probably send you an appointment within the next ten days'.

Tom is very quiet on the drive home, prompting Linda to squeeze his knee in reassurance.

'We're going to fight this thing together, Tom. The doctors don't always get it right. You could go on for years after the chemotherapy'.

'Linda, do you remember what we talked about doing when we retire?'

'Take an extended holiday in America?'

'Yes, but where exactly did we say we'd go?'

'Well, I said I'd like to go to New York. Go up the Empire State building, shop in some of the stores, see everything really. Oh, and you said you wanted to take a train from Grand Central Station.'

'I did. Didn't we say we'd go to San Fransisco too, Lin?'

'Yes. You wanted to see some huge old trees, or something. Actually, I wouldn't mind driving down that hill where they film all the car chases. Tom, we can still do it. I'll take leave from work and we can go as soon as you've finished your chemo-therapy.'

'I'm not going to have the chemo, Linda. If I only have a few months to live, I want to make the most of that time with you and the kids. Speak to your boss on Monday and arrange the time off. We're going to America.'

CHAPTER 28

Maggie's story is published in "The People's Friend" magazine. Although she is pleased that they thought it worthy of publication, seeing it in print confirms Matt's opinion. He was right: she does not want to spend the rest of her life writing saccharine stories, popular as they may be.

Also, she has been doing her job for a long time now and lately she has been thinking that it's time for a change. Although she does enjoy her work, she cannot see herself doing it forever. Her boss is talking about retiring soon and Maggie knows that, should she take on her position as head of department, essentially she would only be doing what she does now, but with more responsibility. nevertheless, she puts all that on one side for now because Lily is staying with her while her parents are away in America.

Maggie is enjoying having a teenager in the house again. When she dropsLily off at her sixth form college it's great to see the experimental outfits and hairstyles of the youngsters as they meet up with friends. It is also nice to have a young female to go shopping with.

When they go into town, Maggie experiences the feeling normally only felt by women who have daughters. It is that moment when you realise that passing men look first at your daughter, not at you. Lily is not vain: she does not seem to realise how stunning she is. Nor is she aware of the attention she attracts from men. Maggie worries that this lack of awareness could make her vulnerable to predatory older men. However, she is safe enough at present because she clearly has no appetite for going anywhere, apart from her Saturday job and college.

Maggie's heart is breaking for Lily. She is trying so hard to be brave and carry on as normal but she is so pale, and her face is pinched with worry. Whenever her parents phone from the States, she makes a monumental effort to appear cheerful, but Maggie knows that she runs upstairs to cry as soon as they hang up the phone.

Tom and Linda are staying in LA at present. They've done all the touristy things like driving up into the hills to see the Hollywood sign and visiting Malibu. Tomorrow they are planning to set off for Arizona to visit the Grand Canyon and the Hoover Dam. Maggie does not think that Tom will manage to walk all round the rim of the canyon. She knows how long it takes because she has been there herself. Michael took her and the boys when they were younger. It was their last family holiday before the divorce and thinking about how happy they were then almost makes Maggie want to cry too, util she reminds herself of the reason their marriage ended.

She knows that Linda was right when she said that Matty gets more like Michael every day; she has noticed it herself. She just hopes that Tom and Linda will come home before the end of term because she definitely would not feel comfortable about having Matt at home while Lily is staying with her. Luckily, there is no need for Maggie to worry because Tom and Linda return to the UK a week before the boys are due to arrive home for the Christmas holidays. Maggie drives Lily to the airport to meet their flight although she is aware that Lily has mixed feelings about the reunion. She is excited at the prospect of seeing her parents again, but she is terrified that Tom's condition may have worsened. Maggie fully understands Lily's conflicting emotions because she feels much the same herself.

When they reach the airport Tom and Linda's plane has just landed so they go straight to the arrivals gate. They do not have to wait long before passengers start exiting with their luggage. 'There's Mum', Lily spots her mother walking behind some of the other passengers.

She appears to have managed to get a tan despite the time of year and the sun has bleached her hair into tawny streaks. Maggie thinks she looks great. Linda waves then moves back against the wall to allow other people to overtake her. She is obviously waiting for Tom, who they can see now. He is seated in a wheelchair and is being pushed by an airport employee. Unlike Linda, the LA sunshine has merely emphasised the yellow tinge to his skin, but his face does light up when he sees his daughter.

Lily pushes aside the barrier and drops down on her knees to throw her arms round her father, prompting smiles from some of the other passengers and frowns from the more impatient ones. Close up, Maggie can see that Linda, far from being the radiant picture of health she seems from a distance, looks drawn and worried. When she moves closer to kiss her cheek, Linda clutches her upper arm so hard that Maggie knows she will find a bruise there later.

Christmas day is very quiet that year. Jonathan wants to spend time with his children and Maggie's parents are staying at home for the first time in years. Michael and Helen join Maggie and the boys for a late lunch, after which thy exchange presents, but it is obvious that Christmas has lost its magic for the twins. All they want to do is get the meal over with as quickly as possible so that they can meet up with their old friends. When Michael points out that most pubs will be closed, they mumble something about a pub in town. On their way out, JJ says 'Don't wait up Mum, we'll probably be late'. Clearly, they are going to a party.

Soon after that, Michael empties his glass and stands up.

'Well, I'd better be on my way too. Thanks for the delicious lunch, Maggie.' Maggie walks him to the door and watches him driving away, wondering if Michelle is the reason he is rushing off. There will almost certainly be a woman waiting for him somewhere, it isn't like him to choose to be alone. She goes out onto the drive to get some fresh air. Down below, the city is transformed by the colourful lights of Christmas; it looks like a miniature Las Vegas tonight. Matt and JJ are down there somewhere, she wonders what they are doing. After only one term they have developed total confidence in their own independence. and ignore questions about where they are going or who is going with them. Although they will always be her boys, she knows that the final cord has now been severed. *This is probably what it feels like to be old*' she thinks as he goes back indoors to get out the scrabble.

CHAPTER 29

Tom passes away quietly just before Easter with Linda and their children at his bedside. He has been virtually house-bound since they returned from the USA. Linda is so grateful that he took the decision not to have chemotherapy. Considerate as ever, he wanted her most recent memories of their time together to be happy ones, and it turned out that he made the right choice. His cancer spread so rapidly that it is unlikely that they would have been able to travel together if they had waited.

Ritchie has been a pillar of strength throughout his father's illness, driving down from London every Friday after work and leaving on Monday at dawn to go straight to the office. He has also helped his mother with the funeral arrangements. It is scheduled to take place at the church where Tom sang in the choir as a boy. When Maggie hears this she is filled with remorse: she had no idea that Tom was a choirboy. Now she wonders what else she didn't know about him. He was always there, so laid-back and unassuming that he was often taken for granted.

Maggie has been to funerals before, but this is the first one she has attended where she was really close to the deceased. She is dreading it. Jonathan plans to attend, but she will not be sitting with him during the service because Linda wants her and Michael to sit with the family. Maggie is worried that this might be awkward but when she tells Jonathan he says,

'It's fine, I understand, Maggie, t's not about me. Linda is going to need your support to help her get through this.' Not for the first time, Maggie thinks that some aspects of Jonathan's personality remind her of Tom.

When everyone files out of the church after the service the sun is shining, but the weather is still very cold. Linda has been so brave, even managing to smile weakly at an amusing anecdote during the eulogy. She also joins in all the hymns, despite the tremor in her voice, but now that they are walking up to the graveyard, she is shaking. Maggie knows that the shakes are not because she feels cold. When the pile of earth comes into view the trembling gets worse, so Michael moves up from behind her and offers a supporting arm. During the prayers at the graveside Linda stands between Maggie and Michael. Ritchie, on the other side of Michael is trying to hold back his tears wyile Maggie has her arm around Lily. When the coffin is lowered into the ground Lily sobs uncontrollably but Linda is silent, frozen. Only Maggie knows that she is squeezing her hand so hard that she can feel the bones in her fingers squashed together.

After the wake Michael and Jonathan both go straight home, but not before Michael takes JJ aside to tell him

'Don't let you mother drive.' For once Maggie is happy to hand over her car keys. She gets in the back of the car next to Helen, who gives her knee a sympathetic squeeze. Once they arrive home Matt goes to the kitchen to make his mother some tea, leaving JJ to draw the curtains and throw a blanket over Maggie's knees.

'Today is the most time I've ever spent with Jonathan, Mum. He's a good bloke, isn't he?'

'I think so, Love. I'm glad you like him'.

'So, do you think you'll marry him, or what?'

'I can't marry him, JJ. He's married already.' Seeing his shocked expression, she adds 'Jonathan separated from his wife years ago. They've just never bothered to get a divorce.'

'But would you like to get married again?'

'I don't know really. I'm quite happy with my life as it is at the moment. Why, would you be upset if I got married?'

'Who's getting married?' Matt, who has given up drinking tea and coffee because his body is a temple, comes back with two steaming mugs on a tray. He has obviously caught the tail end of their conversation.

'No-one's getting married, Matt, we were just talking.'

'Oh, I thought you were talking about Dad'.

Maggie cannot stop thinking about Tom's untimely death. She envies his courage, the way he refused to waste the precious time left to him and Linda. As a young girl she often had visions of doing something heroic heself. She wanted to help to make the world a better place, but life took her on a different path. Now she asks herself whether she has ever done anything for others, apart from her immediate family. Ok, she feels good when she donates to charities or a disaster fund, but actually,all you need to do that is a little spare cash. You don't even have to leave home.

So she makes up her mind that the time has come to do something more meaningful. She just does not know what it will be yet. One thing is certain, writing stroppy letters to the editors of newspapers has not improved life for anyone. Maggie realises that, in order to do that, she needs to completely change her own life, and there could not be a better time for her to make that change. She is lucky enough to be financially secure, and the twins' university fees and living costs are covered by their grants. They are no longer financially dependent on her and she has no mortgage on the house. In fact, most of the rent she receives from Helen goes into her savings account.

In the end, it is Helen who comes up with the suggestion which is to change Maggie's life. They are watching television together when a programme presented by various media personalities comes on. Footage of the celebrities visiting Ethiopia is shown, demonstrating how Live Aid money is being spent there. Maggie sighs,

'Once you're a celebrity, all kinds of doors are open to you'.

'You don't have to be a celebrity. You could do voluntary service overseas, Maggie. My friend Kate's grandson is doing it at the moment. I think the organisation is called VSO.'

So Maggie looks into it. She sends off for information but is disappointed to find that volunteers must be between eighteen and thirty- five years old. *Bloody typical* she thinks and leaves

the literature on the dining room table where Matt, home for the weekend, finds it. 'What's this, Mum, who's going to volunteer abroad?

'I thought I might, but it turns out that I'm too old.

'Are you sure about that? One of my lecturers did VSO last year. He took a sabbatical. Let's have a look.' Matt starts reading and within minutes tells her: 'There's no age limit for professional volunteers.'

'But I'm not a professional, am I? I'm not a doctor, or nurse or engineer. What could I advise anyone about?'

'Mum, you have spent your whole life in business administration. That's your profession. Look, they're looking for Education Management advisors. I would have thought that you fit the bill for that perfectly.'

'What, are you looking for a new job, Mum?' JJ has just come into the kitchen. 'Mum's thinking of applying for VSO'.

'You want to go and work in Africa? You do know you'd have to live like the locals? Don't you think you're a bit old to rough it like that Mum?' JJ's habit of being over- protective of his mother has never been more annoying. Maggie bites her tongue and says only 'We'll see.'

They send her to Cambodia for six months as a business advisor. The flight from Heathrow takes over twelve hours, so she has plenty of time to think about what lies ahead of her. She also thinks quite a bit about the people she has left behind. Despite JJ's reservations about Maggie "putting herself at risk at her age," she can tell that he is really proud of her, as is Matt. Both boys have matured so much since they went to university that Maggie has no qualms about leaving them, and if one of them does get himself into trouble, Michael will always be there for them.

Michael has mellowed recently, becoming much more supportive of his mother as she gets older. It is part of the reason why Maggie isn't worried about leaving Helen on her own. Added to that, Maggie knows she can rely on Maureen to check on her every day while she is away. The thing which mostly occupies her thoughts during the flight is the difference in the way Jonathan and Michael said goodbye.

The main theme of Jonathan's misgivings about Maggie going abroad for so long is that he doesn't know what he'll do without her. He said it again when he bade her farewell yesterday evening. In contrast, Michael's concerns are all for her. He has asked her repeatedly to take care of herself, to be careful and lastly, not to be too proud to come home early if she finds the going too hard. It is an interesting difference of approach which Maggie finally puts down to the fact that Michael already manages without her quite successfully.

She puts further thoughts of home aside and sets her mind on what lies ahead. She already knows that a huge percentage of Cambodians are peasant farmers. Most of them work their own small plots of land, producing mainly rice and vegetables. Every year it becomes progressively harder for those farmers to make a living as the price of fertilizer increases, and now they are also facing a drought. '*Should be a doddle*', is Maggie's last thought as the hum of the plane's engines lull her to sleep.

CHAPTER 30

The day after she arrives s in Phnom Penh he's up early and waiting in the hotel lobby for her driver to arrive. Yesterday evening she slept for hours, then went down to the hotel lobby in search of food. After she finished eating, she went back upstairs and slept some more. Now she is fully recovered from the long flight and eager to get started. At present, she does not know exactly what it is she will get started on, except that she will be driven 'down south'. She knows that the lowlands are in the south of the country, so she assumes she is heading for the rice fields.

The ceiling fan whirring above her head is ruffling the pages of the book she is trying to read, so she gives up and reaches for her holdall. She is bending over to put the book inside when a voice beside her asks:

'You must be Maggie?' The voice belongs to an olive-skinned young man, clearly not Cambodian. He looks about fifteen, far too young to drive. He is wearing what every male appears to wear here, T shirt and baggy shorts, though his have been ironed recently.

'Hi, Maggie. I'm Miguel, the business advice manager. I am here to take you down to your posting. Are you all set? Come on then, let's go.' Miguel may look young, but he is brisk and business-like. He throws her holdall in the back of a dusty jeep, says 'Jump in then' and gets in himself. He whizzes off like a boy racer as soon as her door is closed, making Maggie feel ancient. She wonders how he feels about being landed with someone so much older than he is.

'So, where are we going?' she ventures.

'We are heading south. Sorry, I do not wish to be rude, but you have to really pay attention when you drive here. Once we get out of the city we can talk.' They pull out of the hotel grounds onto a narrow street and Maggie understands what he means. There do not appear to be any pavements or road markings and cars, motorbikes and buffalo-drawn carts are all trying to force their way through what is essentially a continuous traffic jam. They reach a roundabout where assorted vehicles weave their way through the traffic, giving no indication of where they are heading. The thing which Maggie finds most surprising is that it all appears to be very good-natured. There is no honking of horns, no arguments and so far, no accidents. There seems to be some unspoken etiquette governing which person gives way; she can't work it out.

'I don't think I'll ever be able to drive here'.

'Sure you will, you get used to it. You just need to concentrate. Keep watching for a possible gap opening up, then go for it.' He glances over at her, more relaxed now the traffic is not so heavy.

'It's not so bad in the rural areas anyway. Sometimes you can drive for miles and hardly pass any traffic except for buffalo carts. You do need to watch out for those, they can suddenly veer off the road without warning. The driver has no visible means of indicating, so you don't want to be overtaking when that happens.'

'So, how long have you been working out here, Miguel?'

'I first came as a volunteer when I was seventeen. The Khmer Rouge had just been ousted and the entire country was a mess. I stayed for six months then went home to take up a place at university. After I graduated, I did an MBA, which helped me get my present job. I've been back in Cambodia for eighteen months now.'

'You must love it here, then?'

'I do. The people are so gracious. They're kind, gentle and welcoming. Unfortunately, five years of the Khmer Rouge had a devastating effect on the national character, especially on the older generation. It has made them very suspicious, so you need to really work at gaining their trust before you can get anywhere with them. Think you can do that?'

'I can certainly try. I do enjoy a challenge.' Miguel grins.

'I know, I've seen your CV.'

They drive through a small town. It boasts the same narrow streets as the capital but with much less traffic. The main street has a small open market offering vegetables, some fruit and a couple of unidentifiable joints of meat hanging from hooks. Everything is covered by a thick layer of dust. Most of the buildings have corrugated iron roofs and they are all supported on stilts. Maggie shivers:

'Are there a lot of snakes around here?'

'No, not a lot. The main one to watch out for is the green pit viper. It can lurk in the paddy fields, and it will bite if it's disturbed. It's painful, but not deadly. What makes you ask?'

'All the buildings are on stilts.' Miguel chuckles, and the creases which appear on his face make him look older.

'You do know we have a long rainy season and the river frequently overflows, right?'

'Yes. Oh, you mean the stilts prevent the houses from being flooded?'

'You got it.' Sometimes he sounds quite American and sometimes he is definitely Spanish.

'I have arranged a nice house for you. It has a tiled roof so it won't be so noisy when it rains. If it rains. You will be sharing the house with a very nice Cambodian girl. She is the local interpreter, but she also runs the school. She's great, she just jumps in wherever she's needed. Her name is Sophea. I know you're gonna like her.'

They arrive at the house mid-afternoon. It is located in a small, dusty town similar to the ones they passed through on their journey. The weather has been hot and humid throughout the drive, so Maggie is glad she decided to tie her hair back under her straw hat. She does not want to arrive with a frizzy halo of dark hair, but she will soon learn to stop worrying about her appearance: there are far more important things to focus on.

Miguel gives her a quick tour of the tiny house.

'As you can see, you have proper wooden steps up to the house. Some houses around here only have rope ladders'. The inside of the house is divided into four small rooms, separated by woven thatch walls. The floors are unfinished, solid wooden planks. It would cost a small fortune to lay a floor like this in Britain.

Two of the rooms are equipped with a single iron bed, one of which is clearly already in use, and a large chest. The third is obviously used as a sitting room. There are floor mattresses laid out along three of the walls, with assorted scatter cushions and a statue of Lord Buddah. There is also an electric light in the centre of the ceiling which appears to be battery operated.

'Sophea uses this little space at the back as a kitchen' Miguel explains. It contains a wooden table on which sits a small drinks chiller, also battery operated. 'Behind that curtain is the bathroom. Please do not flush any tissues or other objects down the toilet. The plumbing here is not good, but you are lucky to have any at all. Most people around here just dig a hole in the ground. I have to go on to Kampot today, but Sophea will probably be back soon, so make yourself at home. I will return to collect you tomorrow morning, early. Oh, and don't drink the water. You can get bottles from the little shop along the street.'

As soon as he drives away Maggie goes back to the kitchen and pushes aside the heavy woven curtain separating it from the bathroom. There is a tap fitted over a large metal bowl which sits on the ground. It is about six inches deep and resembles a child's paddling pool. Next to it is the toilet, the "hole in the ground" type with an old-fashioned chain. Beside the toilet sits a short hose with a shower head; there is no toilet paper. Maggie is dying to pee after the long drive, so she takes off her hat, throws it into the sitting area and squats. *'This going to be difficult with trousers',* she thinks. *'I'd better make sure I wear a skirt from now on.'*

She goes back outside. It is much cooler now, so she decides to go and look for the shop. It is really just a glass–fronted space. The counter appears to be an old cupboard and an ancient refrigerator stands guard behind it. The shop-keeper, a smiling old man, puts his hands together in the prayer position and bows his head before saying 'Good Morning Madame.' His accent is so pronounced that Maggie can barely understand him, especially since It is now late afternoon. She suspects that his command of English is very limited and she is right. Later, she learns that he once worked as a doorman at a hotel in Phom Phenh, where his only duty was to open the door for guests. Clearly, he must have worked the early shift.

Maggie tries to make him understand that she wants bottled water, pointing to her mouth and smacking her lips. He smiles his understanding and takes a packet of cigarettes from the cupboard. Maggie tries again and is rewarded with an Ahhh of understanding. The old man turns and comes out from behind his counter. There is not enough room to open the fridge if he stays where he is. He gestures towards the open refrigerator to indicate she can help herself from the assorted drinks it contains. Some of them look like they have been there for a long time, but the bottles of water seem OK. She takes out three bottles and is trying to understand how much she should pay when a very pretty Cambodian girl comes along. The girl bows and says something to the shop keeper, before turning to address Maggie. 'Hello, I think you must be Mrs Maggie. I am Sophea, your flatmate. She has such a lovely smile that Maggie takes to her immediately. 'Would you like to come back to the house and I will make you some tea. Let me help you with those bottles.'

They go back to the house where Sophea talks her through the housekeeping arrangements. 'I am sorry we do not have any wardrobes, but you can keep your clothes in this chest. If you need more space, I will show you where you can buy another chest, very cheap.' Maggie explains that she has brought very few clothes with her. At her induction in the UK she was advised that cotton shirts and dresses are very cheap in Cambodia. Also, they are more appropriate for Cambodian society, where women are expected to dress modestly.

After they drink their tea, Maggie says: 'I would really like to have a shower. What do you do about bathing, Sophea?'

'Come with me, I will show you'. Sophea leads the way back to the kitchen, which now contains two plastic bags. Clearly, she has been shopping. In the bathroom she bends over and opens the tap. Water gushes into the vessel underneath and 'Sophea picks up the large jug which is sitting on a wooden stool. While the vessel is filling up, she taps it with the jug. 'When this is full, I sit on the stool and use the jug to pour water over myself. You can stand up if you prefer.'

'But how do you get rid of the water afterwards?'

'If you look at the floor you can see that the wooden planks are not so close together here. Just tip up the bowl and the water will drain away through the floor. But please make sure the door is closed first or the kitchen will be flooded.'

'And what about the boiler, Sophea?'

'The boiler? I'm sorry I do not understand.'

'To heat the water. Do I need to switch it on or anything?' Sophea smiles. 'Fortunately, the sun is always switched on in Cambodia. There is a water tank outside, behind the house. The water it contains is always warm, sometimes it can be quite hot. You can feel it.' Maggie leans over and tests the water, which is indeed hot enough for bathing. 'Would you like to have a shower now, Mrs Maggie? It is more convenient if you take off your clothes and put on a robe. You can hang your robe here.' She indicates a large hook screwed into the wooden door frame. 'I will cook our meal while you are showering. I hope that you like curry, Maggie?'

CHAPTER 31

The next morning Miguel arrives very early, bringing with him another business adviser, Narith. He is probably in his late twenties and has a fairly good command of English, which is essential as Maggie will be working closely with him. He is also plump and slow-moving, totally unlike the brusque, no-nonsense Miguel. '*Careful, don't judge people by their appearance without knowing anything about them, this is a different culture',* she reminds herself.

Miguel tells her that Narith will take her around for the next few days so that she can meet the locals and get an idea of what they are trying to do here, then they all get into his vehicle. He drives for about ten minutes until they reach a house with another jeep parked outside. 'OK, I'll leave you here with Narith. We'll all get together soon to discuss how you have settled in and iron out any problems.' Maggie and Narith get out of the car and Miguel zooms off again, leaving her wondering if he ever puts that car into neutral.

'Would you like to come inside for some tea, Mrs Maggie?' Narith extends his arm in a courtly gesture, palm facing upwards. 'My wife would be most honoured to greet you.' Maggie hesitates. She does not want to get off on the wrong foot with him, neither does she want to offend him or impose on his wife. 'Do we have enough time?' she stalls.

'Oh yes. Mr Miguel had to leave early for an appointment in Phom Phen, therefore he collected me very early. My wife will have breakfast awaiting us. So they climb the steps to where his wife, Mony, is waiting at the entrance. She looks impossibly young to be so clearly pregnant, but she smiles, bows and ushers her indoors. 'You will please excuse my wife doesn't speak English, Mrs Maggie.'

'Please don't apologise. I should apologise for not learning to speak Cambodian before I came here.' They enter a small room much like the one where Maggie is staying, except there is a TV set and a low round table on which to eat. Mony brings bowls of noodle soup, not what Maggie expected, but the soup turns out to be delicious, very aromatic and slightly spicy. She finishes the entire bowl while Narith nods approvingly. 'I think you enjoy, yes? This is one of the most favourite dishes for breakfast in Cambodia. His wife takes the empty bowls and returns with a platter of vegetables topped by crispy fried meats. Maggie has already eaten enough but the food smells so tempting that she cannot resist trying a little. *'I'll get fat if I eat like this every day',* she tells herself.

When they get up to leave Mony comes back into the room. She's smiling and bowing and Maggie really wishes she could thank her in her own language, Kmer. She would also love to give her a hug, but she knows that is not acceptable here. In the end all she can do is to ask Narith to convey her thanks for their hospitality and compliment her on the delicious meal.

Once they are back on the road, Narith gets down to business. 'This week I will help you find your way around and introduce you to the local farmers. They mostly own their land, usually very small plots, and in the present circumstances it is very hard for them to make enough money for their families to live.'

'Oh, I thought that Cambodia is an important exporter of rice to the rest of the world. This is a rice producing area, isn't it?'

'It is, but this year it did not rain enough in the rainy season. Also, the price of fertiliser keeps going up, so many farmers cannot afford to buy it. Without fertilizer, their crop will not be good. This is Kampot, by the way. Our headquarters are here but today we will not stop.'

In this manner, Narith prepares her for the task ahead. All week, he drives her around, stopping to introduce her to farmers on the way. Then, when they are back on the road, he sets out for her some of the challenges which they face. When Maggie asks about small holdings which appear to be farmed by women and children, he tells her how a farmer, struggling to make ends meet, may be forced to take a loan secured against his land. The interest on the loan is often so high that he can only repay the loan by going to Phom Penh in search of work, leaving his wife and children to cope as best they can. 'But can't the government fix the interest rate, make it fairer?'

'Unfortunately, we have a mainly cash economy. It is rare for a small farmer to have a bank account. Often, they are forced to borrow from moneylenders. These are not honest people, you understand, Mrs Maggie. Sometimes they even take the land if the farmer's debt is too high. Ah, here we are. Now you will meet a young man called Kosak. His father borrowed money to pay for doctors when his wife became ill, then he travelled to Phom Penh to find work in order to repay the debt. Unfortunately, his wife died so his son, Kosak, is trying to manage everything with the help of his sisters. As you will see, he is very young to manage such a large responsibility.'

Maggie does see. Kosak can only be about thirteen. She knows that many hospitals and health centres were destroyed during the civil war, leaving local people dependent on private medical care. Still, she cannot imagine what it must be like to be in a situation so dire and her heart goes out to the still smiling Kosak. When they reach his farm they find him trying to repair the roof of the family home. The roof is built in the traditional way using palm mats instead of tiles. Now some of the mats are wearing thin and h have slipped, creating a gap in the roof. Now the Kosak is standing on tip-toe on a ladder in an effort to reach the damaged area. His position is especially precarious because the ladder is fashioned from two bamboo poles, with rope rungs. Narith doesn't hesitate but goes to the aid of the struggling boy. Reaching up he begins to pull off some of the damaged mats, at the same time asking:

'Mrs Maggie, can you perhaps help on the other side?' Working together, Maggie and Narith remove the damaged mats and hook on the new ones passed up to them by a grateful Kosak.

Maggie has already revised her first impression of Narith. She had thought that he would probably turn out to be lazy, but since then she has learned that, although his title is "Business Adviser" he is always ready to help out with any ask, however menial. When the roof is repaired to Narith's satisfaction, he and Kosak have a chat then they all go to say hello to the two older sisters who are working in the rice fields behind the house. When they get back in the jeep Maggie asks Narith,

'Wouldn't it be more sensible if their father returned to manage the farm and sent the older girls to find work in Phom Penh?'

'Unfortunately, those girls cannot find good work in Phom Penh. Now I shall take you home. I think you should drive Mrs Maggie, so you become familiar with this vehicle. I will not give you directions, only in the case that you take an incorrect turning.'

CHAPTER 32

Maggie and Sophea quickly become good friends. As there is no TV in the house, they spend the evenings chatting or listening to music on Sophea's transistor radio. They have agreed to share their expenses, which are minimal, and Sophea does most of the shopping. She also prepares their evening meal because their only cooking appliance is a kerosene-fuelled camping stove. Maggie knows that the only thing she could manage to cook on it would be fried eggs, so she finds it miraculous that Sophea manages to produce apparently complicated dishes on the little stove.

They also help each other with languages. Although Sophea's English is good, it can sometimes be rather stilted, so Maggie is teaching her stock phrases which are not normally taught in school. Similarly, although Maggie soon picks up some Kmer, she doesn't always get the personal pronouns right. Cambodian people are far too polite to correct Maggie, but Sophea is relaxed enough to do so at home. Often, the two women are helpless with laughter when Maggie realises what she has said.

Sophea is constantly worried because the number of children attending her little school keep falling. If this trend continues, she thinks the school will close and she will have to return to her parents' house in Phom Penh.

'I can easily find work there, but I would prefer to remain here if it is possible', she tells Maggie.

'That reminds me, Narith says that girls from here can't find good employment in Phom Penh. Why is that?'

'He didn't explain why?'

'No. Actually, now I think about it, he changed the subject.'

'Well, an uneducated girl from the country can find work in Phom Penh, but her choice is limited. She can work in the garment industry sewing clothes for the export market. The work is very hard and she will be forced to work long hours for very little salary. It is like slavery. Or she might become a maid. The family which employs her will expect her to do all the work in the house; there is no day off. She could work twelve hours every day for hardly any money, only her meameals. If she chooses the third option, she could earn a hundred times more money by becoming a bar girl. Maggie knows that this is a euphemism for "prostitute".

Quite often girls will try the first two, before deciding that becoming a bar girl would in fact be a much pleasanter option. It can offer her not only much more money but companionship, sometimes even love.'

Maggie is silent for a moment, then asks,

'Is that why you get so upset when girls don't turn up at school? Is it because you think they may have gone to Phom Penh?'

'No, not necessarily, but I know how important education is, especially if you are poor. It is the only way to become not poor, especially in my country.' Maggie cannot argue with that, but she can't help wondering about Sophea. Judging by her clothes, she is clearly not poor. Like most young people in Cambodia, she dresses casually in jeans, or chinos and T shirts but Maggie knows that is where the similarity ends. Sophea's clothes are all expensive. She also told Maggie that she never had to do housework when she lived with her parents because they have maids, yet she is clearly content to remain here without even the most basic of mod cons.

The next day, Narith comes to pick her up as usual. On their way to their first visit, hey normally stop to buy breakfast from one of the street vendors. They do so today and when they have finished eating, Narith goes to sit on the passenger side of the jeep.

'I will be the passenger today, Mrs Maggie. You can drive please.'

Maggie is more than willing. She has always found that you get to know your way around unfamiliar areas more easily if you drive yourself. When you don't need to concentrate on the road, you mind tends to wander. She has been in Cambodia for a month now and Miguel has still not appeared to check how she is getting on. Whenever Maggie undertakes a new venture her old insecurities resurface, so she would really appreciate some feedback now. She is not really convinced that there is a point to her being here at all. True, she does accompany Narith every day, but most of the time she just smiles while he carries on a conversation with one of the farmers. She decides to bring this up with Narith.

'I've been wondering why Miguel hasn't been back to check on me. He did say he would return in a week.'

'Mr Miguel is a very busy man. He is trying to persuade all the farmers in this province to join together in a cooperative. This would bring them many advantages. They could ask for better prices for fertilizers and other necessities. Also, when they sell their rice the price could be higher. Unfortunately, the Kmer Rouge government was very bad and my people do not forget that time easily. They are suspicious of all organisations now.'

'I see. It's just that I would like to have a clearly defined role here. I'm not always sure what is expected of me.'

'Mrs Maggie, soon I must take my wife and go to Phom Penh to await my child being born. When this happens, it is important that the farmers in this area know that we do not forget them. You will be my taking carer.'

'Caretaker', Maggie automatically corrects him. 'You mean, just drive around, visit the farmers, do odd jobs.'

'Exactly. I think already you can do that. Where are you taking me today, Mrs Maggie?'

After that, Maggie takes control of the jeep. She collects Narith in the morning and drops him back to his house at the end of the day. Sometimes Mony comes out to say hello to her in the evening. Maggie can now speak enough Kmer to exchange a few words, so when she appears Maggie always runs up the steps before Mony has a chance to come down. Her abdomen looks so huge in comparison to her tiny body that Maggie fears she might topple over otherwise.

Today Mony does not appear, so Maggie goes straight home. When she arrives at the house there is another jeep parked where she normally leaves her vehicle. No-one else has visited Sophea since Maggie arrived, so she hesitates at the door, not wishing to intrude, then calls out

'Sophea, I'm home' before entering. There is nobody in the living room so Maggie goes straight to her bedroom to drop her bag and exchange her trainers for flip-flops before going to the bathroom. She uses the toilet then splashes her face and arms with water. When she goes back to the living room Sophea is waiting.

'Hello Maggie, Miguel is here. He has come to see you'. This is the first time Maggie has heard a Cambodian refer to someone by their first name. They are normally extremely polite and always address people by their title. Miguel enters the room, his face as expressionless as usual, but Sophea looks embarrassed when she invites him for dinner

'I will go to prepare our food. Would you like to stay and eat with us?'

'Thank you Sophea, but I can't. I must go on to Kampot tonight. Perhaps I can have dinner with you tomorrow?' Sophea heads off to the kitchen and Miguel gestures towards the floor cushions.

'Shall we sit, Maggie?' Maggie sits down on the cushions cross-legged and waits for him to go on.

I hear that you've fitted right in here. I am so pleased, you've done well Maggie'

'Where did you hear that? You haven't been here'. Miguel's smile creases his face again, transforming him into an attractive young man.

'News travels fast in this country, Maggie, haven't you learnt that yet? 'Now, is there anything you want to ask or talk to me about? No? Are you happy with your accommodation?' Maggie assures him that she is very happy where she is billeted, then goes on to ask if it is correct that she is to deputise for Narith.

'Yes, that's the plan, so long as you're comfortable with it.' They talk a little more about Maggie's role then Miguel explains why she has been thrown in at the deep end.

'I'm sure Narith has told you that we're trying to set up a cooperative. So far, we haven't had too much success in convincing the farmers. In fact, I realise now that we made a mistake in approaching them first without having anything concrete to offer them. That's why I am spending so much time in Phom Penh. I have been trying to set up meetings with ministers, and I've also been talking to the banks. At present, if a farmer needs finance, he has no choice but to go to a money lender. Without any paperwork so he won't even get through the front door of a bank. If we can get a cooperative off the ground, the banks would be happy to do business with it. Everybody would win except the money lenders.' Maggie asks a few more questions about her role and then Sophea walks Miguel out to his jeep. Maggie watches from the door as they both walk round to the driver's seat, where they stop, presumably to say goodbye. She can't help noticing that Miguel does not get in and shoot off immediately in his normal manner.

Sophea comes back and goes straight to the kitchen to prepare their dinner. Maggie senses that she needs some time alone, so she does not go to help her prepare the vegetables as she usually does. Instead, she sits in the family room thinking about what Miguel told her. Apparently, Narith has been working at keeping the discussion about a cooperative alive when he visits the farms. His wife's pregnancy, although clearly a happy event for him, could not have come at a worse time in their campaign to persuade the farmers to work together. Now Miguel is worried that his absence may well wipe out any progress that they have achieved so far. Maggie makes up her mind; she is going to work harder at learning the language. If she can communicate more effectively in Kmer, she might actually achieve something useful while Narith is away.

CHAPTER 33

Over dinner that evening, Maggie tells Sophea that she has made up her mind to achieve a basic competence in Kmer before Narith leaves for Phom Penh.

'I know it's a lot to ask on top of teaching at the school, but will you help me, Sophea?'

'Of course I will. Actually Maggie, hardly any of the children have been coming to school lately. It's because of the drought. A lot of the children are needed to carry water to the fields, otherwise the crops will fail.' Sophea is quiet for a moment. 'Maggie there is something I want to tell you. I know I can trust you and I have nobody else I can talk to about this matter. Perhaps you have already guessed this. Miguel and I are in love. This is why I remain here in a school with almost no pupils.'

Sophea looks sad, not at all like a girl in love. Maggie knows that love marriages are frowned on in Cambodia, so she needs to tread carefully.

'Well wouldn't it be better if you went back to Phom Penh? You could see each other every day then. Has Miguel met your parents yet?'

'You don't understand, Maggie. My parents would say I am a "dirty girl" if they knew about this relationship. They expect to arrange a marriage for me. It is our custom, and it is my duty to obey their wishes. If they know the school is almost without pupils, they will close it and order me to return home.'

'Surely your parents can't just close the school. How can that be possible?' Sophea explains that the school was set up and is funded by her father. Her grandfather was born in that area and spent his early years in the house that they are sharing now. He went to Phom Penh as a young man and found a job working for a tailor. He learned to sew, and eventually set up a small business himself.

My father started helping out in my grandfather's business when he was very young, gradually learning every aspect of tailoring. When his father died the business passed to him'. Sophea pauses, then goes on:

'Maggie, I admire my father. He inherited a small, one- man workshop and built it into a company with fifty employees. He made enough money to buy for us a nice house in a good area. My family has a very nice life because of his hard work. I could never do anything to hurt him.

Then, when the Kmer Rouge took control of our country, he made sure we all survived by making their uniforms, simple black cotton shirts and trousers with red scarves. He provided them at a very low price. You understand, Maggie, that he is not proud of that. He did it because it was the only way he could keep our family alive.' Maggie is dumbstruck, but she is certain of one thing: Sophea should not continue to deceive her parents.

'I think you've just got to be brave and tell your parents about Miguel. They might be disappointed at first, but what's the worst thing that can happen?' Maggie has a flash-back to the time, so long ago, when she went with Linda to tell her parents she was pregnant.

'They can arrange a marriage for me immediately. They have many friends who have sons; it could be done in a week.'

'But if they know that you love Miguel?'

'They do not recognise love. Only honour and duty.'

'And Miguel, what does he say?'

'He says I should tell my parents about him. If they will not accept him, we can marry in a civil ceremony in Phom Penh and live in his flat in Kampot.'

Maggie thinks: *It's easy for him to say that, he could be transferred to a post in another country tomorrow.* Her first instinct is to tell Sophea to forget Miguel, even though he seems a decent chap. *I wonder if he has actually looked into the legalities of it all. I think I'll do that myself, then I can give her an informed opinion.* So she asks Sophea, 'By the way, I've been meaning to ask, is Miguel Spanish or American? I'm never quite sure.' Sophea smiles wanly,

'You are confused because of his accent? He is American, but his family went to the USA from Cuba when he was only four years old.'

'So, he must have an American passport then?'

'I don't know anything about his passport. It is not important to me.' Maggie sighs, but lets it go. When Miguel said he would come to dinner tomorrow, she originally thought she might go out and give him and Sophea some time alone. Now it does not seem such a good idea. Instead she asks,

'So what are you going to cook for us tomorrow?'

When Maggie goes to pick up Narith the next day he is not waiting at his usual spot on the wooden veranda. She waits a few minutes then goes up the steps and shouts for him. Again, it is a few minutes before he emerges. When he does, he looks flustered.

'Mrs Maggie, I am sorry to make you wait, but my wife is not well. I think you must go alone today. Perhaps you would go first to the centre at Kampot and give them a message. I think I should not delay our journey to the capital much longer. If you wait, I can write to inform them of this fact.'

'Of course, that's no problem, but is Mony all right? Can I do anything?'

'Thank you, but she has recovered now. She had some bad pains and we thought the baby will arrive early, but they have passed. She is feeling normal now.'

Braxton Hicks, thinks Maggie as she goes outside to wait in the sunshine.

She can never get enough of the sun, unlike Cambodians who seem to retreat to the shade whenever possible. Narith returns and hands Maggie an envelope.

'I am very sorry to ask this favour Mrs Maggie. Are you sure you will find your way?'

'I think so, and I've got the map if I get lost. Don't worry about me, go and look after your wife.' Maggie cannot believe her good luck. She was wondering what excuse she could use to get Narith to take her to the centre today.

She does not get lost, but she doesn't go straight to the centre either because she wants to make a phone call. There is a dedicated phone booth available at the centre for the use of VSO workers, but it is still too early to call the UK. She feels guilty about taking the time off, but it is in a good cause. In the meantime, she has about five hours to fill and she has already decided how she is going to fill them. There are several places nearby she would like to visit but, as her time is limited, she decides to take a tuk tuk tour. It will take her round the most picturesque parts of the local countryside, calling at the salt fields and crab market on the way. The tour ends with a visit to a cave temple. Her travel booklet advises her to use one of the many child guides who will be waiting when she arrives at the cave. It also says that, as it is very dark inside the cave, it recommends using a girl as a guide. Maggie doesn't know whether to be amused or scared.by this.

So she finds the starting point for tours and agrees a price with a driver. It costs peanuts and turns out to be money well spent, because he has enough English to make it interesting, sometimes amusing, along the way. He also tells her about a very famous and beautiful waterfall nearby which unfortunately has no water today because of the drought. In view of this, they both agree to give it a miss and go straight on to the cave, where he waits for her outside. The temple is impressive, but it's quite hard to see inside clearly, as it is indeed very dark.

When she exits with the young girl who escorted her round the cave, she calculates that she should be able to get to the centre around three o'clock, local time. If she can do that it would be perfect because she wants to make her phone call at around eight a.m. UK time.

She arrives at the centre about ten minutes early, and delivers Narith's letter to the secretary, a friendly American named Claire. The phone booth is already in use so she and Claire chat while she is waiting. They swap stories about how they came to be working in Cambodia, then Claire says:

'You probably haven't had much time to see the sights while you're here, Maggie. You should take some time to do that before you leave. See as much as you can while everything is still unspoiled because it's not going to stay this way for much longer. The oil companies are already sniffing around'.

Maggie tells her that she plans to return with friends in October to do some sightseeing, then goes to the now vacant phone booth. As she dials, she is willing Julia to be at home. She is, and when she hears Maggie's voice so early in the day she naturally expects bad news.

'Maggie! Are you OK, is everything all right?' Maggie reassures her then tells her the reason she is calling:

'Julia, I want you to do me a favour, and as soon as you possibly can. I want you to phone the US embassy in London and get some information for me.'

'Of course, let me find a pen. OK fire away.' Maggie gives her a list:

1) Can American citizens be married at a US embassy abroad?

2) What if that person is not a US citizen, for example is Cuban but has right of residence in the USA ? Can that person still marry in an embassy?

3) Can a US citizen married to a foreign woman bring that partner to live in the US?

4) What is the procedure for doing so?

After Julia has finished writing it all down, she asks

'You're not thinking of getting married out there, are you?' It has not occurred to Maggie that Julia might jump to that conclusion. She starts laughing, then says

'No, but I want to make sure that a young friend of mine, a sweet Cambodian girl, isn't about to make a disastrous mistake.'

'A modern Madam Butterfly, you mean?'

'That's what I'm afraid of. Anyway, after you've spoken to the embassy can you type up the information and post it to me as soon as you can. Send a couple of extra copies, too. Now tell me, how are the boys; have they been home recently?'

'They're fine. They both came to stay at Michael's last weekend. They all took me and Helen out for lunch, it was lovely to see them.'

'Don't, I'm jealous. So everyone at home is OK then? Have you and Linda booked your flights yet? The later you leave it the more expensive it gets.'

'I know, but I'm waiting for Linda to decide whether she's coming. She doesn't want to make a decision until Lily gets her A level results. We all know she'll do well, but Linda isn't sure anymore. She's really worried about how Lily is l coping with the loss of her dad.'

'Fair enough. Why don't you book your flight anyway? Linda can always join us later, when she's sure that Lily is settled. I'm really looking forward to our girly holiday. We can drive around, see all the temples and historic sites, try all the local food. You'll love it here, Jools.' Julia promises to get the information Maggie requested and also promises to book a flight to Cambodia soon. Satisfied, Maggie decides she may as well just head for home. She can stop and check on Kosak and his sisters on the way.

She arrives home to find Sophea already there. She has been to the market and bought vegetables, shrimps and some pork belly. Maggie's mouth is already watering, she hasn't eaten a thing all day, apart from the spring roll she bought from a roadside vendor on her way to Kampot. Sophea has already prepared the vegetables and shrimps, so Maggie goes straight to the shower. Miguel arrives soon afterwards, so he and Maggie sit in the family room and plan for the time when Narith will be away.

Miguel says all she can do is show her face at the local farms and try to gauge local feeling regarding a cooperative and Miguel seems to agree.

'The most important thing is to keep the dialogue going, I don't expect you to convert them all. I haven't been able to do that myself yet.' Sophea comes in carrying three steaming bowls on a tray and Miguel jumps up to help her. Maggie tries to detect any signs of love between the pair but t when they sit down they both keep their eyes on their food. Sophea is the first to speak:

'I am thinking that I could close the school for the time when Mr Narith is away, then I can be interpreter for Mrs Maggie. What do you think?' Maggie thinks it's a great idea, obviously, but she wants to be sure that everything is above board with Sophea's family, so she asks,

'Won't you have to consult your father before you close down?'

'I can write him a letter asking permission, but sometimes the post takes a longer time here. If Mr Miguel will kindly take it and post it in Phom Penh it will be quicker.' Maggie notes her use of the "Mr" but doesn't comment and Miguel merely says "Sure, I'll post it as soon as I get there.' After that, hey all pass a pleasant couple of hours playing a board game called Tang Prut. At least, the other two play and Maggie tries to learn, but the rules seem overly complex and Maggie has never been very good at games. Afterwards, Sophea writes a quick note to her father and hands it to Miguel as he's leaving. She accompanies him out to the jeep, leaving Maggie to think about the evening. Miguel and Sophea obviously get on well together, but she would never have guessed that they are in love. Despite her concerns about the relationship, she cannot help hoping that the love isn't imagined, or one-sided, for Sophea's sake.

CHAPTER 34

A few days later, Maggie arrives home to find a man seated in the family room. Startled, she turns to leave but he calls to her,

'Excuse me Madame, I am Johal Kim, father of Sophea.' The man speaks limited English, but he manages to convey to Maggie that he has come in response to his daughter's letter. Unlike many Cambodian men, he is wearing a suit. It is well-tailored and looks expensive. He also has the poise that all successful men seem to have. He is clearly charming, and soon engages Maggie in a conversation, albeit a stilted one.

Maggie offers him some tea or a cold drink and is relieved when he goes for the cold drink. There is an elaborate ceremony attached to drinking tea in Cambodia and she would be sure to mess it up. He does not stand up when Sophea arrives, and there is no hugging or kissing between them, just the usual polite bow. Although Maggie knows that public displays of affection are bad manners in Cambodia, she still finds it strange.

She assumes that Sophea's father will want to have a private conversation with his daughter, so she invents a reason to go out.

'I'm going to pick up some more cold drinks from the good morning shop, but I think I'll go for a stroll first,' she announces. The "good morning shop" is the name they use for the tiny shop down the street, because it's clearly the only English the shopkeeper knows. There are bigger and better-stocked shops a ten- minute walk away but Maggie prefers to buy from him if she can. The other shopkeepers are just as polite and obliging as he is, but there's something about his archaic little hole in the wall which Maggie finds endearing.

When she goes back to the house Sophea's dad is preparing to leave. Sophea explains that he is tired after his long journey. He is going to stay with a distant cousin who lives near Kampot, so he still has a fairly long drive ahead of him.

'He will come back tomorrow and we will go to the school together and discuss what will be the next step,' Sophea explains.

'Do you think he will agree to let you stay here as my interpreter for the next few months, Sophea?'

'I don't know. The school is extremely important to him. It is his way of rewarding this area for his childhood, you understand?'

'I do. He wants to give something back. I totally understand that.' They agree that it will be better if Maggie is present to help convince him that Sophea would be more useful as an interpreter for the time being. Maggie will come home early, around mid- day, and meet them either at the school or at home. She desperately hopes he will agree to let Sophea stay on because, although she is trying very hard to learn Kmer, she still has a long way to go before she can carry on a meaningful conversation.

The next day Maggie does not go back to the house but goes straight to the school, where Sophea and her father are carrying on a conversation with two young children. She can make out certain words, "like" and "good". He is clearly asking the children if they like coming to school. "Water" also features in the conversation, so Maggie assumes they are talking about the drought. Sophea tells the children they can go home for the afternoon and they leave, their faces inscrutable. Her father says something to Sophea in Kmer and she looks pleased, her smile dimpling her pretty round face.

'Mrs Maggie, please excuse me, I am rude. I am telling my daughter that I am pleased with her, the children like coming to the school and they all love Sophea. They say she makes it easy to learn.'

'I can believe it, she's helped me so much', Maggie says.

. 'Mr 'Kim, I would like to offer you lunch, but I can't cook here. Would you mind if I bought something from a street vendor?

'Actually, I love street food, but only from this area. It is the best in the country. Also, it reminds me of my childhood.' So they agree to meet back at the house and Maggie goes to purchase the food. While they are eating, they talk about the problems which beset the local farmers. Although he is not involved in agriculture, Sophea's father understands their predicament,. Fertilizers and other necessities are produced by multi-national companies abroad and they are ruthless in their pursuit of profits. Sophea's dad says the textile industry experiences similar problems.

'Foreign companies pay so little for the clothes we export that we can only afford to pay low wages to our workers. They say the clothes we make are cheap because we exploit our employees, but it is they who force this situation to happen. If I do not agree to their price ,they will no longer do business with me'.

'So, is there no hope for the famers, then?' Maggie asks.

'There is always hope, Mrs Maggie, but these farmers are very conservative. They prefer our traditional way of farming. Even my cousin, who is more educated and owns a large amount of farmland, does not understand that the world has changed. He does not want it to change.' Maggie, who has often bought play clothes for the boys because they were ridiculously cheap, feels ashamed. She has never wondered how it is possible to sell quality products so cheaply. 'So, Mrs Maggie, with the help of my daughter you think you can persuade these farmers they must join together to fight for their living?'

'I am certainly going to try, Mr Kim. If you will allow Sophea to act as my interpreter, we may even succeed'.

Sophea sends out letters informing all local parents that the school will close temporarily. It will re-open when the rainy season begins, normally in three or four months' time. Before he leaves, Narith asks Sophea to keep notes of the conversations which take place between Maggie and the farmers. He is specific about the importance of recording any progress towards accepting the cooperative. He also asks Sophea to send him a written progress report every week. He particularly wants to be informed of any objections which may be put forward so that he can prepare a counter argument to use when he returns. Maggie wonders now why she ever thought Narith would turn out to be lazy.

Sophea has not said any more about her relationship with Miguel, in fact sometimes Maggie suspects she might be imagining it. Neither of them gave any indication that they are in love when they all had dinner together. The conversation was mainly in English, and when they did break into Kmer it was to clarify the rules of the game they were playing. At least, she thinks that was what they were saying. At no point did Maggie get the feeling that they were exchanging sweet nothings. She does not want to bring up the subject again until she hears from Julia, so this secrecy suits her, but she cannot help asking herself: *Surely they couldn't hide it so well if they are really in love?*

Narith leaves and a letter from Julia arrives on the same day, delivered by a Tuk Tuk driver. Maggie asked Julia to post it to the centre and Claire the secretary took it upon herself to forward it by this slightly unconventional means. She has written "Please pay the bearer of this letter his fare plus a generous tip" on the envelope and Maggie is happy to do so. She was not planning to go to the centre to check her mail for another week.

Sophea is in the bathroom showering when the letter arrives, so Maggie takes it to the privacy of her bedroom. It is typical of Julia as it gets straight to the point:

1) No US embassy is empowered to carry out wedding ceremonies, nor have they ever had that power.
2) American citizen wishing to marry abroad in a religious setting must also undergo a civil ceremony.
3) He must then take the certificate (or certificates) to the American Consul in order to obtain an affidavit certifying the marriage. Without this certification the marriage will not be recognised in any US state.
4) With regard to taking a foreign bride to reside in the US, the application must be submitted in the United States. In other words, the bride cannot enter the country until her husband has applied for the relevant permission and his application has been approved.
5) Moreover, his wife would be vetted for her moral and political suitability. In the case of a Cambodian, the things likely to be considered are:
    a) Whether she or a close family member has a criminal record
    b) Whether she or a close family member has ever been involved in prostitution, either directly or indirectly
    c) Whether she or a close family member has ever been involved with a communist organisation, either directly or indirectly. I assume the Kmer Rouge would come under that category?

d) Your last question regarding a Cuban without US citizenship is impossible to answer. The ruling would seem to rest entirely on individual situations. Reading between the lines I think it extremely unlikely that such a person could bring a foreign bride to reside in the US, unless she was also Cuban herself.

The remainder of the letter is filled with family news. Michael and Brian have sold all the houses under construction, mostly off plan. They have reserved two of them for themselves. Barry will register one in his in his daughters' names and Michael will do the same for the twins. I think there will be a small tax advantage in doing that. They are set to make a good profit, most of which they plan to plough back into a new project. Michael is already looking for a suitable site.

Linda is trying to carry on as normal but obviously she is finding it very hard. She has not returned to work yet, so I am trying to persuade her to come and work with us. At least she will be among friends on her bad days. Our online business is really taking off now and a new challenge might be just what she needs.

Everyone here is fine and they all send their love. Michael did ask me if I am sure you're not planning to marry some foreign geezer! He still worries about you, he can't help himself. I told him I am going into town at the weekend to book my ticket for our girly holiday, so you had better not have a new bloody husband when I get there.

CHAPTER THIRTY-FIVE

Narith and Mony set off for the capital, leaving Maggie and Sophea in charge. Maggie is biding her time to broach the subject of Miguel with Sophea; she thinks it best to bring it up casually, so she is waiting for the right opportunity. In the event, Sophea makes it easy for her. They have just visited Lap, a young man who recently inherited his farm.

'Lap has more modern ideas than some of the other farmers, Maggie. Miguel thinks he will be a big help in persuading others.'

'That could be big help, we should definitely keep him on side. Actually, I've been meaning to ask, why didn't you tell your father about Miguel when you had the chance?'

'Maggie, I told you, I cannot. He might make me leave his house, say I am no longer his daughter. Where would I go in that circumstance?'

'I assume you would go to live with Miguel. Is that your plan?'

'I cannot live with him. He will lose his employment if the managers know he has a relationship with a Cambodian woman. They will say he has not ethics. Please do not tell anyone, Mrs Maggie.'

'I promise, I won't say anything, but the whole thing seems hopeless to me. Are you sure he loves you? Neither of you seemed to be in love the other night.'

'Miguel cannot show he loves me to other people, particularly if they are in the VSO organisation.'

And it's impolite for Cambodians to show affection in public, so it's second nature for Sophea to conceal her emotions. What a mess,' thinks Maggie. It is clear to her that this relationship is a disaster waiting to happen. They cannot live together in Cambodia and even if Miguel were to give up his job and return to the States, Sophea cannot go with him. She would be alone here without family or any means of support. Even if she could survive in that situation, it seems unlikely that she would ever be allowed to join Miguel in the US. Her father's collaboration with the Kmer Rouge would ensure that.

Part of Maggie knows that she ought to explain all this to Sophea, then try to persuade her to go back to live with her family. Unfortunately, she has undertaken to deputise for Narith while he is away, and she also knows she will do a much better job with Sophea's help. Sophea obviously has a good rapport with the famers, probably because she comes from farming stock herself. Maggie is a great believer in the influence of genetics, despite the nature versus culture debate which still rumbles on in the western world. What makes the situation even more ironic is that Sophea and Miguel would probably make a wonderful team if they worked together. They are both intelligent, altruistic and dedicated to the well-being of the local people. For the time being, all Maggie can do is get on with the job as best she can and hope everything will turn out fine in the end.

She does find it difficult at times because, like most people when they are in love, Sophea can't stop talking about Miguel. She is constantly bringing his name into their conversations, usually to quote what he thinks about this or that, but in the process Maggie learns quite a lot about him. Coming from a poor immigrant background, he had to struggle to complete his education, juggling two part-time jobs between lectures. It is to his credit that he chose that the work he did, joining the fight against poverty, rather than entering the corporate world of global capitalism. Maggie also thinks that Miguel and Mr Kim have a lot in common, if only the older man could set aside his cultural bias, but Sophea is convinced that he will not do that. Perhaps he cannot.

The weeks pass and Maggie is still dithering. Sophea is a dear, kind girl; she does not deserve to be put in the position of having to choose between her family or the man she loves. The problem is, she clearly does not realise just how serious that position is. The crunch comes when Sophea decides she wants to spend a few days with her family, whom she has not seen for some time. Maggie arranges that day's visits so that the last one is near to Kampot; Sophea can get a taxi from there to Phom Penh.

Maggie drops off Sophea at the taxi rank that afternoon and waits while she gaggles with the driver about the fare. That done, he holds the car door open until she is safely inside, Maggie waves rather forlornly as she watches the car drive away. She is surprised at the feeling of isolation which swamps her. She had not realised how much she has come to depend on Sophea's company. *Well, there's no point in standing around feeling sorry for myself. I may as well pop into the centre while I'm here. I can call home and I might even have a chat with Claire.*

She makes her way to the centre, where she asks for Claire, who normally only works three days a week. The receptionist tells her that Claire is rather busy, but she will see what she can do. While she's waiting, Maggie places a call to Helen to check that all is well at home, then Claire comes out to the reception area.

'Maggie, it's good to see you. What can I do for you?'

'Actually, nothing. I just wondered if you had time for a coffee?' Claire hesitates before replying.

'Why not? I need a break'. She ushers Maggie into the office and busies herself pouring hot water from a Thermos bottle onto powdered coffee.

'I'm afraid I can't take long, we're busy trying to avert a scandal here. That's off the record, naturally.'

'Oh dear. What's happened?'

'We're not actually sure about that yet. A young marine engineer working at the deep water port in Sihanoukville has been seeing a lot of a girl who works in one of the bars. He says she is not a prostitute and they are just friends. Either way, the relationship has to end.'

'Why is that?'

'Well, you must know that "bar girl" is normally a euphemism for a prostitute. We believe any association with a prostitute is exploitation and we don't countenance that among our staffers.'

'But what if she is just a decent, hard-working girl?'

'That's unlikely. But if she is the relationship is going to cause trouble with her family. There's no other option for him: he has to end it.'

'What if he refuses to end it?'

'He'll be out of a job, I'm afraid. Our reputation as a charitable institution is too important to risk. Anyway, he is being sent to Phom Penh for a disciplinary hearing and we'll see what happens. Hopefully, he will see sense. So how are things in your neck of the woods?' The conversation becomes more general and Maggie leaves soon after that. On the way home she mulls over what Claire told her. Although she only confirmed what Maggie already knows, it has reinforced her belief that Sophea must end her relationship with Miguel.

Two days later, Maggie walks down to the shops to buy water and something to eat for supper from a local vendor. She did think about cooking something herself on the camping stove, but with cheap, tasty food readily available and close at hand, she decided that it wouldn't be worth the struggle she would have to get it working.

It is just the kind of evening when she would go for a run if she was at home: still warm with a light, fragrant breeze. Maggie does miss running, but it would not be acceptable here for a woman to go out in shorts and a skimpy top. To replace running, she and Sophea practice yoga two or three times a week, but Maggie doesn't find it as relaxing as running.

Her thoughts turn to home, to the boys, Linda and Michael, her parents and Helen. She wonders if Barry still runs up the hill. He may not have time for running now he is taking on larger projects. She hopes he is keeping an eye on her garden, Helen will not be able manage it on her own. Helen was in the garden when she met Jonathan for the first time, Maggie remembers. It does not occur to her that it's odd that Jonathan came last on her list.

She buys a bowl of fragrant noodles with prawns and turns back towards the house, where Sophea is getting out of a jeep. *Surely it can't be Miguel's, how could he know that she went to her parents? Unless she never went to her parents,* thinks Maggie. The jeep drives off before she reaches the house, but Sophea has spotted her and waits outside, smiling.

'Maggie, Good evening. I missed you while I was away.'

'I missed you too. Was that Miguel who drove you back? Didn't he want to speak to me about anything?'

'He was in a hurry, he had to go to Sihanoukville where there is some problem, I think'

'How did he find out you were in Phom Penh?'

'I telephoned him from my parents' house while my mother was at the temple giving thanks for my safe journey. You seem strange, are you angry with me, Maggie?'

'No, I'm not angry. Come on, you can share these noodles.'

Maggie is angry, but not with Sophea. She is angry about the prejudices still prevalent all over the world. *A person's marriage partner should not be determined by their culture; it is so unfair,* she tells herself. But she knows that she cannot delay any longer. Tomorrow she must try to persuade Sophea to give up Miguel, for the sake of them both.

CHAPTER 35

Sophea's tells Maggie that her father obviously approves of her as a house-mate for his daughter.

'He told me he is very happy that you are staying here with me. He thinks it is much better for me that I have you instead of the maid.' Maggie knows that Sophea's parents sent one of their maids to live with her when she first worked at the school. Before Maggie arrived they did not consider it proper for a girl to live alone. Now she wonders if Miguel arranged for Maggie to move in with Sophea so that he could see more of her without being inhibited by the presence of the maid. If that was the case, he must be disappointed that he has been forced to spend so much of his time in Phom Penh since she arrived. Anyway, as a token of their appreciation, Sophea's parents sent her a present: a beautiful silk blouse. The present makes Maggie feel so guilty; she feels as if it is she who is deceiving Sophea's parents.

Next day, when they stop for breakfast at the roadside, Maggie asks,

'Did you and Miguel come to any agreement when he drove you back yesterday?'

'It is too difficult for us to agree. He thinks that, as my parents will not give permission for our marriage, we should just get married without them. He says we can go together to tell them that we are married afterwards. But I don't think I can do that, they would be terribly hurt and angry'.

'Did he tell you what the problem is in Sihanoukville

'Yes. It is because an engineer has a relationship with a bar girl. His employers might send him to a different country. But I am not a bar girl, Maggie. You know that.'

'But if your parents don't agree to your marriage, Miguel could still be sent away. The VSO organisation is in Cambodia to help develop the country, not to cause problems.'

'Maggie, I love Miguel. I will go anywhere in the world that he goes.'

'But it is not that easy. You will need visas, other forms of documentation. It could be years before you can be with him.'

'I will wait. I do not care how long.'

'And how will you live? Where will you live if your parents disown you?' Sophea is quiet, clearly thinking about what Maggie said.

'Sophea, I'm sure Miguel loves you. Any man would love you, you're so beautiful, and sweet, and kind. But I learned something a long time ago: Sometimes love is not enough. Sometimes you have to walk away and leave love behind.'

Maggie cannot do any more. She is not going to bring up the subject again, but she is determined that she won't help Sophea deceive her parents either. If Sophea did lie to Maggie in order to spend time with Miguel, she will make sure that she cannot do it again.

A few weeks later, Narith returns, leaving Mony and their baby girl in Phom Penh. 'Her mother is looking after her and teaching her how to care for the baby. It is our custom. I will collect her when the baby is six weeks old.' Maggie is dying to see Narith's little daughter. Before Mony brings the baby home, she wants to buy her some gold bangles, but Claire told her that most of the jewellery on sale is imported from Thailand and is of poor quality. Apparently

228

only one genuine goldsmith remains in Phom Penh, all the others were murdered by the Kmer Rouge. So she arranges to go with Sophea to the capital to shop for the gift, and Sophea insists that Maggie stays at her parents' house rather than in a hotel.

The long-awaited rain starts while they are on their way to Phom Penh. Maggie knows that Cambodia has heavy rainfall for several months every year, but until now she did not fully appreciate what that meant. The rainwater lashes the windscreen with such force that it makes the wipers redundant: they can barely see the road ahead. After several months of dry weather, Maggie finds the rain exhilarating. She pulls over onto the dusty verge, know turning into a muddy verge, and gets out. 'Come on, Sophea, don't you want to know what it feels like?' Sophea knows exactly what it feels like, and stays put, watching Maggie throw out her arms and turn her face up to the sky.

'Come on, Sophea, it's lovely and warm, you should try it.' Maggie starts to shimmy, then does a little dance. A passing truck driver presses hard on his horn and gestures to indicate she is crazy. Sophea smiles, remembering that, as children, she and her siblings used to dance just like that when the first rains fell. She gives up, gets down from the jeep to join Maggie. They both jump up and down, clutching each other's arms above the elbow, and laughing until they are both out of breath. When they get back in the jeep, still laughing, their T shirts are wringing wet and their hair is plastered to their heads. Maggie reaches back over the seat for her holdall and pulls out a couple of T shirts, then gives one to Sophea.

'Tell the truth, Sophea, wasn't that fun?'

'Yes, it was fun, but I hope you will not do that behaviour every time it rains.' They start laughing again.

When they reach the capital, Sophea directs Maggie to her parents' house. The streets they are passing through now are lined with trees and most of the large, white- painted houses have high gates. They draw up outside one of them and a man of indeterminate age runs to open the gates. He bows and welcomes them in much the same way as people do in the countryside, then a lady who is unmistakably Sophea's mother appears and ushers them inside.

Maggie stays with the family for two days, during which time Sophea's parents and her three younger siblings are always polite and smiling. Maggie finds it hard to believe that Sophea's parents could be the stern and inflexible people she describes them as being. However, Maggie knows that, when it comes to marriage, parents all over the world can often disappoint their offspring.

The rains continue, off and on, for the remainder of Maggie's time in Cambodia, although the novelty soon wears off and she does not welcome it with as much enthusiasm as she did the first time it rained. Sophea is now free to open the school again and, since they are not needed so much on the farms anymore, local children begin to drift back to their lessons. They know how lucky they are to have access to free education, unlike other parts of the country where parents must pay for their children to go to school.

Mony returns with her baby, who they have named Lemal. She is a chubby, delightful little bundle, already smiling and cooing. Sophea immediately falls in love with her and keeps making excuses to go to their house so that she can see the baby. Maggie can only hope that she is not using Lemal as a front for meetings with Miguel. He appears to have made progress with two of the major banks, who have stated their willingness to look favourably on loan applications from their cooperative. The ministry of agriculture is also willing to come on board and provide funding for advisers and technicians. Miguel's future role will be to liase between the various bodies as the project gets under way. Because of this, he will probably spend much more time locally in future.

Maggie is due to leave Cambodia in September and Sophea has still not told her parents about their relationship. She continues to meet Miguel occasionally at the house. When this happens, they behave as though they are just friends in front of Maggie, exactly as they did before. Miguel is clearly determined to keep their affair hidden, so Maggie presumes that he does not know Sophea told her all about it. Or nearly all, she has no way of knowing whether they meet up while she is out with Narith.

Maggie speaks Kmer well enough now to be able to conduct halting conversations with the farmers on her own. Because she can be relied upon to make these visits, she and Narith can cover for each other when they take an occasional day off. Narith, who is suffering the usual sleepless nights of a new father, is grateful for a chance to catch up on his sleep, while Maggie needs some time to go shopping in the capital. By combining a day off with Sunday, she can have two days in which to shop for gifts to take home. That does not leave her much time once you factor in the taxi ride to and from Phom Penh. Luckily, one of the many public holidays falls on a Sunday, giving her three days in which to hunt for presents.

She stays in a hotel while she is in the capital and decides not to contact Sophea's parents at all. She cannot face them because she feels complicit in the love affair their daughter is concealing from them. Before she leaves for home, Narith invites her, Sophea and Miguel to his house for a farewell dinner. Miguel gives a little speech in which he expresses gratitude for the way Maggie held the fort in his, and latterly, Narith's absence. Naturally, she replies that she could not have done it without Sophea's help. The truth is that she feels a fraud. Apart from acquiring a basic knowledge of the language, she does not feel she has achieved much at all during her time in Cambodia.

CHAPTER 36

Maggie takes a night flight back to Heathrow airport. It lands a little after nine o'clock at the newly opened terminal four and. although she's still half asleep, she can see that the spanking new building couldn't be more different from the one she left behind in Phom Penh. There, the departure lounge had such a casual atmosphere that it hardly felt like an airport at all.

She collects her baggage and goes outside to where JJ and Matt are waiting for her. They have both filled out and grown a little taller, but they are still unmistakeably her boys. After they have hugged, the boys take control. They each pick up one of her cases.

'Come on Mum, let's get out of here' and they set off, Maggie hurrying behind, as they make their way to the car park, crossing over a pedestrian bridge to get there. In contrast to the people in Cambodia, everyone appears to be in a hurry, and they all seem to know where they are going, including JJ and Matt. *They've turned into men while I've been away, so capable. I would probably get lost if I had to find my own way out of here,* thinks Maggie. *I probably wouldn't even be able to find my own car.*

'Dad wanted to come with us, but he had a meeting at ten thirty and we didn't know if we would get back in time' Matt says. Maggie is glad, she is relishing this time alone with her sons. JJ gets into the driving seat with Maggie sits next to him.

'Matt drove up here so I'm driving back' he explains. 'We can stop and get some breakfast on the way.'

They stop at a motorway service station where the twins both have a cooked breakfast, Matt exchanging his bacon for one of JJ's eggs, and Maggie has a coffee. Between mouthfuls they pass on news of family and friends.

'Nan and Granddad want to come and see you tomorrow and Dad's arranged a little party at the golf club on Saturday night'

'That's nice of him. Do you know if he invited Jonathan?'

'Shouldn't think so', says JJ. 'Oh, and Lily got into Cambridge to do Biochemistry. She hopes to discover a cure for cancer.' Maggie tries to read his face but it's inscrutable. Matt is avoiding her gaze, giving an unusual amount of attention to buttering a piece of toast.

Maggie is getting a migraine, she can never sleep on a plane. She will probably try to have a nap once they are back in the car. When they get home, she goes straight to her bathroom and strips off. Standing under the shower with a jet of hot water buffeting her body is bliss after six months of pouring water over her head with a jug.

Over the next couple of days, a succession of visitors keep Maggie busy. Her parents arrive first, quite early next morning.

'Maggie, we were so looking forward to seeing you we couldn't wait, so we came by taxi' her mum says. But her dad keeps moaning that he was ripped off by the taxi driver.

'Why didn't you phone and ask one of the boys to collect you Dad?'

'That pair? They're like vampires. They only come out at night.'

'Well, they picked me up at the airport. You know one of them would have come and got you if you'd asked.' Maggie wonders why her father always has to moan when they all know that he dotes on the twins. *He is starting to look really old now*, she wonders why she hasn't noticed that before. Helen comes in with some flowers she picked from the garden.

'Maggie, welcome home, we've missed you. I hope the house was all right, I asked Mrs Jenkins to come in and give it a good clean. I knew the boys would have left it a tip.' Linda and Lily are the next to arrive but they don't stay long. They are going shopping for bedding and other items Lily will need at university. Linda tells Maggie they will have a good natter at the party on Saturday. Linda, who has always been slim, has lost more weight.

'She's too thin now, I'm glad she decided to come with us to Cambodia. We can fatten her up while we're there'

She has still not heard from Jonathan, but knowing how considerate he is, she guesses that he wants to give her time to get over her jet lag and catch up with her family. She will phone him tomorrow while the boys are still in bed. The next day she makes the call and they agree to meet that evening.

'The twins will probably have plans to go out; If they haven't, I'll tell them to make some', she promises. She is still recovering from jet lag, so she hopes that Jonathan will not want to go anywhere. It is more likely that they will order a takeaway then go upstairs, not necessarily in that order.

He arrives on time, as usual, looking exactly as he always does. 'Hi beautiful, you've let your hair grow.'

'I didn't have any choice, there weren't any hairdressers where I was staying.' He puts his arm round her and turns her towards the door, drops a kiss on her forehead as they go inside.

'So come on, tell me. What was it like, what did you do?'

'Oh Jon, it was a fantastic experience. The people are so nice - kind, always smiling. I didn't get much chance to see the country though, apart from the local area. That's why I'm going back next month.'

'You're going back?'

'Yes, didn't I tell you in my letter? Linda, Julia and I are going there on holiday in October.'

'Maggie, do you realise that I've put my life on hold for the past six months, waiting for you to come home?'

'You've hardly put your life on hold, don't exaggerate. I'm sure you carried on working, socialising, all the things you normally do. Just as I would if you went away for a holiday.'

'Six months isn't a normal holiday though, is it? I waited for years for my wife to come back to me. When she didn't come, I promised myself that I would never do that again, not for anyone'.

'So, what if I told you that I'm planning to apply for other jobs abroad?'

'Are you?'

'Yes, probably.'

'Then we may as well say goodbye now. You're a very special lady, Maggie. I'll never forget you.' Maggie cannot believe that he is going to walk away from her like this. No drama, no tears. Later, when she thinks about it, she realises she should have known that. With Jonathan there was never any drama or high passion.

CHAPTER 37

On Saturday morning Maggie has an appointment at the hairdressers. Her hair is now halfway down her back and she cannot control her wild curls any longer. She wants to pop in to see Linda on the way, so she is slightly irritated when a car drives in. She doesn't recognise it so she waits for the driver to park up and get out.. *'It's probably a mate of one of the boys'* she thinks. *There must be something special going on to get him up so early on a Saturday'*. But to her surprise it's Julia who gets out of the car. She almost never comes to the house, and never uninvited.

'Julia, how lovely to see you. But is everything all right?'

'Yes, everything is fine, I just wanted to talk to you about something. Is this a bad time?'

'No, not at all. I have an appointment with my hairdresser later, but I've got plenty of time. Come in, I'll put some coffee on.' Maggie bustles around, spooning coffee into mugs and getting out the milk while the kettle boils. 'You look well, Maggie. Cambodia obviously suited you.'

'It did in many ways. It's a beautiful country and the people are great, but life is terribly hard for them. Now, what brings you here so early on a Saturday morning? I'm betting it's something to do with my ex. What's he been up to now?'

'No, it's nothing like that. Maggie, we've been friends for a long time. Will you promise that, however you feel about what I'm going to tell you, we'll still be friends?'

'You're scaring me now, Jools, just tell me.'

"Well, while you've been away, Michael and I have been seeing a lot of each other.'

'You always see a lot of each other, you work together. What is it he's done?'

'He hasn't actually done anything really. Except', there's a long pause, then Julia blurts out

'He's asked me to marry him.' Maggie puts the kettle down. She didn't expect this, but she has to ask,

' I assume you said "yes"? You do know he won't be faithful to you?'

'I know.'

'And you can live with that?'

'I love him, Maggie. Over the years I've watched him with you, with a string of other women, but I still love him.'

'Then I'm happy for you Jools, in fact I'm ecstatic. I've always thought that, if Michael ever re-married, it should be to you. I just didn't think it would ever happen. Come here.' They hug and Julia sheds a few tears of relief.

'So, what's the plan? When is the wedding?'

'Michael wants to announce our engagement at the party tonight, but I thought you should be told first.'

'And what would you have done if I objected?'

'I don't know, I just hoped you wouldn't. He thinks we should get married in October, after the three of us come back from Cambodia.'

'And I suppose the reception will take place at the golf club?'

'Oh Maggie, you know him so well.' They both start laughing and Maggie says,

'Sod the coffee, I've got a bottle of champagne somewhere.'

Maggie is too tipsy to drive to the hairdressers, so she drags JJ out of bed. He borrows Hellen's car and drives Maggie into town dropping her off ten minutes late for her appointment. After that h , drives Julia home. On the way he asks Julia 'What's got into my mother?' I've never known her to drink in the morning but she's drunk, isn't she?'

'No JJ, she just had a glass of champagne. We both had one to celebrate her home- coming. Lots of people have champagne with breakfast on special occasions. Like Christmas, for example. We're just not used to it.' JJ has time to kill until he picks up his mother, so he returns home where he finds Matt has just woken up.

'What's going on Jay? That's Julia's car outside. And where's Mum? She was supposed to be going to the hairdressers.'

'I drove her there then I took Julia home. They were both drunk.' JJ goes to the kitchen and comes back with the she champagnes bottle, clearly empty.

'Look, they've necked the whole bottle before ten in the morning. Our mother has turned into an alcoholic.'

The combination of jet lag and the unaccustomed morning drinking is too much for Maggie, so when she gets home she goes straight to bed . It was a good move because when she wakes late in the afternoon, she feels normal for the first time since she arrived.

Before she gets ready for Michael's dinner she goes in search of Helen. Her car is not on the driveway where JJ left it, so the boys are obviously out.

Helen is already dressed and ready to go.

'We've got plenty of time, Maggie, we can have a cup of tea first. The boys went to play golf, they said they'll see us there. They've ordered us a taxi for seven. Is Jonathan coming?'

'No, he wasn't invited. Anyway, we've split up.'

'Oh Maggie, I am sorry. When did that happen?'

'Last night. I can't blame him really. I was away too long.'

'But how do you feel about it. Are you ok?'

'Actually, yes. It's a pity, because we got on well together, but I'm not heart-broken. I didn't miss him at all while I was away.'

Except for the sex,' she thinks, but she's not about to tell Helen that.

Michael has arranged for dinner to be served in a room overlooking the terrace. It is the relatively small room normally reserved for committee meetings but the perfect size for a family gathering. The only guests who are not, strictly speaking, relatives are Barry and Maureen, and of course Linda, who has brought Lily with her.

When Maggie and Helen arrive Michael and Julia are speaking to the club manager. *He's probably arranging his wedding reception already,* thinks Maggie. Michael excuses himself and hurries over to envelop Maggie in a tight hug, which goes on for longer than is strictly necessary so he can whisper in her ear: 'Thank you Mags'.

'You're welcome, just don't hurt her. She really loves you Michael.'

240

Linda comes over with Lily.

'I know I'm gate- crashing, Aunty Maggie, but Mum wants JJ to tell me all about Cambridge. I don't think she trusts me to find out for myself.'

'Of course she does, Lily, she's just trying to be helpful. I'm sure JJ would love to tell you everything you need to know'. At eighteen Lily does not need makeup, but like most girls of her age, she experiments with products which are totally superfluous. Despite this, her natural beauty shines through.

I don't blame Linda for being over- protective of her, she'll have every bloke in Cambridge after her, thinks Maggie. 'Come on, let's go and grab JJ now before his grand-dad does.' Maggie takes Lily's hand and pulls her over to the other side of the table.

After dessert is served, Michael stands up to make a short speech of welcome to his guests. JJ says to Lily

'Come on, it's too noisy in here, let's go outside where we can talk. You can bring your drink with you.' Lily picks up her glass in one hand and her Pavlova dessert in the other and follows him out to the terrace. It is still warm enough to sit outside, so they grab an empty table and sit down. Lily picks up a piece of meringue with her fingers, then puts it in her mouth before saying

'The last time I came out on this terrace was at Helen's birthday party. Your mum caught me and Matty snogging. She was furious.' A puzzle piece falls into place for JJ.

'Was that the reason she and your mum fell out? My mum would never say.'

'No, nor mine, but I suspect they did have a row about it.'

'Well, you needn't worry. I promise I won't try to snog you.'

'That's a shame'. Lily smiles and takes another spoonful of the Pavlova.

Indoors, Michael invites Maggie to say a few words:

'I'd like to thank Michael for organising this gathering. I really appreciate it because I missed you all so much while I was away. It's wonderful to have all my family here tonight, so thanks again Michael. I'm not going to say anything more because I know that Michael wants to say a few words. On hearing what Michael has to say, most of the guests swivel their heads towards Maggie as they try to work out how she feels about it.

CHAPTER 38

The three friends start packing for their holiday in Cambodia. Julia is also busy with wedding plans; she has already ordered a silk dress and jacket for the wedding ceremony.

'We're having that at the register office. Michael is organising the reception. He's inviting loads of people, and Michelle is helping him with decorations and stuff. All I have to do is turn up.' Julia is radiantly happy so Maggie crosses her fingers and hopes that she will always be that way.

'Is that the same Michelle who organised Helen's party?' Maggie and Linda exchange looks.

'Yes, she often organises events for us. She planned the decoration and furnishings of the show home for the new development too.'

'*Of course she did*', thinks Maggie, but she says nothing more. She does not want to ruin their holiday and anyway, Julia is a big girl, she knows exactly what she's letting herself in for.

Maggie is taking a completely different wardrobe from the one she took on her previous journey. They will be staying in hotels most of the time, so she needs dresses and shoes for the evening, not just casual things for sight-seeing and hiking.

When they arrive in Phom Penh the rainy season is more or less over, and everywhere they go is picture-book green under the bright blue sky. Maggie hires a car and they drive around, visiting prehistoric temples and staggeringly beautiful ancient monuments. They also head south to the notorious caves where the Kmer Rouge are believed to have murdered over a million people. The air inside is stagnant and heavy, as if weighed down by the souls of the dead. They do not stay long.

There are numerous waterfalls in Cambodia, but Maggie decides to take the others to the one which was waterless only a few months before. She wants to find out if her guide was winding her up. When they get there it is immediately clear that he wasn't. Huge volumes of water cascade down the rocky cliff face, occasionally swirling away from the main body of water to form miniature whirlpools in hollows in the rocks. It's spectacular. Maggie finds a flat-topped rock to use as a seat and Linda flops down beside her. 'You're quiet today Linda, are you ok?'

'I'm fine. I'm just thinking how Tom would have loved all this. We always said we would travel the world when we retired.'

'You still can; we'll do it together,' Maggie promises.

They spend a couple of days at one of the many beautiful beaches, and on the way back to Phom Penh Maggie thinks it would be nice to drop in on Sophea. 'You won't mind if I call in to say hello to my house-mate, will you? She'll probably still be at the school.' Neither Linda nor Julia object, so they take a detour. As they walk down the dusty side street towards the school, they can hear the children chanting. 'They're such cute children', Maggie tells the others,

'They make you wish you could take one home'.

The street door leads directly into a classroom, so Maggie knows that it isn't Sophea leading the chanting as soon as she enters.

'Oh' I'm sorry to interrupt you, I'm looking for Miss Sophea Kim.'

'She not teaching here anymore, she gone.'

'Do you know if she went back to Phom Penh?'

'Sorry, don't know.' The children are beginning to fidget in their seats and whisper to each other, so the teacher to turns her attention back to them. Having three foreign women descend on their classroom is obviously a distraction, so they thank the young teacher and leave. When they are back in the car Maggie says

: 'We'll go round to her house, it will only take five minutes. I can't pass by without saying hello'. When they reach the house the heavy curtains are closed across the doorway, normally an indication that there is no-one at home. Maggie lifts one and calls to Sophea but there is no response

. 'Come on, girls, I might as well show you round,' so they go in.

The sitting area is empty, apart from the statue of Budda. Even the floor cushions are gone. Maggie shows the others the bedrooms, where the bedsteads have been stripped of their mattresses and the storage chests removed. Tongue in cheek, Maggie asks

'Does anyone need the toilet?' and they troop into the kitchen. Go on, it's through there.' She indicates the doorway covered by the curtain. Julia and Linda exchange glances, then Linda lifts the curtain.

'You are joking, Maggie.'

'No. Just be careful you don't fall in.'

'There's no toilet paper.'

'What do you think that little hose is for? I should give yourself a minute to dry off afterwards, otherwise you'll have wet knickers.'

Linda lifts the curtain and goes inside. After a minute they hear a shriek, followed by hysterical laughter. '

You're supposed to aim it, Linda,' Maggie calls. On their way back to the car Linda slips her arm through Maggie's.

'Thanks for persuading me to come here, Maggie, I absolutely love this place.'

'What, the country or the toilet? asks Maggie. But she is secretly relieved. It's the first time that Linda has really laughed since Tom died.

On the last night of their holiday they have dinner at their hotel because they are catching an early flight the next day. Linda is not looking forward to going home to an empty house and neither is Maggie, so she offers

'Come and stay with me for a while, break yourself in gently.' Julia says she is glad she has the wedding to look forward to, otherwise she could stay here forever.

'Why don't we make a pact that we will go away together every year, just the three of us? We could take it in turns to choose the destination, but it has to be somewhere exotic and unspoiled'.

'You'll be married next year. Michael might want to come with you', points out Linda.

'Michael doesn't do exotic and unspoiled', say Maggie and Julia in unison.

CHAPTER 39

Contrary to their expectations, Julia and Michael's wedding takes place at a plush country club. Around one hundred guests attend a formal dinner and are joined by another hundred people for the party in the evening. Maggie declines the wedding invitation but says she will go to the party in the evening, bringing Linda as her guest. Julia still doesn't know where they are going for their honeymoon but she already has a case packed ready to leave the following evening.

JJ and Matty are convinced that Maggie does not want to attend the ceremony because she is unhappy about Michael marrying again. They are too young to understand that relationships don't always end, sometimes they just change. When Maggie and Linda arrive for the evening bash, Julia has taken off the silk jacket with the mannish big shoulders but is still wearing the midi dress that came with it. The calf-length dress is fitted to emphasise her curves and Linda tells her she will have problems dancing in the tight long skirt.

'Don't worry, I've got another dress upstairs to change into 'Julia smiles. Michael has put on a little weight and his hair is going grey now, but he is still an attractive man. *Trust him to carry it off,* thinks Maggie. The bride and groom both seem happy, especially Julia, and Maggie really means it when she congratulates them and wishes them all the best.

Two attractive women on their own at a party inevitably attract any man who is hoping to pull, but Linda is in no mood for dancing and Maggie only wants to spend time with her sons. Unfortunately, there seems to be some rivalry going on among the mature women guests, who are competing for a dance with the twins. The boys clearly find this funny but are happy to oblige. Linda just dismisses them as

'Silly old bags'. Maggie circulates among the guests for a while, chatting to the handful of people she knows. She can't help thinking back to her own wedding, it was so different. *Well it was a different world then, and Michael and I were different people,* she tells herself. Just then Linda comes over

'What do you think, Mags, have we done our duty?'

'Definitely. Come on, let's go back to mine and get plastered. You can stay over.'

The boys are both leaving on Monday to begin their final year of university. Maggie knows that it is also her last year of being the central figure in their lives. After this year, they will come home as visitors. She is looking into going abroad to work again, but this time she wants to make sure she has an appropriate and useful role. She would like to get involved in education management, especially education for women and girls. In the meantime, she is writing an article on Cambodia which she hopes to have published in a travel magazine.

Maggie has written to Sophea twice, but has still not heard from her She knows the postal service in Cambodia is unreliable, so she was not too concerned when her first letter went unanswered, but it seems unlikely that both letters would go astray. The fact that they are addressed to an up- market neighbourhood of Phom Penh should be an incentive for the postman to make sure it's delivered, because people living in posh areas are more likely to come up with a tip.

Maggie worries constantly about Sophea. She asks herself whether she should have spoken to Miguel about their affair and forced the issue. She also wonders whether it would have been better to inform the VSO management. She told Sophea's story to Linda and Julia

248

while they were on holiday. Julia reassured her that she had done all she could and shouldn't feel guilty, and Linda just said Sophea sounded like a drip. Neither of them really understood the tremendous importance of family ties in Cambodia, or the absolute expectation that young people will always comply with parental wishes. She decides to write to Miguel care of the centre at Kampot, just a friendly letter, it would not seem odd to ask after Sophea. If he doesn't reply she will have to give up.

It is funny how merely thinking of someone often triggers an amazing coincidence, because the following day, while she is trying to compose a letter to Miguel, the postman delivers her mail. Maggie is on her way to the kitchen for a coffee, so she picks up the pile of envelopes and flicks through them while she is waiting for the kettle to boil.

Junk, junk, gas bill, airmail. Maggie sits down and opens the envelope with the red and blue border straight away. It is from Sophea and Maggie's stomach flips with both excitement and dread as she starts to read:

Dear Mrs Maggie,

First I should apologise that I have not communicated to you before but I had some problems. After you left, Miguel went back to his own country on leave because his father was very ill. He has not returned until now. While I have been waiting for news from him my parents ordered me that I must return to Phom Penh. They are arranging a marriage for me. The boy they wish me to marry is a doctor and they think it is a very good match for me. When I told them I prefer to choose my own husband my father was very angry. He said it is a big mistake to let me live with a foreign woman, he said I learn to think like this from you. Now Narith is telling me Miguel will not return for a long time because his father might soon be dead. I cannot refuse the engagement any longer because my family will be shamed, so now I am engaged. I think my wedding will be very soon. I remember you told me that sometimes you have to leave love behind, so that is what I must do. I was very happy spending my time with you and I hope you will sometimes think of me. Sophea Kim.

Needless to say, Maggie is deeply moved by this letter. She takes it upstairs and puts it in the little box in which she stores her most treasured mementoes, sending up a silent prayer that the doctor will be good to Sophea.

CHAPTER 40

Since the boys left, Maggie has been monitoring the "situations vacant" pages of the national press, searching for a permanent job abroad, either with VSO or another charitable organisation. She has a vague idea that she would like to work somewhere in Africa, so she goes to the reference section of the central library in town hoping to find out more about individual African countries.

A helpful librarian points her to some relevant reference books, all of them thick, heavy and rather daunting tomes. She has one open on the table and is reading the introduction, which she finds patronising, opinionated and not at all objective. Maggie is wondering if it is worth reading any further when someone asks:

'Don't tell me, Mrs Johnson, you're researching your PHD'. It's Duncan, her old history teacher. He is looking over her shoulder, checking what she's reading.

'I wouldn't bother with him, Maggie, he's a prick.'

'I was just thinking the same thing, Duncan.' She laughs, standing up to give him a hug.

'Oops, librarian's bearing down on us. Come on, let's go to the café and get a coffee.' In the café she takes a seat and watches as he orders their drinks. He is chatting up the girl behind the counter and she's laughing. *He hasn't changed much, even though he has a few grey hairs*, thinks Maggie. He stands out from the other customers, mostly kids escaping from their books for a while, not only because he is well-turned out but also because of his evident good humour: it lights up his face. He turns and gestures towards the snacks on display and

Maggie nods that she will have a cookie. She knows already that she's going to sleep with him.

Afterwards, he pulls her close so that she is lying in the crook of his arm.,

'Well, that was a lot better than last time. You must have been practising.'

'You cheeky bugger. What do you mean?'

'Well, you were so uptight, if I hadn't known better I would have guessed you were a virgin.'

'I was in a way. It was the first time I slept with anyone but Michael'.

'So I took your extra-marital cherry. I'm honoured.' Maggie laughs.

'So who do you usually sleep with, Duncan?'

'There isn't anyone "usual", I wish there was. Do you fancy the job?'

'I'm not sure. Perhaps you'd better give me another competency test.'

Later, back at home, Maggie thinks about Duncan. She has known him a long time, has always got on well with him, and he proved this afternoon that he is good in bed. A friend and a lover rolled into one; she could do worse. She had thought that Jonathan would fit that role, but in retrospect she recognises that he did not try to fit into anything at all. He expected her to be the one to make concessions, to step into his absent wife's shoes. The problem was, if she was always there for him, she could not always be true to herself.

So she starts seeing a lot of Duncan. He would phone her and say,

'A crowd of us are meeting for a drink tonight. Do you fancy coming? You could stay the night at mine'. His friends are mostly college lecturers, though not exclusively. They are good company, convivial, witty and with strong convictions, so there are often heated arguments. She wonders now why she did not notice that she never met any of Jonathan's friends. Also, he never talked about his relatives, except to say that both his parents passed away years ago. She does not even know if he has any relatives. She realises now that Jonathan is basically only interested in Jonathan; she was lucky that she found out so early in their relationship.

Duncan, on the other hand, is interested in everybody with whom he comes into contact. He loves people. He was the first person to actively encourage Maggie's aspirations and when she passed her A levels, he was genuinely proud of her achievement, unlike Michael. He was proud, but only because she was his wife. He was basking in reflected glory, Maggie realises now. Duncan is also always open to new ideas and eager to try new things. Maggie takes him running, initially along the seafront. He is not particularly fit, so he finds it hard at first, but he is determined to improve because he wants to share as much of her life as possible.

By the end of the year, she thinks he is ready to tackle the hill, so they set off together one very cold morning in December. He struggles on the way up but makes it to the style just a couple of metres behind Maggie.

'You're a cheat, Maggie Johnson', he gasps as he bends over to catch his breath. 'You let me spend last night with you so that I'd be too tired to keep up, didn't you?' Maggie grins; last night will be the last time she allows him to stay over until the New Year because the boys are coming home for the Christmas holidays. She has never relaxed that rule.

Matt is the first to arrive. He has grown his hair and tied it back in a ponytail, despite the "new romantics" over-styled look which is currently in vogue. He has also got a black and white chequered PLO scarf wound around his neck. Although his persona is essentially laid-back, Maggie always knew Matt would be the rebel of the family. JJ comes home the next day, looking exactly as he looked when he left. He and Lily travelled back on the train together, giving Matt the opportunity to indulge in a brotherly wind-up.

'I'm glad you're taking your role as surrogate big brother seriously' and is rewarded with a brotherly punch on the arm.

Matt and JJ are spending Christmas day with Michael, Julia, and Helen. The boys were reluctant to leave their mother on her own, but she refused to join them because she wants to be with Linda and her children for their first Christmas without Tom. She knows it is bound to be an exceptionally poignant time for them. After lunch on Christmas day, JJ turns up at Linda's saying he has just popped in to wish them all a merry Christmas. He is driving one of the two brand new Ford Escorts that Michael gifted the boys for Christmas. Maggie knew that the boys were getting a car each because Michael spoke to her about it before he ordered the vehicles. He said they would need their own transport to get to job interviews, and hopefully jobs. Maggie could not argue with that, so she agreed it was probably a good idea. She did not expect the cars to be brand new, though.

Lily and Ritchie get into JJ's car and the three of them go for a drive, leaving Linda and Maggie with the dirty dishes. While they are stacking plates Linda asks

'Is it my imagination, or is there something going on between Lily and JJ?'

'Would you mind if there was?'

'Well obviously not in principle, but when they break up it will be a bit awkward for us. We don't want to fall out again.'

'What makes you think they will break up?'

'Well, they're bound to, they're just kids.'

'And how old were you when you started going out with Tom? You didn't break up, ever.' Linda's eyes suddenly fill with tears, so Maggie puts down the plate she is rinsing and turns to put her arms round her.

Duncan, who is spending Christmas day at his mum's, telephones later in the afternoon. Maggie goes to the telephone in the hallway, but it is hard to hear him because of the noise at his parent's house. It sounds like quite a party.

'Merry Christmas, Maggie. Are you having a good time with your friend?'

'I am thank you, but what's going on there? I can barely hear you.'

'Sorry, it's always like this when my two sisters get together with their husbands and kids. What's your plan for tomorrow, can we meet up?'

'I'm supposed to be spending the day with my sons and mother-in-law, but the twins probably won't be up before mid-day. Why don't you come to tea then you can meet them all.'

In the background, Maggie can hear a child's voice calling

'Hurry up Uncle Dunc, we're waiting.'

255

'Sorry, I've got to go. I've got a hot date with a twelve year-old and a monopoly board. I'll call you in the morning.'

Duncan arrives at Maggie's house in his old Morris Minor. It looks exceptionally dilapidated next to the other cars parked on the drive. When Maggie opens the door he says

'When you said, "the twins" I thought you meant your children, not your cars'.

'Oh, Michael bought them for the boys. They were going to be a graduation present, but then he thought they would need transport to get to job interviews, so they might as well have them now.' Matt comes out, curious to see his mother's new boy-friend. After they have been introduced Duncan, who has never shown the slightest interest in cars, says

'Nice car, a Ford, isn't it? Can I see the inside?' JJ is coming down the stairs when Maggie goes indoors.

'What's going on, Mum?'

'Matt's showing my friend Duncan his new car. They'll be in shortly, I expect'. JJ also goes outside, leaving Maggie and Helen waiting for them in the lounge. Helen says,

'Boys and their toys. Shall we have a sherry while we're waiting?'

In the evening they all watch the news on TV. The main story is the downfall of the last European communist leader, President Ceausescu of Romania, and his wife. They were both put on trial earlier that day and sentenced to death for "crimes against the people." Duncan thinks they've got off lightly. At least they died quickly, unlike the thousands of Romanians who have been left to rot in dungeon prisons'.

In the following weeks, a horrific picture begins to emerge of the appalling conditions endured by the Romanian people. Poverty, hunger and brutal suppression is widespread, but the most horrific information to come out of Romania is the fate of the children in orphanages. TV footage of starving babies left to lie in bare cots without proper clothing is aired around the world. When Maggie sees it she comes to a decision straight away. She Is going to Romania.

CHAPTER 41

Duncan insists that Maggie will only be effective and safe if she goes to Romania under the aegis of a recognised charity. He's familiar with that part of the world because he is writing a book on the social effects of the collapse of communism in Eastern Europe. He puts her in touch with some useful contacts and within weeks her travel arrangements to Bucharest are complete.

'I'll have to include a chapter on Romania in my book now, Maggie, so you could help me with it. I'll try to come out and join you there at Easter and we'll see how it goes.' Her article on Cambodia was printed in Spears travel magazine, following which excerpts were featured in several of the Sunday Supplements. Now Maggie would love to write the chapter on Romania for him.

Before she leaves, Michael comes to see her. She's surprised when his car draws up outside because, although they are now on friendly terms, they do not normally see much of each other. She goes out to meet him immediately, fearful that he's bringing bad news.

'Hello Michael, how nice to see you. Have you come to see me, or your mother?'

'You. I need to talk to you about Mum.' They go indoors and Maggie puts the kettle on. While she is waiting for it to boil her mind is in overdrive. .

'I know I've been busy with the boys, and Duncan, but surely I would have noticed if Helen wasn't well' she thinks.

'Your mum is all right, isn't she Michael?'

'She's fine at present, but I gather you're going off on your travels again shortly.'

'Yes, I am'.

'Well while you're abroad on your crusade to save the world, do you ever think about the old lady you leave behind? She's all on her own here Maggie.'

'Not really. She has friends, and you are here. Barry keeps an eye on her too, and the boys come to see her sometimes.'

'They came once while you were in Cambodia. They're young men, Maggie, they've got their own lives.' Maggie is shocked. Has she really been selfish? Helen has never seemed to mind being left alone here. She has her friends and she still potters around in the garden. Also, keeping an eye on the house makes her feel useful, doesn't it?

'So what do you expect me to do?' Michael sighs and sits down.

'It's my fault really. I know I wasn't very nice to her when I was younger, and I still don't spend much time with her. But at the end of the day, she is my responsibility, not yours. Anyway, I think it's time that Mum moved in with us. If it works out, I'll build her a self-contained annexe, we have plenty of room. Michael now lives in what can only be described as a country mansion.

'What do you think?'

'I think we should ask her what she wants to do. Shall we do that now?' They go next door to Helen's flat where a surprised Helen opens the door to them. She is even more surprised when Michael invites her to move in with him and Julia.

'Think about it, Mum. I worry about you being on your own here. If you were t taken ill it could be days before anyone realises.' After Michael leaves, Helen puts her hand on Maggie's arm and says:

'Maggie, I hope that you won't think I'm being ungrateful, you know that I've loved living here with you and the boys. But Michael and I have never really been close, not like you and the twins. I just think this might be my last chance to make that connection with him. I can't refuse this offer, but I'll always think of you as my daughter and my best friend.' Maggie puts her arms round Helen.

'And you'll always be my second mother. And don't be too proud to say if it doesn't work out. You can always move back here, you know that. Come on, you can make me a cup of tea and we'll talk about it.'

They all agree that Helen will take only her personal belongings when she moves into Michael's house. She can move all her other stuff later, when she is sure that living with him is working out. Hetty the springer spaniel, who is really showing her age now and sleeps most of the time, will go with her. Typically, Michael has a good relationship with local estate agents because of his building projects. He is going to instruct them to find a suitable tenant for Helen's flat, provisionally for six months. By the time Maggie leaves for the airport, a nice young couple who can be trusted to keep an eye on Maggie's house, have moved into the annexe.

CHAPTER 42

Sadly, orphanages are plentiful in Bucharest. Some already have foreign volunteers in place, but the one to which Maggie is sent has only recently come to the attention of the new authorities. After a short induction with the charity, she arrives at the orphanage early one morning with one of their workers, Yvonne, and a Romanian interpreter named Ana. They find an old woman, Maria, sitting on a chair near the entrance. She is apparently in charge, and she tells Ana that she has sole responsibility for the care of all the children, who are housed in two large rooms. There is no heating in the building, and they find none of the toys or equipment normally associated with childcare. The first thing the three women do is help their driver to unload the supplies provided by the charity. They seem pitifully inadequate when they realise the enormity of the task with which they are faced.

There find skeletal children lying in cots, hardly moving, not talking, scarcely a whimper between them. It is hard to tell if they are babies or toddlers because they are all emaciated. Some have rudimentary clothing or covers but these are so stained and filthy that they have taken on the quality of wood and offer no warmth or comfort. Most of their faces are covered in dried snot and scabs and several have faeces stuck to their legs.

The children appear to be separated according to mobility. Those who can walk occupy the larger of the two rooms, while some of the children in cots are not babies but disabled children. The sour smell coming from a couple of old-fashioned chamber pots is overwhelming, and the contents of the pots are overflowing onto the concrete floor.

Maggie says 'Right, shall I get started with cleaning them up?'

'Not yet, Maggie. Most of these children will be traumatised. How do you think they would react to strangers coming in and pulling them about? We'll have to approach them slowly. Ana will go with Maria and speak to the older children. Try to find out their names if you can, Ana. Maggie, stay with the babies. Talk to them but don't pick any of them up unless they make it obvious that they want you to. You can touch them gently if they're not too nervous. Here, put these gloves on. I'm going to try and find out if there is any way of heating this place'. Yvonne pats Maggie's arm reassuringly and goes off in search of a boiler.

Ana makes a list of the children. Most of the boys say their name is either George or Gabriel, while the girls are mostly called Anica or Maria. Some do not seem have a name at all. Maggie thinks shepherds give more thought to the individual sheep in their flocks than has been extended to these little orphans. The most common characteristic displayed by the older children is anger. They lash out at each other for no reason, kicking and sometimes biting, but are clearly fearful of adults. Similarly, the babies hardly ever smile or hold out their arms to invite a cuddle. They rarely even bother to cry.

Over the coming weeks they try to improve the situation for the children, but progress is frustratingly slow. Yvonne locates an ancient boiler in the back yard. It runs on kerosene, and Yvonne somehow manages to get some delivered to the orphanage by the end of the week. There is also a daily delivery of food, mainly soup and dry bread, but there are no feeding cups for the younger children. The older ones drink the soup from bowls, the only dishes available. The charity has provided some feeding bottles and formula for the babies, but they have no quick means of sterilising them and there are not enough to go round.

Maggie asks Yvonne why the charity does not send more supplies, especially warm clothes and bedding.

'We're not the only orphanage in need, and that's just in Romania. We work all over the world, don't forget. There's always someone asking HQ for something, but there's only one pot, unfortunately.'

'How about if I could get someone to send us stuff from the UK, would it get to us?'

'Could you do that?'

'I can try. Do you think I'll be able to use the phone in the office?' Maggie and Yvonne each have a studio flat in a block of flats originally built for Romanian workers. The flats are adequate but without non-essentials such as phone lines. They put together a list of basic supplies for the forty odd children at the orphanage. Two sets of underwear, two track suits and trainers for each of the older kids, vests and baby-grows and cardigans for the babies, plus some plastic plates and mugs. Yvonne pulls some strings with her colleagues in the office and takes Maggie back there the next evening with and her list.

She phones Michael first and up-dates him on the situation at the nursery.

'What I'm hoping, Michael, is that you will donate the money to buy them clothes and bed linen and have it sent here.'

'Well, I can certainly help with the money, but I wouldn't have a clue about shopping for babies. You always did all that.'

'Don't worry about the shopping, I'm going to get Linda involved. All you have to do is hand over the cash. Will you or Julia help her to get the goods shipped?' Next, she phones Linda and tells her that Michael is going to donate two thousand pounds to the orphanage.

'All you have to do is spend it. If you have money left over after you've bought the clothes, get some fun things, games or baby toys, I leave that to you'

'I'll go on the internet to find the best prices. Don't worry, there will be something left over for toys.'

In the meantime, the daily work with the children goes on. Maria, who is not as old as she looks, seems to be reinvigorated now she has co-workers again. She scrubs down the ancient stove, also dependant on Kerosene, and gets it going so that the daily soup can be heated up and feeding bottles can be boiled. She tells Ana that there used to be two other women working with her, but one simply failed to turn up one day. They assumed that her husband had been arrested for anti-government activity, a common occurrence, and she was probably thrown into prison with him. The work became much harder with only two people caring for the children so after a while the second woman stopped coming too.

True to her word, two large parcels arrive from Linda, so the children now have clothes. Thankfully, the weather has warmed up so the clothes they asked for are perfect. There is also enough bedding for all the cots, though laundering the cot sheets is still problematic. Ana says her mother still has her old-fashioned washtub in the back garden. She is going to borrow it and ask her boyfriend to bring it to the orphanage on his bike. He arrives on foot, pushing the bike and balancing a large vessel on the cross bar. It is similar to the container Maggie used for showers in the bathroom in Cambodia. They carry it through to the back yard where Maria can give any soiled cot sheets a rudimentary wash.

Linda has worked wonders with the money because she has also sent some basic toys. For the children there are balls in varying sizes, colouring books with crayons and jigsaws and some brightly coloured building games to improve their fine motor skills . There are also rattles and cot mobiles for the babies and some push-along toys for toddlers.

Now that the children have been cleaned up as much as is possible without the benefit of a bath, they are marginally more comfortable. Maggie wishes now that they had thought to ask Linda for a couple of portable baby baths. When they first arrived, most of the babies had painful sores on their legs and genitals. With gentle cleansing and creaming the sores are disappearing and some of the babies are beginning to respond. Maggie and Yvonne are sometimes rewarded with an occasional babble or smile. They would like to have more time to spend with individual babies, but there is not even enough time to hold each baby while they are being bottle fed. There are just too many of them.

Ana and Maria, who mainly care for the older children, are having less success. The children seem incapable of playing together and fight over the toys constantly, especially the balls. They throw pieces of the jigsaws around and snatch crayons away from other children, only to snap them then discard them. Ana tries to teach them nursery rhymes but without much success because they are so apathetic. Some of the younger ones still ask

'When is Mama coming back?' but the older ones have either given up, or never knew their mothers at all. Ana says that the children are not all orphans. Some of them were brought to the orphanage by their parents because they are just too poor to feed them. Maggie cannot imagine how poor a person must be to make this place seem a better option.

Duncan comes out to research his book during the Easter break. He does not spend all his time in the capital but when he is there he manages to spend the occasional night with Maggie. He tells her that his visit to Romania is premature; it is much too soon after the communist government fell to quantify the impact on society. 'That doesn't matter, I just wanted to see you. I can use this visit for the purposes of comparison later', says the ever-optimistic Duncan.

There is extensive coverage of the plight of Romanian orphans in the world media, and more and more young people are travelling to Romania as volunteers. Yvonne manages to arrange for two of them to be allocated to her and is expecting a third to arrive soon. This is great timing for Maggie because their presence means that she can leave without feeling guilty. She wants to be at home in time for her sons' graduation ceremonies.

When she and Yvonne go home in the evening, she is so tired that she normally goes to bed as soon as she's eaten a frugal supper. She has no idea what Yvonne does, so it is a pleasant surprise when Yvonne knocks on the door of her apartment the evening before Maggie is due to leave. She is carrying a bottle of wine and a bottle of the white spirit named Tuica, Romania's national drink.

'Hi, Maggie. I couldn't let you leave without having a farewell drink with you. What's your poison?' Maggie has not tried tuica previously, so she opts for that. Romanians normally drink it before meals as an aid to digestion, and after a few sips, Maggie can definitely feel it in her gut. It is the sensation one gets from neat Absinthe and one glass is enough for her. They move on to the wine and chat. Although they have been working together for several months, there is little time for personal conversation at the orphanage. All Maggie knows about Yvonne is that she is hard-working, compassionate and very efficient. She knows nothing about her personal life. By the time the wine is finished, Magie has learned that Yvonne's ex- husband is a cheating bastard and she is now in a relationship with a German diplomat. She also has a great sense of humour. Now she holds up the bottle of tuica and asks

'So what do you think, Maggie, shall we move on to this?' Maggie holds out her glass for a refill.

The next morning Maggie wakes with a terrific hangover. It is never a good idea to mix one's drinks, especially when you haven't touched alcohol for months. Luckily, her flight does not leave until the afternoon, so she doses herself with coffee and aspirin before heading for the airport. She is not looking forward to the journey. When she gets to London, she will probably have to take a train and she really isn't up to it. *Maybe I'll just take a taxi home. I wonder how much it will cost for a two hour journey,* she thinks.

Maggie is so relieved when she finds Duncan waiting for her at the airport.

'Duncan, how did you know I was coming back today?' She almost falls into his arms.

'I phoned your friend Julia, Linda gave me her number. You don't look well, what's wrong?'

'Hangover.' He grins and takes her baggage off the trolley. 'If this is all you've brought with you, there's no need for a trolley.'

'I was using it to lean on. Don't laugh, I feel terrible.' In the car park Maggie looks around for his Morris Minor, but Duncan has stopped behind a Ford. The car is just like those Michael gave the twins at Christmas.

'Come on, Duncan, I really need to sit down. ' He goes round to the front of the vehicle and opens the passenger door.

'Sorry, I was trying to get into the boot, I haven't opened it before.' When they are both seated Maggie asks

'How come you changed your car? I thought you loved that old banger.'

'I did, but your sons talked me into changing it. They told me the Morris is an old fogy's car. After that, I felt like an old fogy every time I got in it.'

'If you're an old fogy then so am I. Don't listen to those two, they think they're so cool.' There is a queue at the exit barrier. While they are waiting, Duncan leans over to kiss her, but Maggie says

'I wouldn't if I were you. I think I'm going to be sick'.

CHAPTER 43

The boys will not be home until they finish their final exams and her mother rings to say that they cannot come round because her father isn't well, so Maggie gets a much less effusive welcome than when she returned from Cambodia. She goes to visit her parents and is shocked at how ill her father looks. He has been diagnosed with angina, probably brought on by smoking and his sedentary lifestyle. As usual, Maggie's sympathy is predominantly for her mother. Illness has not improved her father's temper and he views his angina as an excuse to keep her mum running around all day. She is constantly bringing him cups of tea, his newspaper, even his meals on a tray, despite advice from his doctor that he should move around and take gentle exercise. Mary is being ground down by constant worry and tiredness, so she doesn't look too well herself. Maggie knows it would be pointless to remonstrate with her father, so she doesn't stay long.

The young couple who are renting Helen's apartment come round to ask if they can extend their contract. Maggie tells them she will have to consult with her mother- in- law first. She has not seen Helen since she got home but she is going to visit her at the weekend. It will be the first time Maggie has been inside Michael's new home and she is curious to see how Michael and Julia are getting on together now they are married.

Helen answers the door when she arrives and immediately envelops Maggie in a hug.

'Welcome home, Love, I've missed you.' She takes Maggie into a large sitting room. It is tastefully decorated and contains several soft leather sofas. Helen collapses on one of them but, despite the comfy seating, she seems a little uptight. Maggie can tell that the décor was not designed by Michael and wonders if Michelle had any input.

'Sit down, Maggie. Julia will be down in a minute. She's just gone upstairs to change, and Michael should be back any time now. I want to hear all about your trip, I gather the orphanage was horrendous.'

Julia enters the room. Her blonde hair is pulled back into a ponytail and she is wearing jeans and a cotton sweater. Despite her casual clothes she manages to look well-groomed and immaculate.

'Maggie was just telling me about those poor little mites in the orphanage'.

'I know, it's horrific, Mrs J'. Julia sits down beside Maggie and puts her hand on her knee, but she seems ill at ease.

'Welcome back, Lovely. Did Duncan get to the airport on time? He was worried he wouldn't make it.'

'He did, and I was so grateful. I had a terrible hangover.' Julia laughs and says,

'It wasn't all work then. Ah, there's Michael now.' She goes out to fetch coffee and comes back with Michael. He is carrying a large cardboard box which he puts down gently on the coffee table before bending down to kiss Maggie.

'Hi Babe, how are you?' Helen comes over and sits on the arm of the sofa nearest to Maggie.

'I'm afraid we've got bad news for you, Love. 'Hetty was ill while you were away. It was cancer. She was in pain so the vet advised us that it would be kinder to have her put down.' When Maggie left for Romania, the old dog still got out of bed to greet visitors, *d*espite her age and arthritis. *So that's why Helen was nervous, she was going to give me bad news. Poor old Hetty, I should have been there for her.*

'Who went with her? When she was put down?'

'Michael and I took her'. Maggie has an irrational flash of anger: she should have been consulted.

'She didn't know what was going on, Maggie, she just went to sleep.' Michael goes to the cardboard box and takes out a brown and white puppy. He plonks it on Maggie's lap.

'Meet Hetty number two. We thought we could share her with you. She can come to us if you go away again'. The puppy jumps up and begins to lick the tears from Maggie's face.

'I'm having first go', she says.

Later, Helen takes Maggie up to her bedroom. It is decorated in cream and pale blue, with a large window looking out over the garden and the fields beyond.

'Helen, it's lovely. But are you really happy here? You can always come home, you know.'

'I am happy, Maggie, very happy. Julia is lovely, and she can't do enough for me. And I'm company for her when Michael's away' Helen takes Maggie's hand in hers. 'This is my home now, Love.'

Julia has already bought a bed for Hetty, but on the night Maggie takes her home she cries so much that Maggie lets her into her bedroom. After that, Hetty takes it for granted that she sleeps beside Maggie's bed.

Both JJ and Matt graduate with honours, so Maggie and Michael go to their graduation ceremonies together. JJ's takes place first and on their way to the ceremony Maggie feels slightly uncomfortable.

'This is weird, Michael. It feels as though I'm being unfaithful to Duncan.'

'We can do that later, if you like,' he grins and Maggie slaps him on the leg with her clutch bag. JJ already has a job as a trainee with a firm of architects in Southampton. He is going to move back to Maggie's house, but only until he finds himself a flat, he keeps reminding her. Matt has enrolled on a Masters course at RADA, something to do with technical theatre. He is going to Los Angeles until the course begins in September He says he wants to explore the reality of trying to make it in Hollywood, but Michael says he would be better off exploring the reality of earning a living. Matt just smiles and tells him:

'I'll be fine, Dad. I'm going to get a job as a barista.' A panicking Michael asks what a barista is, but Maggie doesn't know either; they have to look it up.

CHAPTER 44

The house seems empty with Matt gone and JJ out all day, but this does leave Maggie free to write the article she has been planning. Although much has been written about the plight of the Romanian orphans, no-one has described in detail the day-to-day difficulties of trying to improve their conditions. In the article Maggie discusses not only the practical problems but the adverse psychological effects upon the children living in the orphanage. She is delighted when a mental health journal agrees to publish it and even more delighted when Duncan refers to her article in his book.

Linda has not forgotten their holiday pact and chooses South Africa for their next excursion. When Michael hears that Julia is going away with Maggie and Linda, he wants to go with them, but Maggie points out that, if he does, she would have to invite Duncan too.

'Linda would be the only one on her own, Michael. Anyway, we want it to be girls only.'

While they are in South Africa they visit beautiful beaches, take the causeway up to Table Mountain and, most memorably, go on Safari. One night their guide wakes them up around midnight.

'Come with me, quickly ladies. No need to get dressed'. He signals that they must be quiet, so they follow in silence until he stops behind some bushes.

'Look' he whispers. They crouch down in their pyjamas and peer through the foliage. Breathless, they watch as three baby leopards lap up water on the other side of a pond.

The day after they fly home, Maggie's father dies following a heart attack. It is a very sad homecoming, especially for Matt and JJ, who have always been fond of their grandfather. Maggie is also upset but privately she knows that the main reason she feels sad is because she is not as upset as she should be. Her mother, on the other hand, seems to have gone to pieces. She looks lost, rudderless, and she keeps telling Maggie how empty the house feels without him. *Of course it feels empty without his overbearing presence,* Maggie thinks, but all she says is

'Come on Mum, let's pack your case. You're coming home with me tonight.

Mary never goes back to live in the house she shared with her husband for over forty years. After the funeral, she tells Maggie

'I think I might sell the house and buy a nice little flat'. Maggie tells her not to rush into anything when she is still grieving.

'There's no hurry to sell the house now, Mum. You're still in shock. Wait until you can think straight before you decide anything'. Actually, Maggie quite likes having her mum to stay. It is so nice to be able to spoil her a little without having her dad moaning in the background. And Mary is so fond of the puppy. She makes such a fuss of her that Hetty deserts Maggie and goes to sleep in Mary's bedroom every night.

One weekend, JJ goes to visit friends from university, so Duncan stays over. Maggie is afraid that her mother will disapprove, so she asks Duncan to get up early next morning and slip out of the house before she wakes up. Unfortunately, she is already in the kitchen and making tea when he goes downstairs.

'Oh, I was going to take Maggie a cup of tea in bed for a change, she's been bringing me one every morning since Brian passed away.'

'Well give it to me. I'll take it up to her and then we'll have ours together, shall we?' Later, Maggie asks her mum whether she minds Duncan staying the night.

'Of course not, Maggie, it's your house. Anyway, I really like him, not like that Jonathan.'

'Oh, but I thought you liked Jonathan?'

'I did when I first met him, but he wasn't genuine. He put on a good act but underneath he was cold, selfish. Duncan's different, here's no side to him.'

Well, if you want to learn how to choose a man, ask your mother' thinks Maggie.

JJ finds a flat in Southampton and moves out, and Mary says she should be thinking about leaving too.

'Why not just stay here permanently, Mum? I thought you liked living here?'

'I do, Maggie, but I don't want to be in the way. I expect Duncan will be moving in now that JJ's gone, won't he?'

'Mum, Duncan and I have never discussed living together. We are quite happy as we are. Please stay Mum. I can empty your house and put it on the market for you. You don't even need to go there if you don't want to.' But the conversation raises a question for Maggie. *Why have Duncan and I never talked about living together?*' She decides she will bring it up at the earliest opportunity, and in the meantime, she has a job to do. She takes her mother back to the house to clear out her father's meagre wardrobe and possessions and to collect the things her mother wants to keep. Once that is done, she arranges a house clearance company to take away the furniture. There is no question of selling any of it, it's too old and rickety.

The house is put on the market and its poor condition and correspondingly low price make it an appealing investment for developers. It sells within weeks, leaving Mary with much more money than she ever imagined she would have. On the advice of her solicitor, she also makes a will. By the time everything is settled it is nearly Christmas. Matty will be coming home, but JJ says he will only be able to spend Christmas day with Maggie. He will probably go to Michael's on Boxing day and he is due back in the office the day after that.

Apparently Lily, now in her final year, has been offered work in Southampton as a lab assistant. It will be good experience for her, so she tells Linda that she is going to stay with a friend there. Naturally, Linda suspects that the friend is JJ.

'Why don't you just ask her?' Maggie suggests.

'It's difficult. What if she isn't going to stay with JJ? She would be really offended. And she does have friends who live in Southampton'.

'Well, make sure you give her the contraception talk again, just in case', Maggie has been worrying about something herself recently. In fact, ever since she spoke to Duncan about moving in together. It happened when they were sitting on his couch, watching an old movie. They were holding hands, their fingers entwined. The vibe was so companionably domestic that it felt quite natural to ask,

'Duncan, why have we never talked about moving in together?'

'Would you like to move in here with me then, Maggie?'

'No, I've got Mum to think about now, haven't I? But you could move in with us.'

'Maggie, I really love you, but if I moved into your house I'd feel like a gigolo. You must understand that?'

'No, I don't. Anyway, we could both sell up and buy something together. Why not?'

'Because I know how much you love your home. You do, don't you? Think about it. And this flat isn't worth half of what your house would sell for. Even if we both put in the same amount, you would end up with a much smaller house. Would you be happy with that?'

'But I wouldn't mind contributing more than you. Between us we could buy a lovely house.'

'You're not listening are you, Maggie? Anyway, where is this coming from? You've never said anything before.'

'It was just something Mum said. Forget it, I wish I hadn't mentioned it now.' But Maggie can't forget it. She knows that Duncan's jovial, laissez faire exterior conceals some very old-fashioned values. He never lets her pay when they go out for a meal or to the cinema. But what worries her most is his assumption that she values her house more than him. *Is she really that mercenary? What was it Linda called her when they had that row? Her majesty? Is that really how people see me?*

Maggie knows that people assume she is wealthy because of the house. Actually, the opposite is true. Now that Mum has settled in she will have to start job hunting again because her savings are rapidly disappearing. It is flattering when one of her articles is published, but she is paid peanuts for her efforts. In the meantime, she will have to sort things out with Duncan. She could not bear to lose him now.

CHAPTER 45

Now that her mother is living with her, Maggie has to give up all thought of working in Africa, so she takes a job with a very prestigious charity instead. It is mainly office –based so she gets home in time to share an evening meal with her mother. Duncan often joins them, normally staying overnight after supper. Maggie doesn't raise the subject of living together again. She does not want to rock the boat.

The young couple buy a house at last and move out of the annexe. They are replaced by an older lady, a widow named Alys. Within a few weeks she and Mary are fast friends. They walk Hetty together, play cards on the kitchen table on rainy afternoons, and share a taxi to the local day centre every week. Now that she is no longer under the thumb of her bullying husband, the real Mary re-emerges. It is much like the time when she first began to baby-sit the twins.

The local Polytechnic where Duncan now teaches is going to be awarded university status, which means the status of the teachers there will also be elevated. Duncan will have time allotted for research, which is welcome news because he recently started work on a second book.

Lily enrols on a Masters course at Southampton university and she and JJ announce their engagement. When she hears the news, an ecstatic Maggie gives JJ the engagement ring Michael bought her. Not the original ring but the expensive one he bought her later. Maggie rarely wore it herself, but it is a beautiful ring and she wants Lily to have it now.

'Didn't I tell you those two would never split up?' Maggie tells Linda, and they go out to shop for wedding outfits together.

Matty finishes his course at RADA and goes back to LA to work in a theatre off Broadway.

'What does that mean, "Off Broadway?" Maggie asks Michael.

"A flea pit, probably" is his dour comment. Like actor Michael Caines's father, Michael is still hoping his son will" shape up and get a proper job."

A few months after JJ and Lily's wedding, Barry the builder passes away, closely followed by Helen, who slips peacefully away in her sleep a few weeks later. Maggie is so grateful that Helen was able to go to at least one of her grandsons' weddings, and as Michael sourly points out,

'You couldn't expect her to hang on forever waiting for Matty to tie the knot. Sadly, Maggie is forced to recognise that she has reached that stage in life when funeral attendances inevitably occur more frequently. She is so grateful that she has this chance to spend time with her mother in her final years.

At work Maggie has become increasingly disenchanted with the charity. She understands that sound business practices are imperative for any organisation, but she has begun to think that the profitability of the business sometimes takes priority over the charity's stated aims. Moreover, Maggie cannot understand why the directors are paid such large salaries when they do so little. A board meeting reads like a gathering of the Eton old boys club and is just as likely to promote real benefit worldwide, thinks Maggie. Disillusioned, she hands in her notice and takes a job with a local women's refuge. She knows from her first day there that she has made the right decision because the centre provides hands on help to the abandoned and abused. In some ways it reminds her of her work at the orphanage

Over the years, Maggie, Linda and Julia continue to take an annual holiday together. They go to India and watch the sun come up over the Taj Mahal, turning it from white to a soft pink, The following year they visit the Forbidden City in China and struggle up the Great wall. Every year Michael, and later Duncan, ask to go with them but they always refuse. The reason they give is simple:

'Linda would be on her own, the odd one out.' In the end it is Linda who gives in: 'Oh, let them come, Mags. I don't have to be banished to a tiny room, we could rent a house. Do you know what I really fancy doing? I'd like to go back to Spain. Do you remember that first holiday? When Ritchie was only a baby.'

'Of course I remember it. I had to tell Mum and Dad that Michael and I would have separate rooms. But won't it upset you to go back without Tom?'

'Probably, but I'd like to go anyway. We don't have to stay where we went before. We could spend a few days there then move around. We could do Barcelona, Madrid, maybe even Seville, just play it by ear. What do you think?' So they all head off for Spain. When they arrive at their villa It is quite late, too late to go for dinner, so they decide to have drinks and snacks on the terrace instead. Linda is the first to turn in for the night, leaving the other four to finish off their duty- free alcohol. Maggie had thought it would be weird to see Michael and Julia sharing the same bedroom, but when they all say goodnight and Duncan steers her gently into their room, it doesn't feel weird at all.

The next day Linda and Maggie try to find the restaurant on the beach where they used to go in the evenings, but there are so many now. They all look the same and the beach can only be reached by a walkway under the seemingly endless rows of apartment blocks.

'I give up, let's go and look for our hotel, Maggie'. The hotel is much easier to find. It looks exactly the same, except it has been given a coat of paint. Michael, always sensitive to Linda's feelings, puts his arm round her and tells her

'Come on, let's go inside and have a drink in the bar. You and Maggie got drunk on Babycham here, if I remember correctly.' The interior has not been given a coat of paint and is looking very tired. Most of the other occupants of the bar are elderly. *'They've probably come here on a coach trips', thinks Maggie.*

'We thought this place was so glamorous, do you remember, Michael?'

'I remember every detail of our holiday here'. Michael, grinning, locks his gaze on Maggie until she starts to blush.

They go down to Marbella where they walk along the golden mile every evening, then drive up to Granada, stopping on the way to visit the gardens of Al Hamra. They all want to visit Barcelona before they leave, so they catch a plane there from Malaga. They are standing on the pavement, staring up at Gaudi's unfinished cathedral when Linda's mobile phone rings. She moves away a little so she can hear above the sound of traffic.

'Hi Lil's, what's up? I'm fine. No, not at all. Of course I'm sure. What? Are you winding me up? Is that definite? Well you take care, Darlin. I'll call you tonight.' Linda puts her phone back in her bag, re-joins the others to announce

'Lily's pregnant. She's expecting twins.'

Lily sails through the pregnancy and gives birth to a girl and boy right on time . Thanks to the roll-out of foetal scanning, they have already been named Eliza and George by their doting parents. Eliza

282

is fair-haired like Lily while George is dark, with a hint of red in his hair. Apart from JJ, heir two grandmothers are the first to meet the new arrivals. They stand on opposite sides of the hospital cot, both entranced by the tiny babies, then they squabble good-naturedly over baby-sitting rights. JJ, amused, settles the matter.

'Stop it, both of you. We won't be going out for ages yet and anyway, Dad has already declared first dibs .

CHAPTER 46

Maggie is worried about her mother. Mary always seems tired these days and she also complains of abdominal discomfort but refuses to see a doctor.

'It's probably just indigestion, Maggie. You're bound to get it as you get older.' Maggie asks her tenant, Alys, whether she has noticed any change in Helen recently. She hasn't but she tells Maggie,

'She's bound to get tired at her age, she's not getting any younger. I fall asleep in front of the TV myself most nights. '

So Maggie puts her worries aside and concentrates on work and her beautiful grandchildren. And Duncan, of course; he is always there, supporting and encouraging her. There is nothing Maggie can't do in Duncan's estimation. Matty comes over to see the babies with an American girl in tow. They all drive over to JJ's together, squeezed into Maggie's little Peugeot 205. Matty greets JJ with a laconic 'Nice one, Bro' then grabs Lily and kisses her, hard. JJ tells the American girl, 'Ignore him, he's just trying to wind me up.'

The girl, Lindsay, is attractive, friendly and confident. She works as a producer at a TV station and is clearly besotted with Matt. When Maggie asks if they are planning to get married Matt says he doesn't believe in marriage. Lindsay doesn't say anything.

Mary is starting to lose weight; she also seems to have lost her appetite. She fobs off all Maggie's anxious questions, saying that she's been off her food lately. 'Duncan tells Maggie to stop pussy footing around her and do something positive. 'Make an appointment for her with your GP and make sure she goes. In fact, take her there yourself. I'll help you get her in the car if you like.' So

Maggie makes the appointment and drives Mary to the surgery. After examining her, the GP says he is going to send Mary to the hospital for some tests. An anxious Maggie asks what they will be testing for.

'The usual things, bloods, kidney function and so on. Let's wait and see what the tests tell us before we start worrying, shall we?'

The tests show that Mary has ovarian cancer. She will need Chemotherapy but with treatment her life could be extended by anything up to five years. Mary undergoes several courses of chemo and various drug therapies. She never complains, always managing a smile and a word of reassurance for Maggie. The treatments do slow down the spread of the disease, but they take a terrible toll on her, both physically and emotionally. She can no longer walk Hetty, so Alys or Maggie take her out in the afternoons now. In the final year of her life, Mary is in considerable pain. The morphine helps but most of the time she is barely conscious, but Maggie doesn't mind, she just wants her to be free of pain. However, life is precious and Mary fights for every breath right up to the second that she passes away.

After the death of her mother, Duncan stays with Maggie almost every night, but she knows she cannot expect him to do that forever. Maggie still loves her house, but now it holds too many memories and there are too many empty rooms. The time has come to sell it, memories, and all, and find somewhere smaller.

JJ and Lily are also house-hunting. They need more space and a bigger garden for their boisterous four year–old twins. So when Alys gives notice that she is leaving, saying she feels lonely without Mary living next door, Maggie has an idea.

She phones JJ that evening.

'I've had an idea, love. Why don't you and Lily buy my house? I could move into your Gran's old flat, it would be just like old times.'

'I'm sure Lily would love that Mum, but we couldn't afford it. Your house is way above our budget.'

'Not if I gift you half the house. Then you would only need to raise enough money to buy Matty's half.'

'Can you do that, give away half of a house?'

'Of course I can, it's my house, I can do what I like with it. You might have to pay some stamp duty, I'm not sure what the rules are now, and naturally we'd have to ask Matt first. But I can't see why he would object, he lives abroad anyway. And he wouldn't have to wait for me to die to get his share of the house.'

'Mum, that's a horrible thing to say.'

'You know what I mean. You and Matt might even avoid some of the inheritance tax'.

While they are sorting out the details, Maggie has an unexpected visitor. She is upstairs when she sees a taxi pulling onto the drive. A woman gets out, followed by a young girl. *They've got the wrong address,* she thinks and runs down to open the front door.

'Mrs Maggie?' The woman asks hesitantly. The girl comes forward to stand beside the older woman; she looks familiar, but Maggie can't quite place her. The woman speaks again.

'Don't you remember me, Maggie?' Now that she can see her face, there's no mistaking the woman. It's Sophea, older, not quite so slim but definitely Sophea.

'Sophea! Come in, send your taxi away, come in. Is this your daughter?' Maggie is so delighted that she keeps firing questions at them without giving them time to answer.

Eventually they go inside and Sophea explains her visit. Her husband is here for a medical conference at Southampton University. She has always kept Maggie's letters, so she has her address. When she searched for it online so she realised her husband would be staying near to Maggie's old home, so she decided to accompany him.

'I knew it was possible that you no longer reside here, but I wanted to try. I always speak about you with my daughter, Dara.' Maggie brings tea and while they are talking Dara pets the dog. She appears fascinated by Hetty and Maggie understands why: Cambodians do not keep dogs as pets.

'Would you like to take her out to the garden and throw her a ball, Dara? She'll bring it straight back to you.' Dara goes outside and Sophea understands that Maggie wants to talk in private.

'You want to ask me about my marriage, I think? At first it was very difficult for me, I cried for Miguel whenever I was in private. My husband was forced by his parents to marry too, but he is very kind man. He said to me that we will learn to love each other one day. I always asked myself how Miguel could leave without even a letter, and I realised he is not kind like my husband, so I decided it is better to forget about him.'

'And have you been happy, Sophea?'

'Yes. We have also a son; he stayed in Cambodia with my parents. We are a very happy family. My parents are old now, but my father told me if I see Mrs Maggie, he wants to send his regards. Maggie, I am so happy I could find you and tell you this, I know you were sad for me.' Later, Maggie drives Sophea and Dara back to their hotel where her husband is waiting in the lounge. He is clearly, eager to meet his wife's old friend.

'I am so happy to meet you, Mrs Maggie, my wife has often told me about you. I will be tied up at the university for most of the week, but I would like to take you for dinner the day before we leave, if you are free? Maggie agrees to meet them for dinner at their hotel the evening before they are due to leave for home. Sophea's husband is urbane and charming and clearly enjoys hearing stories about the time she shared a house with Maggie. It is also clear that the couple are happy together. Maggie is so relieved, she has always wondered if she could have done more to help Sophea . Now she feels that a burden, previously unacknowledged, has been lifted.

CHAPTER 47

Matt comes over to sign the paper-work for the house sale. He is going to invest his share of the proceeds in a production company. Lyndsay will remain in her job for the time being but once the company takes off she will give it up and work with Matt. Maggie asks why Matt didn't ask Michael for a loan when he needed money.

'I wanted to do it on my own, Mum. Dad might have lent me the money, but he has never taken my career seriously, you know that. It would only have confirmed his opinion if I'd gone to him for money. But are you sure you want to go ahead with the deal? It's not too late to change your mind, Mum.' Maggie assures Matt that she has never been surer of anything, and the papers are signed.

'A few months later, Maggie is standing at her kitchen window in in the annexe. While she's washing the breakfast dishes, she is watching the twins playing on the slide in the garden. They start off by whizzing down on their bottoms, next they come down head-first, but more carefully. When George gets to the bottom for the third time Lizzie shouts,

'Let's make a train'. She tries to walk back up the slippery slide, clutching its sides for support, leaving George to take the more traditional route up the steps. When he gets to the top he waits for Lizzie, who tucks in between his legs and they slide down together. After that they both race back to the steps and there is a tussle at the bottom: both twin wants to be first to climb back up. From behind her Duncan, who slept over last night, says

'You go and get ready, I'll sort them out'. He goes out and picks up Lizzie, swinging her off the ground up into the air. She squeals with delight, leaving George free to climb up the steps.

Maggie knows that she can rely on Duncan to keep an eye on them, so she goes into the bedroom of the cosy flat to change her clothes. Linda is coming over later. The two grandmothers are going to take the twins out for the afternoon. While she is getting ready, she thinks: *What an unexpected journey life takes you on. After all those places and people, I've come full circle and now I'm exactly where I'm meant to be.*

EPILOGUE

The dreams are so real to Maggie now that she is totally immersed in them. She can smell and feel and touch. She feels the sand between her toes on the day that she first saw Michael, feels his body hot on hers as they make love in the back of his car. She feels his tears of joy on her cheek when the twins are born and burns with rage when she learns he has betrayed her once more.

She holds her tiny twins in her arms, inhales their fragrance. She re-lives her pride at their graduation, mingled with sadness that they are no longer "her boys". She feels Linda's hand squeezing her fingers numb at Tom's funeral, hears Lily's uncontrolled sobbing loud in her ears. She welcomes the silence after her mother's last rasping breath, grateful that she is finally at peace.

She feels the warmth of Duncan's hand on hers and knows that he has come to say goodbye.

Printed in Great Britain
by Amazon